"[A] taut and ⬛⬛⬛⬛⬛⬛⬛⬛⬛⬛⬛⬛⬛⬛⬛⬛⬛ eception [and] satisfying ⬛⬛⬛⬛⬛⬛⬛

"Intensely grippi⬛⬛⬛⬛⬛⬛⬛⬛⬛⬛⬛⬛⬛⬛⬛its at our deepest fears about the safety of children and ⬛⬛⬛⬛ve readers hooked until the last page." —*Romantic Times* (Top Pick)

"An action movie in print . . . There is no shortage of twists and surprises." —*Publishers Weekly*

"A thriller lover's dream of white-knuckle action . . . Ms. Lewin is an author whose star is on the rise. . . . Bravo!" —*Rendezvous*

"Patricia Lewin provides a fast-paced thriller that leaves her audience breathless keeping up with the speed." —*Affaire de Coeur*

Praise for *Blind Run*

"From its sharply etched opening in the desert to its gripping finale—and I won't tell you where—*Blind Run* is the work of a writer with a genuine talent to thrill. Bravo, Patricia Lewin!" —*New York Times* bestselling author Tess Gerritsen

"Spellbinding . . . Packed with white-knuckle action, daring chases and breathless escapes." —*New York Times* bestselling author Iris Johanson

"Lewin's taut thriller is filled with hair-raising car chases and complex double crosses." —*Booklist*

"Brilliant, breathtaking suspense. *Blind Run* starts with a bang and maintains a blistering pace right down to the nail-biter ending." —*New York Times* bestselling author Lisa Gardner

"*Blind Run* is edge-of-your-seat entertainment from a terrific new voice in suspense." —*Romantic Times*

"[A] fast pace [and] abundant action. —*Publishers Weekly*

Also by Patricia Lewin

Out of Reach
Blind Run

OUT OF TIME

A Novel

PATRICIA LEWIN

BALLANTINE BOOKS • NEW YORK

Out of Time is a work of fiction. Names, characters, places, and incidents are the products of the author's imagination or are used fictitiously. Any resemblance to actual events, locales, or persons, living or dead, is entirely coincidental.

A Ballantine Books Mass Market Original

Copyright © 2005 by Patricia Van Wie

Published in the United States by Ballantine Books, an imprint of The Random House Publishing Group, a division of Random House, Inc., New York.

BALLANTINE and colophon are registered trademarks of Random House, Inc.

ISBN 0-345-47962-9

Cover design: Carl D. Galian
Cover illustration: Don Sipley

Printed in the United States of America

www.ballantinebooks.com

OPM   9   8   7   6   5   4   3   2   1

For my nieces and nephews: Jolene, Cheri, Jennie, Tom, Christine, David, Christine, Brian, and Sean. And for my daughter, Andrea.

For all the times you've come to my book signings, brought your friends, bought my books, then read them. You all are the best.

ACKNOWLEDGMENTS

I don't believe in coincidence. So I know it was more than chance that I moved in across the street from a remarkable woman with the knowledge to guide me through the medical and biological maze I'd created for myself in this book. I simply could not have come up with this scenario and made it real without her.

So, a special thanks to Jean Marie Houghton, MD/PhD, for the hours of brainstorming and for reading my medical scenarios and scenes, for answering my endless questions—via e-mail, or when I'd dash across the street with "just one more"—and for giving me a better understanding of my character, Jean Taylor, telling me she "had" to be a woman. Oh, and, of course, for the use of her name.

All mistakes, or literary license, are mine.

Thanks also to Nancy La Cross, who on our daily walks listened to me rattle on about my latest book, then gave me Cuba. And to the rest of the NGE ladies, who lent me their first names.

As always, thanks to Sharon Reishus for setting me on the CIA path and always being ready to answer my questions.

Also, thanks to Virginia Ellis for reading the complete manuscript. You know how much your comments and suggestions meant to me.

As for my location research, the Florida sections of this book came easy. Although I no longer live there, Florida will always be my home, its sights, sounds, smells, and feel of the air are permanently embedded in my psyche.

Unfortunately, however, I was unable to visit Cuba. U.S. citizens are forbidden by law to travel to Cuba without permission from the Justice Department. Although I did apply, my request was denied. So my research on Cuba consisted of many hours of books, Internet, and interviews with people who'd visited or lived there. I can only hope I got it right, because the more I discovered Cuba, the more fascinated I became with it. I sincerely hope that someday I'll be able to see that beautiful island in person.

DAY SEVEN

PROLOGUE

Casa de la Rosa, Cuba

Death pressed against her temple.

Chilling, hard steel, small caliber, but still lethal at this range. Sudden and unexpected, the gun and the man holding it had caught Erin off guard.

"Breathe," said the familiar voice behind the weapon. "While you still can."

"Moss," Erin whispered his name and tried to steady herself against the certainty of her own death. A gun to her head made it too easy to forget her years of training, made everything but fear slip away.

A second man came into her field of vision, a thick stripe of tape across the bridge of his swollen and discolored nose. Erin shivered when he looked at her, hate ripe in his eyes. One of Moss's hired killers, the last time she'd seen him, he'd been sprawled at her feet, cursing and grasping at his shattered face. Now he seemed ready to return the favor, or worse.

Where was Alec?

Had Moss killed him? The only way Moss would have gotten past Alec was if he was already dead. The thought settled like a weight in her stomach, making breathing once more a difficult task.

Moss nudged her with the gun, just a little left of her spine, sparking her anger. Better than fear or grief, it was an emotion she could handle. And use. Except she didn't see how.

"On the floor," Moss said.

Erin hesitated. Once they had her on the ground, it would be too late. If she was going to do something, it had to be now, while she still had her feet beneath her.

"Don't even think it, Erin." Moss must have read her mind, because she looked into his eyes and saw her own death.

He was right. It was all over.

DAY ONE

CHAPTER ONE

Miami, Florida

August in Miami.

Alec Donovan knew hotter and more humid places existed. He'd once spent an interminable July in Austin, where the dazzling, dry heat had sent thermometers twenty degrees higher than those on the Florida Gold Coast. He remembered the intense sun, baking against his skin, as he worked with the local FBI office to locate a missing toddler. They'd found the boy, but not before the Texas heat had nearly sapped the last of their strength and pushed tempers to a ragged edge.

Then, just last year, he'd given a seminar to the field office in New Orleans, a city known for its summer months of heat and humidity. He would have picked a different time of year if he'd had a choice, but as one of the FBI's leading CAC (Crimes Against Children) authorities, Alec's expertise was in high demand. Both in the field and out. Timing for either was seldom up to him.

Thus, he'd experienced firsthand the stifling Southern

heat. That didn't make him feel better, or cooler, as he started across the University of Miami campus.

It spread out in neat shades of green. Grass, unlike its Northern cousins, spiky and stiff, but dense and carefully trimmed. Trees, some tall and slender with feathery leaves, others massive, their twisted trunks and roots reaching toward the walkways, heavy branches draping overhead. A variety of palms, familiar and not, with metal plaques naming the plant and its origins. Ferns, scattered in bunches, alone or around the base of trees.

All a little too manicured for his taste.

He'd first visited Erin here in January, when the wind and streets of D.C. had been icy, and the South Florida weather a sunny seventy degrees. He'd told her at the time he could live here. She'd simply laughed and suggested he come back in six or seven months before jumping to any conclusions. He suspected, then and now, that her response had been more about fear of letting him too close than any concern for his ability to adapt to the Miami summers.

Still, she had a point. It was damn hot.

The thick air stirred, fluttering around him like a damp blanket. A distant rumble drew his eyes to the western horizon and its line of dark clouds. He picked up his pace and darted beneath the overhang of the Learning Center, just as the first fat drops darkened the sidewalk.

Within seconds, a sheet of rain blurred the daylight.

"Welcome to the tropics," he said, and turned to continue his search for Erin.

He found the room number he was looking for on the far side of the building. Through the glass door, he saw an auditorium-style classroom with lines of empty seats descending toward a podium and desk. About a dozen students sat scattered in the first two rows. In front, sitting on the edge of the desk facing them, sat Dr. Erin Baker, PhD not medical, and ex-CIA intelligence officer.

Alec opened the door and slipped into the shadows at the back of the room. Frigid air slapped against his heated skin, stinging and soothing at the same time. He took a deep breath, relieved, and wondered how anyone had survived living in this climate before the invention of air-conditioning.

He worked his way down a couple of rows and took a seat.

No one noticed him, or so he would have believed if he didn't know better. Erin wasn't the type of woman who missed much, and though she'd made no move to acknowledge him, he didn't doubt she'd seen him.

From a distance she looked young, as she had the fall night he'd first met her, nearly a year ago. Like then, something caught inside him at the sight of her, some elemental awareness of her that he hadn't understood at the time.

She'd told him a crazy story about a man with a magician's hands and a string of missing children. Any other investigator would have dismissed her as a nutcase. Instead, Alec had believed her—though the why of that still escaped him—and had followed her down a dark path neither of them could have predicted. In the process, he'd discovered a woman with so many layers he thought he could spend a lifetime exploring them all. The problem was convincing her to allow it.

Today, she wore her usual jeans and a slim, fitted

shirt, her dark hair still short, a bit mussed, and more functional than stylish. According to her secretary, the class was a senior seminar on U.S.-Cuban relations, and one of the last of the summer semester. But Erin didn't seem much more than a grad student herself.

Unless you looked closely.

For anyone capable of seeing, it was her stillness that gave her away. The stillness of a warrior, unafraid and certain of her own skills and abilities. The stillness of a predator, knowing her prey would eventually cross her path. The stillness of a woman, waiting for something . . . something more than this seemingly small and fettering classroom.

Then Alec shook his head and bit back a snort of impatience at his own fanciful thoughts. Erin was just a woman, and she'd chosen this life. She'd left the CIA of her own accord and become a full-time academic.

At least for now.

Which was the crux of his dilemma as he watched her address her students. He full-heartedly approved the safe path she'd chosen, but he'd seen another side of her, at her best or worst, depending on your perspective, with blood on her hands, the light of victory and revenge in her eyes. And he knew that long-term, she'd never be content in a classroom.

CHAPTER TWO

Miami, Florida

Erin saw Alec slip into the back of her classroom.

Suppressing the automatic smile that filled her, she kept her expression neutral, seemingly oblivious to his presence. Though nothing could be further from the truth. Instead, she was suddenly conscious of her less than feminine attire and lack of makeup, and fought the urge to fidget, smooth down her hair, or adjust her clothing. It was unnerving. She wasn't a woman who normally fussed over her appearance.

With an effort, she focused on the heated discussion between two of her students, a young woman and man who'd been on opposite sides of every issue the entire semester, especially the U.S. trade embargo against Cuba.

"The embargo is a failure," said Darlene, a Florida blonde, who was every bit as bright as she was pretty. Though she didn't seem to know it. "It has been forty years, and the trade restrictions against Cuba aren't working. Seems to me it's time for our government to admit they made a mistake and move on."

"Who says the embargo's a failure?" asked Tim, her male adversary.

"Phuleeze." Darlene rolled her eyes. "All it's done has made the U.S. Castro's scapegoat. He can blame all his country's problems on us."

"Let him." Crossing his arms, Tim sprawled back in his chair. He was tall and lanky, his long legs taking up a lot of space, and had the look—awkward, glasses—of a student none of the others acknowledged outside the classroom. Here, however, he was in his element, seemingly smarter, or at least more informed, than the rest, and his body language dismissed Darlene even more effectively than his words.

She didn't back down, though. "Sure, and meanwhile the Cuban people are paying the price." As Tim relaxed, she came forward, sitting sideways on the edge of her seat, facing him. "They're the ones the embargo is hurting, not Castro or his government. It's unfair."

"Was it fair when Castro confiscated more than a billion dollars in American property and assets?" Tim's response was flip, again dismissive.

"That was a long time ago. It's—"

Tim cut her off. "And the hardships to the Cuban people are due to the fall of the Soviet Union and their support. Not the U.S. trade embargo. Besides, Cuba imports very few of its staples, so why is there such a shortage? Could it be that the Cuban government, which dominates the distribution of goods, is corrupt?" He widened his eyes in feigned surprised. "What a concept."

"Don't be a jerk, Tim. I'm not—"

"Whoa," Erin interceded, just barely resisting the

urge to check Alec's reaction. It made her uncomfortable knowing he was watching her. "Let's keep this civil."

"Darlene, you've made valid points, as has Tim. But don't let him push your buttons." Her gaze jumped to Alec, saw him smiling, and she quickly refocused on Tim, giving him a behave-yourself frown. "It's the fastest way to let him win." She glanced around at the others, again avoiding Alec's eyes, knowing his grin had broadened. Pushing other people's buttons was one of Erin's specialties, something Alec knew all too well. And here she was admonishing a student for using the same tactic. "Okay, let's hear from someone else?"

Another of the male students gave Darlene a puppy-dog grin. "If the government lifted the embargo, the U.S. could make money in the Cuban sugar industry."

Darlene smiled back, acknowledging his support, which Erin knew stemmed more from his wanting to impress Darlene than anything else.

"The only money to be made in the sugar industry would hurt our own exporting," claimed another young man. "Besides, we'd end up taking the place of the Soviet Union and subsidizing the Cuban government with credit. And since Cuba hasn't paid off any of its creditors so far, why would we do that?"

"We wouldn't," added Tim, jumping back into the discussion and finally leaning forward in his chair. "In fact, if nothing else, the embargo has saved the U.S. millions of dollars in unpaid debts." He paused, then sat back again. "But you all are missing the main point. Cuba is a communist state, and we cannot allow communism to take root."

"What about China?" Erin asked, inserting another

element into the mix. "If we trade with China, why not Cuba?"

"Cuba isn't nearly as important to our national interest as China," Tim said. "China's size, power, UN affiliation, and trade influence determine its diplomatic status. Cuba has none of that."

"So the Cuban people are paying the price of U.S. international politics," said Darlene, obviously still disgusted with Tim and anyone else on his side of the fence.

"Politicians have always chosen causes for their own purposes, sanctions included," Tim answered.

"And that makes it right?" she challenged.

"Right or wrong, it's reality."

For a moment, no one else spoke. Tim's grim views were putting a damper on the discussion.

Then, "So who's right, Dr. Baker?" asked a student in the front row.

The question amused Erin. She couldn't blame them for trying to get the answer out of her. They always did. "You tell me."

"Oh, come on," said Tim. "You're Cuban, you've got to have an opinion on this."

"My father was Cuban," she acknowledged, "but this class isn't about me. It's about exposing you to the facts, so you can draw your own opinions." She looked pointedly from one student to another. "You need to make up your own minds which side is right."

"Oh, come on, give us a hint."

She laughed. "I don't think so. If I did, I'd get twenty essays reflecting my opinion." She paused, considering. "One thing I will say, though. This is not a black-and-white issue. There is no one right answer to Cuba's problems. There are only shades of truth and partial lies. Rationalization. And opinions." She paused again, letting her words sink in. "So I want those papers to tell me what you think, where you stand on the issues, and what each of you came away with from this semester." She smiled. "And of course, I want you to back up those beliefs with facts."

Good-natured mumbling drifted through the room. This wasn't the first time they'd had this particular discussion. They were a good group, bright and engaged in the topic. It made her job so much easier.

"Okay, I think we're done here." Erin pushed to her feet. "Have those papers to me by noon tomorrow or take an incomplete for the course. Then enjoy the rest of your summer. You've been a great class."

The students responded with light applause. Then the noise level rose as they stood and gathered their belongings, the usual three or four heading straight for her.

She chatted and smiled, answering their questions when appropriate. Most of her attention, however, was on the man at the back of the room. Over their heads, she watched Alec stand and start toward her. She knew it should annoy her when he showed up unannounced like this. Instead, the unpredictability of his visits teased her senses in a way she didn't want to think about too hard. Despite her initial resistance, Alec Donovan had stepped into her life, and fighting the smile that filled her at his presence was no longer possible.

CHAPTER THREE

Santa Clara, Cuba

Joe Roarke had always known he'd end up dead in a place like this, alone in some Third World alley, where his death would go unnoticed, and certainly unacknowledged. He just hadn't expected that death to come in Cuba, less than a hundred miles from the home his parents had fled shortly after his birth. The irony of it didn't escape him.

Around him, a late afternoon storm had emptied the streets of Santa Clara and reduced visibility to a few feet. He'd taken refuge in the shadows beneath a balcony, the crumbling stucco at his back still warm from the day's heat. The rain had bought him time, throwing off, or at least slowing down, the men following him.

This mission was supposed to have been a boondoggle.

One of the CIA's foreign agents in Cuba, a man named Padilla, had gotten spooked, and Langley had sent in Joe to check it out. His Cuban heritage had been part of their reason for choosing him, but mainly he'd been in the vicinity, already en route to the Caribbean for an overdue vacation.

He'd almost refused, except the suits had promised him a two- or three-day—tops—excursion into the heart of Cuba. Posing as a freelance photographer contracted to produce a coffee table book, he could take his time and extend his vacation for a week or so. He just had to check out a medical aid facility near Santa Clara, a city in central Cuba. A prodigal son returning home. Nothing to it.

Except something had gone very wrong.

He'd been to the camp, talked to the administrator, a Dr. Diaz, and had arranged to return the next day for pictures. It had all been very civil, pleasant even. He'd been on his way back to Santa Clara to check in with Padilla and send a preliminary report to Langley. Then, on a narrow mountain road heading into town, all hell had broken loose.

Three men with AK-47s had ambushed him. He'd escaped, barely, and lost them in the dense woods. This was their turf, but years spent in the world's jungles had honed Joe's skills and given him the advantage. Or so he'd thought.

The funny thing was, he hadn't seen anything of interest at the camp. The place had felt off a bit, but then everything in Cuba seemed skewed to him. Someone at the camp, however, had considered him a threat.

Why? Was there a hole in his cover? Or had someone recognized him? Or even worse, known he was CIA? He'd spent his entire adult life working the back streets of the world's underbelly. If he'd somewhere, some place, crossed paths with someone at the camp . . . well, that might explain it. But who?

The rain was letting up now, and he was out of time. He'd have to make a decision and move soon, either deeper into the city or back the way he'd come.

Padilla's shop was only a couple of blocks away.

If Joe could reach it before his pursuers picked up his trail again, he could send a warning to Langley and tell them Padilla had been right. Something was wrong at that camp. Getting to him had been Joe's plan, the singular goal that had kept him moving through the jungle for the last forty-eight hours, working his way out of the mountains.

Get to Padilla. Get word to Langley.

Another good plan. Too bad it too had failed. He'd underestimated his pursuers and their resources, acknowledging now that he'd escaped them in the jungle because they'd let him. They simply hadn't followed him into the dank underbrush. Instead, they'd been waiting on the outskirts of Santa Clara. And for the last four hours they'd be trailing him, toying with him like a rat in a maze, running him to ground.

Now, getting to Padilla wasn't the problem. It was getting to the man without exposing him.

Joe knew Langley would be waiting to hear from him. He was two days overdue, and soon his disappearance would raise a red flag. Then they'd send someone after him. The CIA may not acknowledge their covert officers, even in death, but they wouldn't leave them behind, either. If for no other reason than a captured CIA officer was a security risk.

Thinking back, Joe knew he should have stayed in the

mountains, climbing further into their heights and down their southern slopes. He might have been able to make it to Guantánamo as a possible way off this island. As it was, he fully expected to die here.

Hindsight was a real bitch.

His best bet now was to get back out of the city, though he expected it was already too late. They'd be on him the moment he made a move. But he couldn't lead them to Padilla and buy the other man's death with the slim hope of getting word to Langley. He would just have to take comfort in knowing that his disappearance would draw attention to the situation and bring others, better prepared, to find out what that camp was hiding.

Slipping from the shadows, he worked his way along the edge of the narrow street, away from the center of the town and Padilla's shop. He'd made it a few blocks, slivers of hope blossoming with each unchallenged step.

Then he saw the first of them.

A lone man stepped into his path from the doorway of a nearby building. Joe stopped. The man made no aggressive moves, but Joe recognized the man's eyes, stupid pig-eyes, filled with cruelty and gleaming with the triumph of a feral predator who'd cornered his prey. Joe had seen eyes like this on a hundred faces, in dozens of holes around the world.

Joe turned and started back the way he'd come, resisting the urge to run. A second man blocked his path.

Behind him, someone chuckled. "You lost?"

Joe knew that voice and swung back around. As he did, he caught sight of movement off to the side. Two, maybe three more men. They'd surrounded him. His focus, however, was on the man now standing before him. It was a familiar face.

"It's been a long time, Roarke."

Joe couldn't pull a name from memory, but he didn't often forget faces. And this one, he knew. They'd served together, Special Forces, Desert Storm, a million years ago it seemed. Before the Agency had claimed Joe's life. Still, if this man had been at the DFL camp, it explained a lot.

Except why Joe wasn't already dead.

No one in this dingy street would challenge or question these men if they put a bullet in his head. No one would dare. So they wanted him alive. Otherwise he'd already be lying in a pool of his own blood on the watery streets.

"Come with us," said that familiar voice, "and no one will get hurt."

Fuck that.

Better to die here. Because if they had any idea who he was, information would be what they wanted. And he wouldn't give it up, no matter what they did to him. So he'd make them kill him here, though he wouldn't go down easy. They'd pay dearly for his life, and he'd take one or two with him in the process.

Joe charged.

CHAPTER FOUR

Miami, Florida

The kids liked her.

The thought made Alec smile. It didn't surprise him that she was a good teacher, or that at some level, students responded to her underlying strength. Or maybe, they too sensed she was theirs for only a short time.

Alec stayed put until the first group had passed him on their way to the door. Then he started down toward the front of the room, stepping aside for three young women who looked him over unabashedly, one of them throwing him a flirty smile. When he reached the bottom level, he waited for the last two girls to finish their conversation with Erin.

Once they had, they grinned broadly at him, then back at Erin. "All right, Dr. Baker."

As they hurried off, up the stairs, Alec followed them with his eyes, wondering what that was all about.

"I think you've just improved my student evaluations for the semester," Erin said as the glass doors closed behind the young women.

He turned back to Erin, confused.

She crossed her arms. "Are all men so dense?"

"Obviously."

"They think you're hot."

He grinned at that, moving closer. "What about you? Do you think I'm hot?"

"I think," she moved out of reach, putting the desk between them, and started to gather papers, stuffing them into a briefcase, "that if you'd have let me know you were coming to Miami, I would have told you I have plans for the weekend."

"That doesn't answer my question." Though her actions, the quick jerky movements and refusal to meet his gaze, belied her words, he wanted to hear her say it. The chemistry between them was something she couldn't control, or deny. And it made her nervous. Edgy. He wanted her to admit it.

"I'm taking Claire and Janie up to Disney World," she said. "We're leaving tomorrow afternoon."

He laughed softly at her refusal to even acknowledge his question. "Boy, you really don't like the tables turned, do you?"

She stopped filling her briefcase and looked at him, her expression carefully blank.

"You're the queen of throwaway lines," he said. "But you can't handle them coming at you." It was one of Erin's favorite tactics to toss out a line that disarmed and confused, rather than answer a question directly. She'd kept him off-kilter for days when they'd first met, using his attraction to her to keep distance between them.

"What are you talking about?" she said, as if she didn't know exactly what he meant.

He moved to her side of the desk, and this time she stood her ground. He really hadn't expected her to back up again. It wasn't in her nature. Reaching up, he ran the back of his fingers down her cheek. "Do you think I'm hot?"

Her answer was visible, in her eyes and in the slight quiver of her lips. "I think," she said, obviously fighting her own reaction, "that touching me without permission is a good way to end up on the floor."

"Kinky." He moved closer still, feeling the heat of her, *and* her rigid control.

"I could break a bone or two for you on the way down." Her voice sounded ragged, like she was having trouble breathing.

"It might . . ." He lowered his mouth to within a whisper of hers, until his words were a breath against her lips. ". . . be worth it."

She could no longer hide her response, nor the way her body leaned toward his in anticipation. And he felt a small thrill of triumph. Eventually, she'd stop fighting him. And herself.

Smiling, he stepped away. Better to keep her guessing, wanting. It was the only leverage he had, the only thing that kept her from running scared. "But then again, I'm not really into pain."

For a moment she stood motionless, unbelieving. Then she let out a snort of laughter and put more distance between them. "You know, Donovan, you're a real pain in the ass."

"That's why we get along so well." He picked up her briefcase, because it would piss her off. "And I know all about Disney World. Come on, I'm buying dinner."

"I don't—"

"I've already cleared it with Marta." An old friend of Erin's mother, Marta helped care for Erin's troubled sister Claire and Claire's eight-year-old daughter, Janie. And from what little interaction *he'd* had with Marta, he knew who ran things.

"You talked to Marta?" Erin, obviously, knew as well.

"Sure. How do you think I found you?" He started up the stairs, figuring she had no choice but to follow. He had her briefcase, and since she never carried a purse, he expected he also had her car keys. And maybe her wallet.

"Marta said to tell you not to worry about getting in early, something about taking Janie for pizza." He couldn't resist glancing over his shoulder, just to be sure she was coming.

Erin was right behind him.

"So, you see," he said, "it's already arranged. They don't expect you home for dinner."

"That child is going to turn into a pizza."

"But not tonight." He held the door, though he knew it would bug her, a man treating her like she needed his help when nothing could be further from the truth. Erin was the strongest woman he knew, which was saying a lot. Women in the FBI generally didn't lack self-assurance or confidence, and his own partner, Cathy, could give any man a run for his money.

Erin, though, was in a class by herself. That was why he couldn't walk away no matter how hard she pushed back, and why he enjoyed pulling her strings. It was his way of evening things out between them, turning the tables, and keeping *her*—if even slightly—off balance for a change.

Funny that a woman like Erin, who was unafraid to face the most violent and vile of men, feared letting anyone get too close. He knew it probably had something to do with her sister Claire's disappearance when they were children. But Alec wasn't about to accept that excuse.

"So how about we head over to The Wharf?" he said. "I like watching the boats cruise up and down the Intracoastal."

She hesitated, then laughed lightly, softening, as they stepped outside. "And we have perfect weather for it, too."

The rain and wind lashed the trees and sent small branches and shredded palm fronds skittering across the manicured grounds. Heavy clouds churned overhead, blocking the sun and hiding the summer sky. They hung back, close to the wall beneath the breezeway, as windswept rain reached for them.

"We could be here awhile," he said.

She shook her head. "No, it'll be over in a few minutes."

Thunder crashed, its power trembling through the building at their backs, as a flash of lightning momentarily illuminated the darkened world beyond the concrete overhang.

He found that hard to believe. "If you say so."

She laughed again. "This is just a normal afternoon summer storm. They pass quickly. Fifteen, twenty minutes tops. You'll see." Then, crossing her arms, she leaned back against the concrete wall.

For a few minutes they watched the storm, Erin's stillness and an awkward silence building a wall between them. He searched for a way to breach it while thinking things should be different between them. They'd been through hell together, faced death and walked away. It should have made them more comfortable with each other. Instead, it hovered between them like a nightmare neither wished to revisit.

Then Erin said, "Did you come straight from Seattle?"

He looked at her, a bit surprised that she knew about Seattle. Their only contact since last fall had been the three times he'd shown up in Miami unannounced, like he had today. And then, they hadn't spoken about the CIA, the FBI, his cases, or the one they'd worked together last year.

"I got in a couple of hours ago," he admitted. And had come straight from the airport. Unplanned, even on his part. The need to see her stronger than his orders to report back to Quantico.

Erin nodded, her eyes still on nature's tantrum, as if this was the answer she'd expected. "I followed the Hanley case."

Of course. The hunt for the missing teens, a sister and brother, twins, not yet sixteen, had received national media attention. It was an explanation of sorts, how Erin knew he'd been in Seattle.

"It was . . . rough." A deep well of sadness opened within him, catching him unawares. He thought he'd locked away the guilt and grief, compartmentalized it behind the steel door in his head labeled DON'T GO THERE.

"I'm sorry." She met his gaze then, understanding in

her eyes. And he realized that's why he was here, why he'd run to her straight from a case gone bad. When Erin was twelve, her younger sister Claire had been taken from a playground while under Erin's care. If anyone knew how he felt, the way his failure tore at him, it was she.

"You can't save them all," she said.

Though it was what he'd told himself at least a hundred times in the last twenty-four hours, what he told himself every time, he didn't like hearing it. "Fuck that."

She shifted her weight against the wall. "Yeah." Again, she got it. The desperation to make things better, safer, and the anger and frustration over those who could not be helped. "Any chance of finding the guy?"

"The locals are working it." But they both knew that not all cases turned out like the one they'd worked together. The bad guys weren't always caught, the innocents not always saved. "They have a good profile and a few solid leads. These guys get caught." Maybe saying it would make it true. "Eventually."

Just not always before they'd claimed more victims.

Silence again. Easier this time as the memories circulated between them. His. Hers. And those they shared. Together they'd exposed an international slave trader and his supplier—a man called The Magician, who'd been evading the authorities for two decades. Neither Erin nor Alec had come away from the encounter unscathed, but they'd saved one boy's life and set another free. And who could say how many families had been spared the future horror of a missing child?

"Alec . . ." He heard the hesitation in her voice. "You can't quit."

The statement surprised him. It was the one thing he'd never admitted to anyone, not even her. The temptation to quit, leave the CACU and possibly the FBI, came at him more and more often lately. Especially at times like these, when he'd failed so miserably. He thought maybe it was time to let someone else take the reins. Someone younger. Smarter. Someone who didn't feel each loss as if someone had thrust a knife in his gut. But it wasn't something he wanted to talk about.

Not even to Erin.

So he ignored her statement and nodded toward the weather beyond the overhang. The worst of the storm had passed. "Looks like you were right. It's letting up."

For a few seconds she hesitated, and he thought she would say something else about Seattle. Or his thoughts of quitting. Instead she smiled, though it looked forced.

"Of course I'm right," she said. "I grew up here. Remember?"

He let out a short laugh and followed her down the walkway, avoiding the puddles that had gathered at the grassy edges. Everything was brighter, greener. The western sky was once again a brilliant blue. And it even felt a few degrees cooler.

"Strange weather," he said. This was nothing like the summers he'd known in western Massachusetts, or even Virginia.

"It's just . . ." She broke off, slowed, suddenly tense.

Alec followed her gaze to the nearly empty parking lot, where a man sat in a car across from hers, motor running. Seeing them, he shut off the engine and climbed out.

Physically, he looked like your average guy on the

street, medium build, height just under six feet, light brown hair. That's where ordinary stopped. He stood like a soldier and moved with precision as he turned to face them, his gaze sweeping over Alec before settling on Erin.

"Someone you know?" Alec asked, fighting the urge to step between her and the stranger.

"Yes."

Alec glanced at her, a surprising streak of jealousy shading his thoughts. "A friend?"

She kept her eyes on the other man. "He's from Virginia."

Langley. She didn't have to spell it out. The man was CIA.

"Go on to the restaurant," she said. "I'll meet you there."

"I'll wait."

"Alec, please. He won't talk to me with you here."

"That's okay by me."

She looked at him then, finally, her expression determined. "But not with me. I won't be long, thirty minutes. Max."

Alec glanced at the stranger. He'd known the CIA would come for her sooner or later. That didn't mean he had to like it. "Okay," he said. He really had no choice. "Thirty minutes."

"The Wharf, right? On the Intracoastal."

·"Yeah." Alec kept his eyes on the other man. "Are you sure you don't want me to stay?"

"I'm sure." She reached up, turned his head toward hers, and kissed him lightly. Then she said, her voice soft, pleading for understanding, "And yes, I think you're hot."

His reaction was automatic, almost possessive. He slid an arm around her waist and pulled her hard against him, changing the gentle kiss to something else, something desperate. Then he let her go, abruptly, before he could change his mind.

She stepped back, her voice a bit breathless. "Go now. I'll see you at the restaurant."

"I'll be waiting. A half hour." He backed as well, then stopped. "Whatever he wants, Erin." He paused, hesitating. "Tell him no."

CHAPTER FIVE

Miami, Florida

Erin dumped her briefcase inside the car, the ghost of Alec's kiss still lingering on her lips. Unsettling. And untimely. At the moment she didn't have the luxury of reacting to his touch. She needed all her wits to face the man walking toward her. So she buried her thoughts of Alec and turned, arms crossed, to face Bill Jensen.

"Hello, Erin."

"You're a long way from home," she said.

"Aren't you going to say how good it is to see me?" He kept his voice light, but it wasn't real humor. Feigned. Company manufactured to fool the uninitiated or unwary.

Erin was neither. "That depends on why you're here."

"Don't people vacation in Miami?"

"Not usually in August." She glanced past him, as if looking for someone else. "Unless you have kids with you."

He grinned. "You got me. No kids. No vacation. I'm here to see you."

"A personal visit, then?" Though she knew the answer to that one as well.

He hesitated, his first genuine reaction. "It could have been, if I'd thought you were interested." The last time she'd seen him, he'd made *his* interest clear. All Erin had to do was say the word. "But it looks like Donovan beat me to it."

It didn't surprise her that he'd recognized Alec, but she wasn't going to let that sidetrack her. "That's not why you're here, though, is it?"

A shade of disappointment touched his eyes. "We need to talk."

Erin glanced away, sighed. Though she would have liked to say no, what was the point? "Okay. Let's walk." She started back down the path she and Alec had just left, and Bill fell in beside her.

The rain had eased the summer heat and left the air damp with the smell of earth and cut grass. A strange off-color light, like that of a fading bruise, lingered in the storm's wake and sharpened the greens of the surrounding foliage.

The campus was eerily empty, void of the usual bustle. Evidently, the few remaining students were either holed up in cramped dormitory rooms finishing last-minute projects, or getting ready for one last night on the town before they headed home for what remained of the summer.

"How's your current class of CTs?" she asked, filling the gaping silence with a safe topic. Bill was the lead martial arts instructor at the Farm, the CIA's yearlong school for new hires. With each class he had a whole new group of students—CTs, or career trainees—to work with.

"Not bad. I have one girl who's really good. Holds a black belt in tae kwon do." He glanced at Erin. "She's not as good as you were, but not bad, either."

"Did you find out about her black belt before," Erin couldn't resist teasing him, "or after, the first class?"

"Very funny." He let out an abrupt laugh.

On Erin's first day as a student in his class, she'd taken him by surprise in a sparring session and put him on the mat. It had made him the brunt of both instructor and trainee jokes for weeks.

"I learned my lesson," he added.

She grinned. "So reading student files has become more of a priority these days?" She'd been training in the martial arts for years and held three black belts. A fact he would have known if he'd bothered to read *her* file.

"Don't push it," he said, his light tone matching hers.

They walked on in companionable silence for a bit. They'd been friends once, more than friends for one brief night. Then she'd given martial arts demos for his classes, showing them that size didn't mean strength. Or skill.

"Have you found another demo queen?" she asked.

Bill smiled. "I'm working on it, but no one can replace you."

"Yeah," she said, "I'm irreplaceable." Nine months ago, when she'd handed in her resignation, her immediate supervisor had agreed it was the best thing for everyone. Though Erin had told herself that leaving the CIA was what she wanted, needed, it stung that they'd let her go so easily.

She wondered how much Bill knew about any of that. Did he know about her involvement in Alec's search for Cody Sanders? Or the Magician, who'd taken Claire when she was seven, along with countless other children over the years? What about the money man who'd financed the entire operation?

She suspected all of it had been kept quiet, revealed only to those with a need to know. Bill, however, had been with the Company a long time. It wouldn't surprise her if he'd known the whole story way before they'd sent him down here.

"Erin . . ." His voice brought her back to the present. "We need your help."

"We?"

"Don't be obtuse. It doesn't suit you."

Of course she knew who he meant. From the moment she'd seen him waiting in the car, she'd known they—the Company, the Agency, the CIA, whatever name you put on it—wanted something from her. "You're wasting your time. The CIA no longer issues my paychecks."

"That can change."

She glanced at him, the confidence in his voice irritating. He'd always claimed to know her better than she knew herself, and sometimes he'd been right. Usually it amused her. Today, it didn't. "I enjoy teaching."

"There's nothing new in that."

Which was true. While working as a covert officer out of Langley, she'd taught at Georgetown. It had been a dead-end assignment, but she'd had her sister Claire to care for and Claire's daughter, Janie. It had kept Erin tied to the States when she would have preferred working overseas. Still, she'd loved working with the students; all those bright young minds gave her hope for the future.

"Did you know Claire was home now?" Erin's sister had spent years in and out of psychiatric hospitals, and other than her supervisors, Bill had been the only one of Erin's CIA colleagues who'd known about it.

"Of course you knew," she said before he could answer. The CIA had obviously kept tabs on her and would have fully briefed Bill before sending him south.

"Just hear me out, Erin. Before you tell me to get lost."

Her first impulse was to send him packing. She had responsibilities. And whatever the Agency wanted from her, it would undoubtedly interfere with the life she'd begun to build with Janie and Claire. Yet, despite that, Erin wanted to know why they'd sent him, what they wanted from her.

"You have five minutes," she said.

"That's fair." For several steps he said nothing more, then, "Have you ever heard of Doctors For Life?"

She thought a minute. "It's an international aid organization, isn't it?"

"Yeah, it's an all-volunteer group. Primarily, they supply medical care to Third World and economically depressed countries. But they do other things, too, disaster relief, and some education where it's needed." He slipped his hands into his pockets, pausing as if to gather his thoughts or consider the best way to draw her in.

Erin waited.

He threw her a sideways glance. "Several weeks ago one of our foreign agents in Cuba reported suspicious activity in the DFL camp."

"Cuba?" She stopped walking, her interest piqued despite herself. "What kind of suspicious activity?" The phrase could mean anything. Or nothing.

He turned to face her. "We didn't think much of it at first. But apparently there is a new armed presence in the camp. Nothing really unusual for Cuba, but our agent insisted we look into it." He started walking again, evidently expecting her to follow. "What's the use of paying these people for information if we don't listen to them?"

One of the primary functions of a CIA intelligence officer was to recruit and handle foreign agents, people willing to sell information about their governments to the United States. She wondered how hard it was to find people in Cuba to spy on the Castro regime. It would be dangerous, but probably no more than in any other country. No government smiled on treason.

"It was a pretty low priority," Bill said, "but we ran background checks on all the current personnel and staff at the camp." He pressed his lips together in a frown, as if that research had been particularly distasteful. She couldn't imagine why. So far, he was describing standard CIA behavior. "We got one hit. A man on the FBI watch list."

"And you thought of me?" Which didn't make a whole lot of sense. At least, not with the little information Bill had revealed so far. Her specialty had been Middle Eastern cultures.

"We want you to infiltrate their facility in Cuba," he said, finally.

Even knowing it was coming, the actual words jarred her. The CIA wanted her back, and they wanted her to go into Cuba. Of all places. Without even knowing why they'd selected her, she was tempted. As the Agency knew she would be.

Her ties to Cuba ran deep. She'd grown up in Little Havana, where Cuba's presence permeated every aspect of life. Her friends had been Cuban, her teachers, the clerks at all the local stores she had frequented. Even the politicians. In many ways the city belonged more to the island ninety miles to the south than to the Florida geography it occupied. Overriding all of that, however, were blood ties to a father she hadn't seen in twenty-seven years, a man she sometimes hated but couldn't evict from her memories.

Still, going to Cuba really was out of the question.

She couldn't leave Miami now. What about Janie? And Claire? Sometimes she thought things were going well with Claire now that she was once again living at home. Janie adored her mother, and Claire seemed more stable than Erin could ever remember. Other times, however, Erin wasn't so certain. She feared the smallest event could jar them and shake apart the fragile structure of their lives. Erin's. Janie's. But mostly, Claire's.

Besides, there had to be more that Bill wasn't telling her, some reason why the CIA had approached *her* instead of using an active officer. Something beyond her language skills and Cuban heritage. And whatever it was, she didn't want to know about it. She'd been used and discarded once by the Agency and didn't need to learn that lesson twice.

"You're wasting your time, Bill," she said. "Send someone else. Someone who works for the CIA."

"We did send someone else." He hesitated. Briefly. "Five days ago."

She knew better than to ask but had to know. "And?"

"He's disappeared."

She sighed, closing her eyes. "How long?"

"He's more than forty-eight hours overdue."

Too long. When an officer went missing, there was always a reason, and very few of those were good.

"You think DFL is involved?" she asked.

"The organization?" Bill shook his head. "No. Certainly not voluntarily. We've been in contact with their headquarters, and they're cooperating with us at the highest levels. That doesn't mean, however, that all the individuals within the camp are clean." He threw her another sideways glance, seeming a bit anxious. Nervous maybe. Again, she wondered what had him on edge. "And we are talking about Cuba here."

"Castro?"

Bill shrugged again. "It *is* his island."

Erin fell silent. The temptation was there, taunting her

from the sidelines. She'd never been to Cuba, to the island she'd felt a part of all her life.

"Someone has to go in after him," Bill said, pulling her from her thoughts. "And you're the best person for the job."

She stopped again, searching his face for answers. Why her? Why now?

Bill answered her unspoken questions with a name. "Joe Roarke."

Erin sucked in a breath, then dropped onto a nearby bench, not caring that it was still damp from the earlier storm.

Joe Roarke.

She hadn't heard that name in years. He'd been with her in Cairo, her first and only overseas assignment, as her mentor and handler. He'd showed her the ropes, helped her recruit her first foreign agent, and taught her how to survive. Erin owed him her life.

"Roarke was supposed to file a preliminary report through our agent in Santa Clara after visiting the DFL camp," Bill said. "He never showed."

"And your man in Santa Clara doesn't know anything." Though she knew the answer before asking.

"He can't even make inquiries without risking exposure. If Roarke's been compromised . . ." Bill let his voice trail off, the possibilities hanging between them. With Joe possibly in enemy hands, the agent could sign his own death warrant with a single question.

"I see." Erin stood and started walking again, angry and suddenly unable to stay still.

Joe was probably dead. Or worse, alive and wishing he was dead. She shuddered, the weight of what she owed him resting heavily on her shoulders. Conflicting loyalties, to Joe and to her family, and anger at the CIA, tore at her.

The Agency was playing her. Again. As they'd done last year. They'd sent Bill, a friend, to recruit her and were using her loyalty to Joe Roarke to reel her in. They weren't even being subtle in their manipulation. She hated it, as well as herself for considering the mission.

Still, she didn't understand why they'd come to her. The CIA had other well-trained active officers to send into DFL. Even other officers who knew Joe and would willingly go in after him.

Stopping abruptly, she turned on Bill. "Why me?"

He looked away, guilt playing across his features. And she knew she was right. He'd been nervous, anxious, about this meeting.

"Why me, Bill?" she repeated. "There has to be a reason why they want me to go into Cuba rather than someone else."

He hesitated, sighed, then met her eyes. "You're right, there *is* something else. Some*one* else. Someone who solidifies your cover at the DFL camp."

Again, she waited, but only for a second this time. Her patience was gone, and she feared she knew the CIA's final card. "Who?"

"It's the head doctor at the DFL camp. Emilio Diaz. Your father."

CHAPTER SIX

Casa de la Rosa, Cuba

Tired, Dr. Emilio Diaz rubbed both hands over his face.

He'd had enough for one day. His eyes burned and his back and shoulders ached from hours of bending over a desk. He'd spent the afternoon on paperwork, filling out the endless DFL requisition forms and the equally numerous reports for the Cuban government.

Cuba had more doctors per capita than any other country in the world, close to six hundred per hundred thousand, but suffered from a severe shortage of medicine and medical equipment. His people were sick, and he had to beg for drugs from foreign governments and international aid organizations like DFL. Then he had to justify his requests to his own government.

It grated on his already frayed nerves.

Nor did it help that these would be the last DFL requisitions he would fill out, the last supplies they would send him. Pushing back from his desk, he stood, deserting his office and stepping out onto the second-floor balcony of Casa de la Rosa.

Once a great plantation, the surrounding land and

house had been confiscated by the Castro regime after the revolution. Emilio didn't know what had happened to the original owners, nor did he want to know. They might have escaped to Miami with the scores of others who'd fled the island as Castro scoured the land. Or they might be dead, too slow or too late to avoid his wrath. Either way, the land was now state-owned and leased to local farmers. Meanwhile, the house had stood empty and forsaken for years, a symbol of all that had been defeated, or, depending on your point of view, lost.

Then DFL had needed a location for its relief efforts after Hurricanes David and Frederic swept the island within weeks of each other in 1979. The government had given them Casa de la Rosa. It had been in bad shape, but the DFL team had managed. Something they'd learned from the Cubans, who were experts at making do.

That had been twenty-six years ago, and the DFL camp had grown up around the old plantation house. Emilio had watched it, first the repairs that had turned the house into a clinic, then the conversion of the barn for storage, office space, and eventually classrooms. In the early days the staff had used the mansion's second floor for their quarters. As their numbers grew, however, DFL had supplied large sleeping tents that resembled those used by the military. Then just last year, using DFL materials, the people of Santa Rosa had helped build cabins for the volunteers.

The best thing that DFL had brought, though, was access to equipment and drugs most medical facilities on the island lacked. Other international aid organizations had pulled out years ago, frustrated with the Cuban government's red tape and interference. DFL, however, had stayed. Largely due to Emilio's efforts.

Now, DFL was leaving Cuba as well.

Emilio had received the notice eight months ago. They had given him one year to shut down. He'd fought the decision, making multiple trips to the New York office to plead his case. It had done no good. The decision was final. They told him he should be satisfied that his efforts had kept DFL in Cuba years longer than many other aid organizations. Instead, if he allowed himself to dwell on it, it only angered him further.

Tonight, however, he was just tired.

He took a deep breath, willing his tired muscles to relax. This was his favorite time of day, when the island hovered between light and dark, bright heat and satin night. The earth held still, air thick and fragrant, light softening. Even the camp was quiet.

A pair of volunteers crossed the yard, speaking in hushed tones, as if they too hated to disturb the peace. They nodded as they passed him, heading toward the mess tent, where most of the other volunteers were already at dinner.

In the end, Emilio *had* found a way to save the clinic.

It had come in the form of Gregory Moss. A case of mutual need. Emilio needed money for medical supplies and equipment, and Moss needed the DFL facility. In saving his clinic, however, Emilio had damned himself. Of that, he had no doubt.

Another group of volunteers passed him on the way to dinner, and Emilio realized he was hungry. But he'd already decided he'd get something in town. Moss wouldn't like it. He insisted Emilio eat with the rest of

the staff and keep his ears open to their gossip. He suspected, however, that Moss's motives had more to do
with keeping track of Emilio himself than any concern
about the volunteers.

Moss trusted no one. Especially Emilio.

Deserting the porch, he descended the stairs, then
headed out of camp. He didn't much care what Moss
liked or didn't like. Tonight Emilio had to get away from
this place and the people who populated it. He needed
to forget DFL and their impending departure, and he
needed to forget Gregory Moss.

He passed a couple of men, smoking and lounging on
the rough wooden steps of the old caretaker's cottage.
Guards. Though they wore no uniforms and displayed
no weapons. They could be members of Castro's PNR
(Policía Nacional Revolucionaria) or some of Moss's
men. It amounted to the same thing. They watched, they
reported. The only difference was who they reported to,
though even that was questionable. For all Emilio knew,
Moss could be here at the bearded one's direction.

Emilio nodded as he passed the men, knowing they
wouldn't stop him. Not without a direct order from
Moss, who didn't dare pull the reigns too tight while he
still needed Emilio's facility.

Emilio wasn't sure how much longer he could put
up with Moss and his men. They dodged his every step,
watching over his shoulder and breathing down his
neck. They were the worst kind of parasites. Vultures.
Yet he had no one to blame but himself for their presence.

As he left the camp behind, he felt the tension of the
last few days start to ease.

Santa Rosa was a half mile down the road.

It was a small agricultural village, set at one end of a scenic valley. Behind it, the Sierra del Escambray, home of the revolutionary movement led by Castro and Che Guevara, rose dramatically. The townsfolk claimed that Castro and his followers had often come to Santa Rosa in those prerevolutionary days. Whether the story was true or not, Emilio couldn't say. But the distinction gave the residents a certain pride that they might not otherwise claim.

As Emilio got closer, he heard music. It was a bit early for the local music hall, but the musicians were warming up on the square. The classic Cuban rhythm—part Spanish, part African—called to him, drew him in, and offered to heal his weary soul.

This was worth saving, he reminded himself. His island, his people were worth any sacrifice on his part. Including cutting a deal with the devil himself.

On the outskirts of town, a group of children played baseball using a wadded-up roll of tape and a homemade bat. He stopped for a moment and watched, stung by their inventiveness and saddened by the necessity. None of the children's enthusiasm for the game was dimmed by the lack of equipment. But it cut Emilio deeply.

The Americans, and their attempt to punish Castro with their embargo, hurt only the people. Emilio's people. It was not just medicine or medical supplies that they lacked, but other necessities that made life easier. These children, and others like them, did not even have a simple baseball or bat to help usher in a summer night.

Then one of the children spotted him, and the game

was forgotten as they surrounded him. "Doctor, doctor," they called. "Where is the candy?"

Emilio's mood lifted at the sound of their innocent voices, and he slipped his hands into his pockets. "Candy? What candy? I have no candy for you. Run along now."

The children giggled, all too familiar with this game.

"Candy, candy," they chanted, bouncing up and down, not the least frightened by the frown he'd pasted on his face.

"Go away now," he said again. "There is no candy."

In response, they chanted louder. One of the little ones grabbed on to his arm, and Emilio's feigned displeasure evaporated. He couldn't resist the laughter that bubbled inside him, nor the pleasure he took in swinging the little girl up into the air. She squealed in delight. After setting her back on her feet, he pulled out a handful of hard candy from his pockets.

"Here, is this what you want?"

The children cheered him.

"One each." He doled out the treats, pleased that none of them snatched more than their share. He'd bought a large supply of the candy the last time he'd visited Miami, but it wouldn't last forever. When it was gone, he'd find some other sweet for these children, because sugar was the one thing Cuba had in abundance. For now, though, the children enjoyed the novelty of American candy, brightly colored and individually wrapped.

"Teresa." He motioned to one of the older girls. "Where is your little sister? Where is Maria? Still with the cold?"

"Sí."

"Take this." He handed the child a bright red candy. "Tell your *madre* I said it was okay and have her bring Maria to the clinic tomorrow."

"Gracias." Teresa beamed. "I will make sure she gets it."

"And . . ."

"I will tell *Madre* to bring Maria *mañana*."

"Bien."

Finally, with the candy gone, and the night too close to continue their game, the children drifted away. Home. Back to their small, run-down houses and apartments. With their departure, the depression that had been creeping up on him all day welled up again.

Hands back in his pockets, Emilio pushed on, passing the group of musicians on the square. They'd already gathered a small audience, and several people waved to him as he passed, but he kept moving.

In the town's only restaurant and bar, he took one of the back tables and ordered rum and a plate of food. Then he sat with his back to the wall, lost. The rum came first, then the food, and he ordered another drink. The music started, and couples took to the floor.

That's when he saw the two men. He recognized them immediately, though he didn't know their names. They stood just inside the door, searching the dark, crowded room. Emilio felt the tension creep back into his shoulders and eased himself from his chair. He could slip out the back door, and they might not see him.

Then, before he could move, one of them caught his eye. Nodded. Said something to his companion. And they started toward him.

Emilio forgot his attempt to run. He could not escape Moss's men. Or his own fate.

CHAPTER SEVEN

Miami, Florida

Erin needed to run, to clear her head so she could think.

Instead, she walked with Bill back to the parking lot, her thoughts jumbled and unfocused. Some part of her knew he was still talking, trying to convince her or give instructions. She didn't know. Or care. Her thoughts had taken a different path.

They were with her father, with Emilio Diaz.

For twenty-seven years, she'd tried to put him out of her mind. Yet sometimes at night, just before sleep claimed her, she could still hear his voice with its soft melodic accent. Faded and muted by time, those memories rose up now unbidden.

When she was little, Emilio would put her to bed, telling her stories about Cuba, always in his native tongue. She'd fall asleep, his lyrical words in her ears, the image of a tropical island paradise behind her closed eyelids. She had adored him. Then, he'd left.

Now the CIA was offering her the chance to ask him why.

"I know it doesn't give you much time," Bill was saying.

Erin realized she'd totally shut him out and forced herself to refocus on his words.

"I need an answer by midnight," he said.

Around them, the Florida night crept in, the light fading and the sweet smell of night-blooming jasmine stirring the air. It must be close to seven. Not much time to decide.

Less than five hours.

In the years since her father had left, she hadn't seen or heard from him. She knew he'd returned to Cuba, but that was it. She realized she hadn't even known whether he was still alive. Until now. She had so many unanswered questions. How could she turn down the chance to see him again?

How could she not?

Claire was doing well, but she was still fragile. How could Erin expect Marta to take care of her alone?

"Hire someone if you need help at home," Bill said, obviously well prepared for her every argument and hesitation. "Or we'll find someone for you. Someone qualified. And the Company will cover all expenses."

As if having a stranger in the house would make everything okay for Claire. The stability she'd found since Erin had moved them back to Miami had come from family, from living with Erin, Janie, and Marta. How much damage would it do if Erin suddenly started running off to do the CIA's bidding?

No. Erin stopped that thought.

She wouldn't be returning to the life of an active CIA officer, taking off at a moment's notice whenever the Agency demanded. This was a onetime deal. For Joe Roarke. Dead maybe. Or not. Either way, Erin owed him her life. And she wasn't sure she could trust someone else to find out what had happened and bring him home. And there was her father, a hazy image beckoning to her from the past, her emotions mixed and unsettled at the thought of seeing him again.

"We have a narrow window of opportunity to get you into the DFL camp," Bill said. "One of their teachers has just returned to the States due to a family emergency. You'll take her place."

"Teaching?"

"English. To children from the nearby town. It's one of the things DFL does."

She couldn't digest it all, much less make any decisions.

Again, her thoughts slipped to her father. She had spent most of her life suppressing not only her memories of him, but also the questions and the hurt. And the anger. He had left his family without looking back. She wanted to know why, and might never get another chance like this.

"We have no reason to believe . . ." Bill hesitated. "We don't know that your father is in any way involved with Roarke's disappearance."

Erin knew he wouldn't tell her even if the CIA did suspect her father. Not when they wanted her to go in, dig around, and possibly expose him as a conspirator. Better to let her discover the truth for herself.

"Of course." Bill slipped his hands once again into his

pockets, obviously uncomfortable with the situation. "If Diaz is involved . . ."

"You expect me to ignore the fact he's my father." It wasn't a question. They were playing one connection against the other: her loyalty to Roarke against her confused feelings about the father who'd deserted her.

Bill's jaw tightened, and she knew she was right. First and foremost he would always be a Company man. Complete the mission, no matter the cost. And don't let a little thing like blood ties get in the way. He may as well have said it aloud.

In a way it surprised her that they'd come to her at all, even with all the factors that made her a good candidate. When it came to family, people were unpredictable. And she'd already proven herself capable of breaking the rules when it came to hers.

Of course, she had none of the normal feelings for her father. How could she when she didn't know him, wouldn't recognize him if she saw him on the street? Something the CIA knew only too well. They were gambling on her sense of justice, and her loyalty to Roarke, to override whatever lingering attachment she still had to the man who'd once been her father.

"There's a charter flight to Havana at noon tomorrow," Bill said. "We need you on that plane." They'd reached his car and stopped, and he looked her over, an expression of genuine concern in his eyes. "Are you okay?"

It set her off, the fresh roll of anger finally clearing her head. She'd like it better if he stopped pretending to care, to worry about how she was taking this. He was here, following orders like a good little soldier.

"Does it really matter? As long as I accept this mission?"

She saw a flash of hurt in his eyes, but it was quickly squelched. "We all do what we have to."

"Spare me the platitudes, Bill. I've heard them before."

"Then you—"

She cut him off. "I'll let you know what I decide." She needed to think. She had the facts. She would make her decision, and nothing else he had to say would make any difference one way or the other.

For a moment he didn't say anything, and she thought he'd make another plea for understanding, for friendship. Instead, he handed her a blank business card with a number written in black ink. "I'll be waiting to hear from you."

She nodded, and he hesitated before saying, "It was good to see you, Erin." Again, there was that flash of regret. "No matter the circumstances."

Erin backed away, not ready to grant him the absolution he sought for his part in this. Besides, her mind was already racing down paths she didn't want to travel. And as she watched Bill pull away, she turned to her car and the duffel bag she kept in the trunk. The beach was a short five-minute drive away. She needed to move.

To run.

At the best of times, it kept her fit. At the worst, it kept her sane.

CHAPTER EIGHT

Miami, Florida

By 7:30, Alec knew Erin wasn't going to show.

He sat at a polished horseshoe bar, nursing a beer and waiting. Like dozens of other restaurants along the Intracoastal, The Wharf perched at the edge of the water, its dock catering to a steady stream of boaters stopping in for a drink or a casual meal. From the outside tables, the restaurant rose in three levels, each farther from the canal and more protected in case of inclement weather. The bar was situated on the top level, and thus, always open.

Alec liked the place.

It felt tropical, relaxed, and he'd looked forward to spending an evening with Erin. Casual conversation. Banter. In this kind of environment, with people around, they would be easy with each other. She'd lower her guard and let herself be a woman. Afterward, they'd go back to his hotel and make love. It would only be later that she would shut down. Erin wasn't afraid of sex, but true intimacy? That was something else entirely.

None of that, however, was going to happen tonight.

Maybe he'd known she wouldn't show from the moment he'd seen the stranger in the parking lot. The guy had CIA written all over him, and he'd come to pull Erin back into his world.

Alec ordered another beer.

Okay, so maybe he had known that sooner or later she'd end up back with the CIA, in one capacity or another. She was too well trained, too good at covert operations for the suits at Langley to let her go—even if they *had* let her resign. They'd use her again, and she'd let them. Because a part of her loved the action, the danger that working for the CIA promised.

Knowing that it had been inevitable, however, didn't make it any easier to swallow. Alec had thought, at least, he'd have more time with her. Time to heal the distance between them. Time to explore his feelings for her and convince her she had them for him as well. Time to make her understand that they were stronger together than apart. Now the Agency would put her in harm's way again, and they might not have any time at all.

At 8:00, he settled up with the bartender.

Outside, the temperature hovered in the low nineties, and a breeze came in off the ocean, thick and salty. Though still warm, the heat was less intense without the sun. He climbed into his car, rolled down the windows, and considered his next move.

A part of him wanted to say the hell with it. He'd head to the airport and catch the next flight back to Virginia. The CIA was back in Erin's life, and whatever they wanted from her, it was none of his business. He had his own problems, his own bureaucracy to appease with a report of how he'd let two children die before he'd found them. His own demons to wrestle to the ground.

He should leave Erin to hers.

Then his cell rang, the sound jarring in the car's stuffy interior. Flipping open the phone, he recognized the Miami exchange. "Erin?"

"I'm sorry," she said, her voice distant and hollow.

Relief washed over him, and he realized he'd been worried about her. Erin could take care of herself, but who knew what enemies she'd made while working for the CIA? No one was invulnerable, and he had only her word that the guy in the parking lot was a friend. "Are you all right?"

He heard her hesitation. "I'm fine."

"Are you sure? You don't sound—"

"I'm fine," she repeated. "Just a little tired."

He closed his eyes, nodding slightly as he rested his forehead against one balled fist. So he'd been right. The CIA wanted something from her, something that had put a strain in her voice and more distance between them. He wanted to ask her about it, but knew she wouldn't tell him anything—especially over the phone.

"I'm sorry I missed dinner," she said again, trying to sound upbeat. "I was looking forward to it. But . . ." Again that hesitation. "Things took longer than I expected."

He didn't know how to respond to that. She was talking about missing dinner, when the problem ran so much deeper. They seemed to want different things, from their lives and from each other. She wanted sex, he wanted intimacy. She wanted the thrill of physical danger, and he wanted her safe at his side. He wanted to love her, while she continued to hold back, protecting her heart in a way she'd never think to safeguard her life.

"Are you still at the restaurant?" she asked.

Alec glanced back at the building. "I just left."

"I'm really sorry, I—"

"It's no big deal, Erin." He put a nonchalance in his voice he didn't feel. "You got delayed. It happens. Besides," he tried to make his voice light, "I showed up unannounced, remember?"

"You did." She laughed lightly. "Another night, then?"

"Sure." There was an awkward silence as he searched for something else to say. "Where are you now?"

Another brief pause. "The beach. I needed to clear my head."

If he hadn't already known something was wrong, he would know now. For Erin, running was as much therapy as exercise. "Will you be home later?"

"Yes, but—"

"We need to talk."

"Alec . . ."

He could almost see her shaking her head. He didn't let her finish. "I'll see you in a little while," he said, then broke the connection before she could voice another objection.

He waited, wondering if she'd call back, while the temptation to leave Miami nudged him once again. Instead, he started the car, and it seemed to move of its own volition in the opposite direction. Southwest. Toward Kendall. Toward the house Erin had bought when she'd moved her family back to Miami. It was probably hopeless, but he had to try to stop her from accepting the CIA's offer.

CHAPTER NINE

Miami, Florida

It was after 10:00 by the time Erin arrived home.

Alec was waiting for her. He sat in a white rental car in front of her house, while behind lowered shades, light leaked from the windows.

She'd been halfway through her run, two miles along packed sand from where she'd parked, when she'd stopped in her tracks, guilty and angry at herself. Her conversation with Bill, and the resulting turmoil of emotions, had driven Alec from her thoughts. All she could think of was her father. And Joe. It had only been after her head had begun to clear that she remembered her promise to meet Alec at The Wharf.

Regret struck her, as it had earlier.

If the CIA had waited one more day to come after her, she would have spent the evening with Alec. It was a tantalizing thought, tempting, along with the knowledge that she did not have to send him away. The night wasn't over. And she wanted to see him, for a myriad of reasons she didn't want to examine too closely. She'd welcome the feel of his arms around her, relaxing for a few minutes in their circle and drawing from their strength. Tonight, even more than before.

However, that wasn't why he was here. Not anymore.

On campus, she'd practically admitted Bill was CIA, and even if she hadn't, Alec would have figured it out. Plus, she knew he'd picked up on her agitation over the phone. It amazed her how well he'd gotten to know her in such a short time. It also frightened her. So obviously, he knew something was going on. The only question was how much to tell him.

There was, of course, the security issue, but that wouldn't stop her. Alec was an FBI agent, with a security clearance that matched her own. The Company would claim he had no "need to know," but considering her involvement with him, that was an arguable point. Besides, she realized, she trusted Alec more than she trusted Bill Jensen or anyone connected to the CIA. Alec would not betray her. Or use her.

Finally, she got out of her car. As she crossed the yard, he climbed out of his as well and leaned against the door.

"What do they want from you?" he asked without preamble.

She stopped a few feet from him and folded her arms. "You know I can't tell you that."

"You can." There was an edge to his voice, a challenge. "Or I'll find out on my own."

He probably could, too. At least he could find out enough. He had extensive resources, both within and outside the FBI, that would get him close to the truth.

Still, she didn't like being backed into a corner, and although a few minutes ago she'd considered telling him everything, her own stubbornness reared its head. Lifting her hands, palms out, she said, "Don't do this, Alec."

"Do what?" He spoke quietly, though it did little to diminish the impact of his words. "Worry that the Company will suck you back into their world?"

"You don't have a lot of room to talk, you know. You're not exactly a Sunday school teacher yourself." She went on the offensive, her automatic defense. "But since you're a man, that makes it okay, right?"

"Don't play that game, Erin." He kept his voice low, not rising to the bait. "That wasn't a sexist comment, and you know it. My work is far less dangerous than whatever they want from you. Besides, they're using you, just like they did before."

She knew he was right, but they were offering her something she wanted as well. Her father. "No one's forcing me. I can always say no."

"But will you?"

She hesitated, lifting her chin to look him in the eye. She didn't need to justify herself to him. He had no hold on her.

"*Are* you going to tell them no, Erin?"

She looked away, suddenly angry. With him. With herself.

Until that moment, she hadn't acknowledged her decision. Not even to herself. Or maybe there had never been any question of what she'd do. Maybe she'd known from the moment she'd seen Bill in the UM parking lot that she'd go back to the CIA.

And yes, she was going to Cuba.

She would find Joe and bring him home, safely if she could, but home either way. And she'd confront her father and ask him where he'd been all these years. The fact that tipped the scales, however, the self-understanding that bothered and angered her, was that she wanted to go, wanted, no needed, the excitement of going back undercover.

"You're accepting the assignment," Alec stated, and she heard the controlled anger in his voice. "Aren't you."

She looked at him again. "Yes."

"What about them?" He nodded toward the house. "Are you just going to leave them alone?"

"Go to hell." Spinning on her heels, she started toward the house. She wasn't going to let him put a guilt trip on her. She did that well enough on her own.

Alec grabbed her arm. "Erin."

"Don't," she swung around, breaking his hold with a defensive sweep of her free arm, "touch me."

He backed away, hands up. "Okay. That was uncalled for."

"You think so?" Sarcasm dripped from her voice, and for a moment she glared at him, her own fear about leaving Claire in Marta's care stirring her temper.

Until she saw the concern in Alec's eyes.

She forced herself to relax, to ease off. He'd only voiced what she'd been thinking since she'd first seen Bill Jensen. Although Claire seemed to be adjusting well, no one knew if her current stability was real, or how long it would last.

"I'm going to bring someone in to help Marta," she said, though she owed Alec no explanation.

He looked ready to argue further, then nodded, looking away. When he finally met her gaze again, resignation had settled on his face. "What are you going to tell them?"

She sighed, tired, and relieved that he seemed ready to let it go. "Just enough."

"Then tell me, too." He softened his voice. "Please."

She studied him, knowing she shouldn't say anything more. Bill, however, had opened this door by showing up at the wrong time. Unintentional or not, it couldn't be undone. Alec already knew too much.

"They've found my father," she said, her voice catching on an unwelcome tightening in her chest.

"Your father?" Concern and doubt etched Alec's features. "I didn't know he was missing."

"Only since I was five." She looked away, unable to meet Alec's gaze. She never talked about her father, had never told anyone how badly his desertion had hurt. "One morning I woke up, and he was just gone." She pressed her lips together, shrugged, as if it had meant nothing. Though she expected she wasn't fooling Alec. "I haven't heard from him since."

There was a pause while Alec said nothing. Then, reaching out, he traced the line of her cheek and lifted her chin until his eyes caught hers. "I'm sorry, Erin."

His gentleness was her undoing. Tears burned her eyes, unchecked, almost unnoticed. Until Alec stepped closer, and she instinctively backed, wrapping her arms tightly about her waist. If he touched her again, she knew she would lose what little control she had left.

A flash of hurt crossed his features, but he didn't push it. After a moment he cleared his throat, then asked,

"What about your mother? Didn't she give you any explanation?"

Erin laughed abruptly, bitterly. "Mom refused to talk about him, other than to say he'd returned to Cuba and wasn't coming home." She took a deep breath, determined to regain control. For years she'd protected herself with anger. It worked now, as always. "About a year later, Mom married Claire's father, and it was as if Emilio Diaz had never existed." Erin shrugged, almost convincing herself she didn't care. "Mom even had my last name legally changed to Baker."

Alec leaned back against the car, obviously thinking about her revelation. When he spoke again, his voice was distant, quiet, like he wasn't quite done mulling it all over. "And the CIA told you where to find him."

She hesitated. If she answered his question, no matter how she phrased it, she'd be stepping over the line. According to the CIA, she'd be giving Alec information about her mission he had no right to know. She told him anyway.

"He's a doctor, working for an organization called DFL, Doctors For Life." Pausing, she took the last step. "In Cuba."

His eyes acknowledged what she'd just told him, where the CIA was sending her.

"I have two weeks before the fall semester begins," she said. "If I don't go now, I won't be able to go again."

He nodded, and silence settled between them like the heavy night air.

Erin spoke first. "Go back to Quantico, Alec. I'll call you when I return."

"*If* you return." Again, it was as if he was thinking aloud.

"I have to do this, Alec." She paused, honesty winning out. "No, that's not true. I want to do this."

He refocused on her. "That doesn't mean I have to like it."

"No," she said. "It doesn't. But it does mean you have to accept it. Or," she hesitated, "walk away."

He went very still, and she could only guess at the thoughts behind his frown. Maybe this was what he'd been waiting for, the point when he'd finally disengage from her life.

"Is that what you want, Erin?" he asked, as if reading her thoughts. "Do you want me to walk away?"

She could say yes and be done with it, with him. But the word, the simple one-syllable word that would send him away, caught in her throat. She couldn't say it. Because if he left, he'd take a part of her with him.

"No." She released the breath she hadn't realized she'd been holding. "I don't want you to walk away."

He didn't move, didn't respond, standing perfectly still as if weighing his options. To go. Or stay. Then he reached for her, stepping closer while slipping an arm around her waist.

Erin's breath again caught in her throat, but she didn't fight as he pulled her flush against the long line of his body. She felt caught, unable to resist. He lowered his mouth to hers, at first a mere brushing of lips, a soft petal stroke that banished her resolve. Her resistance.

Why had she fought him so long?

Then, with a suddenness that vanquished all thought, he tightened his hold and deepened the kiss, softness turning to urgency. Need.

Her response was instantaneous. Sliding her arms

around his neck, she drew him closer, revealing more with this kiss than she could say with words. If he asked, she'd put off going inside with news of her upcoming departure. She'd go with him back to his hotel. Everything else could wait. She wanted him. Not just now, but in whatever future they could find together. The realization hit her hard, as his kiss melted the cold places inside her, softened her with a desire she'd never known. The desire to love a man for more than one night.

Finally, he broke away, slowly, reluctantly, without releasing his hold on her waist. And with his free hand, he reached up and touched her cheek again, just one light caress with the back of his fingers. She waited for the invitation, for him to ask her back to his room. Instead, he said simply, "Well then, I'll be here waiting when you get back."

CHAPTER TEN

Casa de la Rosa, Cuba

Emilio was needed immediately. A medical emergency.

That's what Moss's men had claimed in order to get him out of the café without a fuss. Although he would have gone with them, anyway. What choice had he?

When you dealt with the devil, you didn't argue with his soldiers.

Outside, they climbed into an American Jeep, a rare vehicle for this island, and another indication of Moss's favor with the Cuban authorities. Driving toward the DFL camp, Emilio expected them to turn into Casa de la Rosa. They passed it instead.

"Where are we going?" he demanded, the first niggling of fear nipping at him.

"The lab."

"What? That's ridiculous. Everything I need is at the clinic."

The man shot Emilio an impatient look. "Moss's orders."

Emilio stopped asking questions. Obviously the medical emergency, if there really was one, had to do with someone or some *thing* Moss wanted kept hidden. Either that, or he no longer needed Emilio. After all, he had the facility, and he had Jean Taylor. Killing Emilio would require some explanation, but would it really cause enough of a stir to derail the man's plans? Emilio didn't know.

A half mile past the entrance to Casa de la Rosa, they turned off the road. One of the men jumped out and cleared away a camouflage screen of brush that hid an old, overgrown mountain trail. They pulled under the trees, waited as the man replaced the concealing foliage and rejoined them, then started off again, navigating through the dark woods.

Emilio had known Moss's men used an alternate route to supply the lab, but he'd never been on it himself. His path to the lab from the camp was more direct, and by default, much too visible for Moss's purposes.

Finally, they stopped behind the building covering the entrance to the lab. The driver stayed with the Jeep while the second man led Emilio inside and down the stairs.

As always, the presence of the lab jarred Emilio.

A despicable reminder of the bargain he'd made, it shouldn't exist here, so near a place devoted to healing. Before he could go further with that thought, however, the guard led him past the glassed-off room, down the hall to a section of the underground facility Emilio had never seen.

They entered a passkey-protected area, obviously meant for storage, which had been turned into a make-shift examining room. Emilio didn't want to think too hard about the room's usual purpose. Dr. Jean Taylor did not practice medicine, did not treat patients. And this was her domain.

Inside, two battered men lay on gurneys.

Jean Taylor hovered over the one farthest from the door, taping his ribs. Looking up, she nodded toward the first table. "That one's critical."

Emilio moved to the man's side, observing his pale, dia-phoretic face. What was she doing binding cracked or broken ribs when a man's life hung in the balance?

"Looks like massive internal injuries, most likely a lacerated liver or ruptured spleen," Jean said from across the room. "He's not going to make it."

Anger curled in Emilio's gut at her callowness. Jean Taylor was brilliant, but totally void of compassion. She'd already declared this man dead, though he still breathed. Whether she believed that attempting to save him wasn't worth her time and the ego blow if she failed, or whether she was simply incapable of human feelings, Emilio couldn't venture to guess. He hated to agree with her, hated her coldness, hated that she was probably right.

The man had taken a beating. His face was a mottled pulp of bruises and cuts, but it was the other symptoms that foretold death. Pressing his fingers to the man's neck, Emilio felt the man's pulse, rapid but weak.

"What happened?" he asked while running his hands over the injured man's chest. He had two, maybe three broken ribs.

"A bar fight?" Jean answered with a half laugh.

Emilio knew better and ignored her. He'd moved on to the man's abdomen, which was rock-hard, a sign of peritonitis, internal bleeding. The man groaned, pain reaching him through the fog of unconsciousness.

"How long ago?" Emilio asked.

This time the guard answered. "About an hour. In Santa Clara."

Emilio shot the man an accusing glare. "Why didn't you take him to the hospital there?"

"Don't be stupid, Emilio," Jean said. "Moss wanted these men here. Both of them."

He glanced back at her, barely containing his anger. "This man needs to be in a hospital."

She shrugged. "So he does."

"I don't have the equipment to save him." With the proper treatment the man might have survived his injuries. "He needs to be in an operating room, not in some damn corner of your lab."

"He's not exactly an innocent, Emilio." Finished with her patient, Jean snapped off her latex gloves and tossed them in a refuse bin. "He does work for Moss."

Emilio glanced at the man she'd chosen to treat and recognized him immediately. They'd talked two, maybe three days ago. He didn't belong here, didn't work for Moss.

Following the direction of his gaze, and maybe his thoughts, Jean added, "Don't worry, he's alive. I gave him a sedative. Though considering he's responsible for that," she nodded toward Emilio's patient, "I expect his life span will be rather short."

Her hard words snapped Emilio back to the dying man. "He needs fluids. What do you have here? Saline? Ringers lactate? Either will work. And I need tubing and—"

"What's the point? You can't save him."

"Damn it, Jean. Get me what I need."

She sighed and stepped over to a supply cabinet.

Emilio turned back to his patient, keeping one hand on the pulse-point at his neck. "Hang in there," he said. Behind him, he heard Jean rifling through the shelves. "Hurry." Though he knew she was right. It was too late, had been too late the moment they'd decided to bring the man here rather than the hospital in Santa Clara. As Emilio waited for her, the pulse beneath his fingers slowed, slipping toward stillness. Then stopped.

Emilio felt the loss like a blow to the gut.

Turning, he saw Jean standing beside him, everything he needed for an IV drip in her hands. "I told you it was a waste of time," she said.

His anger flared, and he barely resisted the urge to

throw her against the wall. She was a cold, heartless bitch who deserved to die. One move toward her, however, and the guard at the door would end Emilio's life. Moss might need Emilio's facility, but he needed Jean Taylor's brilliance more.

So with an effort, Emilio turned away and walked to the other gurney, where a man still lived. If not for long. "He was here the other day."

Jean said nothing.

"I talked to him," Emilio added absently, wondering about the man's involvement with Moss. "He told me he was a photographer." Which must have been a lie, or at least Emilio hoped it was a lie. He couldn't stomach the idea of another innocent death. There would be enough of that in the days and weeks to come.

Behind him, he sensed the door open, but he didn't look up.

"And you believed him?" asked a new voice to the room.

Now Emilio did look, a chill wrapping itself around his spine. He'd known and dealt with dangerous men most of his life. Small, angry men. Weak and power-crazed. One could not live in Cuba and avoid them. However, the man standing in the doorway was a different kind of horror. Totally sane. Totally ruthless.

Gregory Moss.

"He's not a photographer," Moss said. "He works for the American government, either military, DEA, maybe even CIA."

Emilio didn't believe it. Moss saw enemies where none existed. "How do you know that?"

"Does it matter?"

Yes, it mattered. Life always mattered. And if Moss believed what he said, the injured man's life was over. Whether there was truth to the accusation or not.

"I'm moving up the schedule," Moss said, oblivious to Emilio's internal turmoil, or simply not caring. "We're going out at the end of next week."

"What?" Jean stepped forward. "You can't—"

Moss turned those cold eyes on her. "You have a problem with that, Dr. Taylor?"

"You promised me three more months."

"Things change." He nodded toward the unconscious man. "*He* just changed them."

"I'm not ready."

"Then I suggest you get ready." He turned toward the door, stopped, glanced back at the man on the gurney, then focused on Jean once again. "You have five days. Don't waste them."

DAY TWO

CHAPTER ELEVEN

Miami, Florida

Alec awoke.

It seemed like barely minutes since he'd stretched out on the stiff hotel bed. Opening his eyes, he glanced at the bedside clock and its iridescent numbers glowing yellow-green in the dark room. 5:00 a.m. He'd been asleep all of four and a half hours. Not the minutes it felt like, but not nearly long enough, either.

Damn.

He rubbed a hand over his eyes, the ghost of a dream still chasing him. He'd been in a mist-shrouded forest. And Erin, a gossamer shadow in the trees, had called to him even as she ran in the opposite direction, leaving him alone and disoriented. He didn't need a degree in psychology to interpret the eerie scenario, or to know he'd gotten all the sleep he was going to get for the night.

He took a shower, banishing the last of the dream, then ordered breakfast. Still, it was too early to make his first call of the morning. At one point during the sleep-deprived night, his thoughts had traveled down paths they shouldn't take, forming a plan he should just forget. So at 6:30, he couldn't wait any longer. He dialed the number for his partner's home in Virginia.

On the fourth ring she picked up, sounding half asleep. "Cathy Hart."

"Did I wake you?"

"Shit, Donovan." Her voice went from sleepy to grumpy with two words. "What the hell time is it?"

"Sorry. I wanted to catch you before you headed into the office."

"Well, you succeeded, so what do you want? And where the hell are you, anyway?" He started to reply, but she cut him off. "Never mind, I know where you are. How *is* Erin?"

Alec laughed lightly. Cathy knew him too well. "She's good," he lied. "In fact, that's why I'm calling. I'm going to take a few days off and spend some time here."

"I'm happy for you." Her voice dripped with sarcasm. "So that's what you woke me to tell me?"

"Well—"

"Wait," she was on a roll now, and there would be no stopping her, "you know Schultz is going to want your report on Seattle. You're not going to ask me to do that for you, are you?"

"No. I'm heading over to the Miami field office in a little while, and I'll write up the report from there. But I do need you to cover the face-to-face with Schultz."

She sighed. "He's not going to be happy about that."

"Hey, he likes you better than me anyway."

"That's exactly why he'll want to hear from me. He enjoys torturing you."

Alec laughed again. "You're probably right."

Schultz had a love/hate relationship with his top agent.

On the one hand, he considered Alec a pain in the neck, a prima donna who demanded and got resources other agents couldn't touch. However, Alec's case success rate made Schultz look good. So they both knew Schultz would put up with a lot.

"So," Alec said, "will you cover for me?"

She sighed, again. "You owe me for this one. Big-time."

"I owe you more than one." He grinned. "Thanks."

"You're welcome." Her voice softened. "Just promise me one thing, Alec."

"Anything."

"Promise me you're going to get a little R&R while you're down there. That you and Erin aren't going to be getting into any . . ." she paused, maybe searching for the right word, ". . . trouble."

"Sure." He felt a bit guilty about deceiving her. "No trouble. I promise. And I'll let Erin know as well."

Cathy laughed shortly. "Okay, then. I'll handle Schultz."

Alec hung up, knowing it was better that he'd lied rather than involve Cathy in his plans. Last year she'd climbed out on a limb for him when he'd let Erin become involved in the Cody Sanders case. He'd sworn when it was over, he'd never put her in that position again.

Ten minutes later he was in his car, heading north.

Miami's FBI field office was located on Second Avenue in North Miami Beach. Under the best conditions, it was a thirty-minute drive from Alec's Coral Gables Hotel. Instead, it took him close to an hour. He didn't even want to think about making the drive during the week, when rush-hour traffic would be at its worst. He'd have to move to a hotel closer to the FBI location. Or, if he was smart, head for Virginia where he belonged.

When it came to Erin, however, he'd never done the smart thing.

As he pulled into the parking lot adjacent to the building, a sense of déjà vu washed over him. A few years ago he'd been called in to help with a serial kidnapping case. After ten intense days of searching for the fourth missing teenager in as many months, they'd found all four girls alive. It had been one of those cases that had kept him from quitting.

Now, he was about to call in a marker or two.

Inside, he showed his badge to security and told them he was there to see Special Agent Mathews, the man who'd been the lead agent on the kidnapping case. After verifying Alec's identity, the security guard gave him directions to Mathews's office. Evidently the guard had called ahead as well, because Mathews met Alec halfway.

"Donovan." He grabbed Alec's hand and pumped it. "What brings you to the Sunshine State? Don't tell me we've misplaced another kid?" Though said in a joking manner, a trace of worry shadowed Mathews's eyes.

Alec smiled to reassure him. "Not this time."

"Great to hear." There was actual relief in his smile, and his jovial manner became real. "Come on, I just brewed a fresh pot of coffee." He led Alec down the hall, waiting until they were both settled behind closed doors, cupping steaming mugs, before asking the inevitable question. "So, what can I do for you?"

"I need a desk and computer for a few hours." The Miami field office consisted of over seven hundred special agents and support personnel. There would be a vacant office or two.

Mathews sipped at his coffee, waiting no doubt for some explanation. Alec offered none.

"Sure," Mathews said finally. "One of my team members is out for a couple of weeks. You can have her desk."

"I appreciate it."

"Is there anything else I can help you with?" It was another request for information, which Alec wasn't ready to supply.

"Maybe later."

Mathews seemed ready to say something else, but evidently thought better of it. "Okay, then. I'll show you to your new office."

A few minutes later, Alec sat behind the desk of Special Agent Georgia Reed, currently vacationing somewhere in Mexico.

As he'd promised Cathy, he put together his Seattle report first thing. He did it quickly, refusing to let himself feel anything about those three futile weeks of searching. Just put down the facts, he told himself, and extrapolate his conclusions, like he'd done a hundred times before for finished cases. The ones that ended well. And the others.

With that out of the way, he was free to do what he'd come for. That was, find out what the FBI had on Emilio Diaz.

Erin had claimed she hadn't seen her father in over twenty-five years. Alec wanted to know what the man had been up to, how and what the CIA knew about him, and why they'd used him as leverage to send her into Cuba.

Yet Alec hesitated.

A part of him realized he was about to tread on dangerous ground. Once he started looking into Diaz, he'd be moving from concern to interference. If he and Erin were going to have any kind of long-term relationship, he couldn't go digging around whenever the CIA came calling. Because if she survived, they would come calling again. And again.

Yet he couldn't leave it alone, couldn't walk away without knowing what she was up against. Besides, he rationalized, he was just going to take a look at a few files. Nothing more.

So, with a few keystrokes, he crossed the line.

What he found didn't surprise him. The FBI had an extensive folder on Diaz. The basic stats read like those of a thousand other refugees who'd fled to the States in the wake of the Cuban revolution. His father, Carlos, had been a wealthy landowner in the Santa Clara area, east of Havana. Sugar plantation country. In 1960 he'd lost everything when Castro nationalized his land. He and his family had just barely escaped to Miami with their lives. Emilio had been sixteen.

Like so many other Cuban refugees, they'd quickly adapted to life in their new country. With the help of federal aid, Carlos started a restaurant in Little Havana and prospered. Determined to see his son educated, he sent Emilio off to the University of Florida in Gainesville. In 1966 the young man graduated in the top 5 percent of his class with a degree in biology. The following fall he started medical school at the University of Miami. By this time Carlos's business had taken off, and he prided himself on sending his only son to the expensive private school.

Then in 1972, after Emilio had completed his medical training, he met and married Elizabeth Baker, a blond, blue-eyed beauty queen from Fort Lauderdale. Two years later they had a daughter: Erin Josephine, born November 6, 1974.

That's when the Diazes' file became more interesting, and probably when Elizabeth's world fell apart. She almost certainly must have expected her life to take a different course from the one it followed. She'd snared herself a doctor, an ambitious man who would support her in style. Or so she must have believed.

Instead, all of their lives changed in 1979.

In the wake of Hurricanes David and Frederic's rage across the Caribbean, Emilio closed down his private practice, joined DFL, and went into Cuba with the DFL relief effort. That's also when Emilio Diaz had been put on the FBI's Watch List.

CHAPTER TWELVE

En route—Cuba

Erin hated flying.

Whether in a big commercial liner or a small commuter flight like the one she was on now, it didn't matter. She would rather be almost anywhere else.

It wasn't so much that she was afraid as she hated the loss of control. Putting her life in someone else's hands went against every instinct she possessed. Unfortunately, there was no choice. In the twenty-first century, flying was a fact of life she couldn't avoid. So she dealt with it. She closed her eyes and feigned indifferent sleep while consciously avoiding the white-knuckle clutching of other unhappy travelers. Then she imagined herself somewhere else, preferably running on a long stretch of empty beach.

The exercise usually worked.

As far as she knew, Joe Roarke had been the only one who'd ever figured it out. While working together in Cairo, they'd been called back to Langley for an emergency meeting. They'd hopped a military transport to Germany, then a commercial jet back to the States. It had been a long, arduous trip, and evidently her iron control had slipped. When they finally landed at Dulles, Joe had suggested she get a pilot's license.

"At least that way," he'd said, with all the rye humor she'd come to expect from him, "you'll have the illusion of control. You can reassure yourself by knowing you could take over for any pilot you decide isn't doing a good enough job."

"You're real funny," she'd responded before walking away.

Still, joke or not, getting a pilot's license wasn't a bad idea. Except it involved more flying. A catch-22.

Fortunately, Havana was a quick one-hour flight from Miami.

As usual, Erin put her head back and closed her eyes. Instead of a calming beachfront, however, her thoughts slid back to the night before.

Breaking the news to Claire and Marta had been much easier than Erin had expected. She'd feared resistance. After all, they had plans for the weekend. Claire, however, seemed genuinely thrilled that Erin had the opportunity to reconnect with her estranged father. Which made her wonder if she'd been worrying about her sister for nothing. Maybe Claire was stronger than any of them knew. As for Marta, Erin sensed the other woman's suspicions, but she, too, agreed this was an opportunity Erin couldn't pass up.

Still, Erin felt a streak of guilt. Though she hadn't lied to her family, she hadn't told them the whole truth, either. Which brought her to Alec, and their conversation on the front lawn.

The memory settled uneasily, as did her feelings for him.

Last fall in Virginia, when the man who'd kidnapped her sister had finally been stopped, Erin had thought everything would change for her. Life would be better, more normal. She'd let Alec into her life and, maybe, allow herself to love him. But old habits die hard, and nothing was ever as simple as it seemed. She'd been keeping people, men especially, at bay for too long, and she didn't know how to do anything else.

Alec, on the other hand, seemed to have no doubts. He showed up unannounced, making her smile and ache for something she couldn't define. He'd made his interest clear from the very beginning, stating without words that he wanted to be a part of her life.

Until last night, when he'd been ready to walk away for good. She'd known it, read it in his eyes. And in that instant, she'd realized that if he left, he'd take a part of her she'd just discovered and might never find again.

So she'd asked him to stay, and it scared her to death.

The plane hit an air pocket, shuddered, then settled down.

Erin opened her eyes, forced air into her lungs, and refused to grip the hand rests. Another breath, and the plane stayed steady, and she once again closed her eyes.

She needed to stop thinking about Alec Donovan. She was heading into a dangerous situation, and she couldn't lose her focus. It was a sure way to end up dead. Later, she'd sort out all the confusing emotions he aroused in her. But not now.

Instead, she forced herself to concentrate on her mission.

Which wasn't exactly what she'd been led to believe.

Her briefing had started at 5:45 this morning, a little over six hours ago. Bill and his team had set up a temporary command post in a sleepy, run-down strip center on Federal Highway. It was the end storefront, the windows covered and sealed off with brown paper. A sign in the window claimed that Bill's Computer Repair would open soon.

She'd parked in back, then knocked at the service entrance.

Bill opened the door. "Good, you're early. We have a lot of work to do."

Without waiting for a response, he led her through a small storage area into a wide-open room humming with activity. Three men and a woman were setting up computers, stringing cable, and checking phone lines.

"Heads up," Bill said to his team. "This is Erin." Nodding to each of the others in turn, he added, "Rob, Zeb, Rhonda, and Al." Use of first names only was common practice within the Agency, and Erin suspected even those were false. "They'll keep us hooked up to Langley and to you."

"Your backup team's already on their way to Santa Rosa," said one of the men. "They won't go near the camp or make contact, but you'll be connected to us through them."

"How?" Erin asked.

"You'll have a Pocket PC," Bill explained. "Before you leave, we'll key it to your fingerprints, so to anyone else using it, it will be nothing more than a language translator."

"Don't worry," the woman said. "We won't lose you."

Erin smiled at the other woman's confidence. The CIA hired only the best. "I know you won't."

"Okay, folks," Bill said. "Erin has a noon flight. So she needs to be fully briefed in the next . . ." He glanced at his watch. "Five hours. So get the computers up and running."

The support team returned to their work, and Bill led her into an adjoining conference room.

"Before we get started," he said, "I want to make a couple of things clear."

Erin settled into one of the chairs around a scarred table that looked like a refugee from a garage sale. "Okay."

"This is not a rescue mission."

She sat straighter, wary. "Excuse me?"

"Your job is to gather information." Bill crossed his arms, looking formidable and unmoving. "We need to know what we're up against. What, if anything, is going on in that camp, and who is involved. That's it. That's all we want from you."

"Wait a minute—"

He interrupted her. "Find Joe if you can, but you are *not* to attempt to pull him out on your own. You get the information and get out. Then we'll send in an extraction team."

"That's not what I agreed to," Erin said, angry that he'd used Joe to involve her, then changed the rules, tying her hands.

"We've already lost one officer—"

"You don't know that." Until she saw the body, she wouldn't believe Joe was dead. "He could—"

Bill held up a hand to stop her. "I hope I'm wrong, but we both know the possibility that Joe's alive is pretty slim."

She wouldn't admit that. Not aloud.

"I'm not going to lose a second officer to that island," Bill said into the silence. "Understood?"

When it came right down to it, Erin had no choice but to agree. She knew, however, that if she found Joe alive, there was no way she was going to leave him behind. No matter what her orders.

So for the next few hours, she reviewed the information the CIA already had on the situation—which wasn't much.

DFL had supplied the CIA with files on their current and incoming personnel at the Cuban facility. Like many aid organizations, volunteers signed up for a particular length of time. DFL was on a six-month schedule, with half the participants rotating out every three months. That way, there were always volunteers with a minimum of three months' experience working at the camp.

The facility was now at the end of one of these cycles, so there would be a shuffle of personnel over the next week. It worked for Erin's cover, because she'd be only one of many new faces showing up in the days to come. However, it also doubled the number of files and photographs she needed to study, committing to memory as much as possible.

Besides the DFL files, she memorized the information she would need to remain in contact with the command center. So by the time Bill had driven her to the airport and put her on a charter flight to Cuba, she knew the code words and phrases she would need to contact both her backup team and the agent Padilla in Santa Clara.

Now, as the pilot announced that they were fifteen minutes out of Havana, Erin braced herself for the days to come. This was what she'd trained for, but she wasn't a fool. No amount of planning or preparation could prepare an operation for every eventuality. In this case, they had very little information, so the chances that something could go wrong were good. Joe, one of the best covert officers she knew, had disappeared on a routine mission. Now the CIA was counting on her cover as a volunteer and as Emilio Diaz's daughter to keep her safe.

It was thin, very thin. However, she had no regrets about accepting the assignment. Live or die.

As the plane started its initial approach, Erin looked out the window and caught her first glimpse of Cuba. It took her breath away. She thought she'd been prepared for the island's beauty, but none of the words or pictures had done justice to the reality.

At first it was like a sparkling emerald dropped in an indigo sea. Then, as they lost altitude, the vision shifted, gaining detail. White sand beaches rimmed the shore and stretched beneath an ocean that rolled away from the land in shades of blue, running the gamut from palest powder, to aqua, to the midnight of open waters.

Though she'd never been here, Erin had been surrounded by Cuba her entire life. Just living in Miami, where the street signs were in Spanish and the department stores hired only bilingual clerks, was a constant reminder of this small island just ninety miles off the southern tip of the U.S. mainland.

For Erin, though, like so many others, Cuba was more than the idiosyncrasies of the predominantly Latin Miami. It was her past, her heritage. Or at least, part of it. Erin had never voiced her desire to visit her father's homeland, but she'd held the wish close for years.

If nothing else, Marta, who'd grown up in Cuba, was an ever-present reminder.

She sometimes spoke of Cuba's lost beauty, and Erin would see the wistful look in the older woman's eyes and hear the yearning in her voice. More often, though, Marta cursed Castro and the poverty and desolation he'd brought to her people. She told Erin about the grim days following the revolution, the executions and confiscation of property, and the fleeing masses.

As Erin had gotten older, she'd discovered there were two sides to the story, as was true for all stories. Still, Marta's early influence left a bitter taste in Erin's mouth for all things Castro, and it made her reticent, ashamed maybe, to admit her desire to see Cuba for herself.

Still, every time Erin looked in the mirror, she saw Cuba in her dark eyes and hair. And now, as the plane touched down, its wheels bouncing on the hard pavement, she had the oddest feeling she'd just come home.

CHAPTER THIRTEEN

Little Havana, Miami, Florida

Alec turned on to S.W. Eighth Street—better known as Calle Ocho—the main artery running through Little Havana.

He had thirty minutes before he was to meet Jose Mendez: a local cop. But Alec wanted to get a sense of the rendezvous point and surrounding area beforehand. So he drove from one end of Calle Ocho to the other.

The road stretched from Twenty-seventh to Fourth Avenue, vibrant and alive with splashes of color and music. A series of small stores fronted the street, their rainbow awnings eye-catching. Here and there a cluster of umbrella tables clung to the front of a small café or espresso shop. Foot traffic populated the sidewalks, Cuban Americans mainly, but some obvious tourists as well. They gathered in small groups around street musicians—guitar player on one corner, a guitar-drum combo a couple blocks down—and tossed dollar bills in cigar boxes at their feet.

The street had an almost Caribbean feel, with a large dose of something that could only be called big-city commercialism thrown into the mix. It produced an interesting and unique blend of ethnic and homegrown culture. Miami and Havana. The U.S. and Cuba. All mixed together in a neighborhood like no other in the country.

On his second pass down Calle Ocho, Alec spotted the prearranged meeting place: a parking lot next to Café Cubana. Turning, he backed into a space and shut off the engine. Mendez's instructions had been simple and clear. Wait for him. He'd come to Alec.

Mathews had set up the meet. Not only had he given Alec a desk and computer without question, Mathews had gone a step further when Alec had asked for yet another, more unusual, favor.

"I need more information on this man," he'd said, placing the tear sheet on Diaz in front of the other agent. "He's a Cuban American with U.S. citizenship living in Cuba. And he comes and goes freely between the two countries."

"That's pretty unusual." Mathews took the summary. "Castro's not real forgiving when it comes to his people claiming U.S. citizenship."

"I think Castro looks the other way in this case. The guy likes to stir up trouble."

Mathews studied the sheet, then handed it back. "Sorry, I've never heard of him. But then, this isn't really my area of expertise. Give me a minute." He flipped through a small notebook on his desk. "I know someone who can help, a cop on the Miami force. He grew up in Little Havana and knows the streets. We exchange favors occasionally, and if he doesn't have the information you need, he'll know someone who does."

So Mathews had made the call, pulling in a favor without bothering to ask why one of the FBI's most successful CAC investigators was interested in a Cuban American dissident like Diaz. A half hour later, Officer Jose Mendez had agreed to meet Alec in the heart of Little Havana.

Now Alec watched as a young man in jeans and a white muscle-shirt approached the car. Leaning down to rest his arms on the open passenger window, he said, "You Donovan?"

"That depends. You are?"

The younger man smiled and opened his fist to reveal a badge. "Detective Mendez. Miami PD."

"Then I'm Donovan."

"Great." Mendez opened the door and slid inside. "Let's drive." He motioned toward the street. "Take a right out here and head toward Fourth."

Alec did as instructed.

Once moving, Mendez said, "Mathews says you're the agent who found those girls out in the Glades a few years back."

Alec shrugged. "It was a team effort. And we got lucky."

"I'd say those girls got lucky."

That much was true. Thanks to a tip from a local fisherman, they'd found all four girls in a shack about ten miles from Alligator Alley. Although physically unharmed, the girls had been held hostage by a man who claimed God had told him to start gathering wives before the second flood. He'd kidnapped them one by one over a two-year period, locking each in a fetid shed until he'd broken their spirit and drive to escape.

Even without that, there was, in fact, nowhere for them to run, except through ten miles of alligator-infested swamp. Eventually all but the last girl, whose disappearance had brought Alec into the case, had accepted her fate and the madman's dominance. During the day they tended his squalid homestead, while at night he kept them in chains.

It was a case that filled Alec with both hope and despair. Hope, because the girls were once again with their families, and despair because, without that tip, they might still be lost.

Alec changed the subject. "Where are we going, Detective?"

"For the moment, we're just driving." Mendez sprawled in the passenger seat, his eyes on the street beyond the window. "Ever been in Little Havana before, Agent Donovan?"

"Can't say that I have." Though he didn't know why, especially considering the time he'd spent in Miami over the years.

"Havana may be the heart of the Cuban people," Mendez said. "But this is her soul."

It was an interesting distinction, implying a people waiting for a time when they could return to their native soil.

Mendez, however, didn't give Alec time to think it through. "You're looking for information about Emilio Diaz."

"That's right. What do you know about him?"

"Not much more than the FBI." Mendez shrugged. "Maybe not as much. He's in Miami a couple of times a year, supposedly to gain financial support for the DFL program in Cuba. Which he does. But he also comes to rally support against the U.S. trade embargo against Cuba."

Alec threw him a quick glance. This much was in the FBI file on Diaz. Alec needed more. He needed details. "How so?"

"Gives talks, passes around petitions, that sort of thing."

"Violent?" Alec asked.

Mendez shook his head. "No. And he keeps everything aboveboard and legal. Hell, he even gets permits for his rallies."

"So how successful is he?"

"Not very. Sure, there are some people here who are unhappy with the U.S. government. But hey, I bet there are a few all-American types in Iowa with grudges as well." He grinned. "Basically, most Miami Cubans fled their homes to get away from Castro. He doesn't have many sympathizers here."

"So that's why Castro allows Diaz to come and go?"

"That, my friend, would be my guess." He sat straighter, following something beyond the window with his eyes, then turned back to Alec. "Though, to be honest, who knows what's in the mind of the great bearded one?" Mendez pointed toward the next intersection. "Turn left here. We're going to talk to one of my contacts, a kid by the name of Stephen Raoul. He might be able to give us some answers."

Alec followed Mendez's directions to Domino Park, a landmark along Calle Ocho. They parked and walked in, past older men playing dominoes or chess. Across the park, however, was a younger set, a group of late teens at a picnic table. Alec detected the scent of marijuana.

"Just a word of warning," Mendez said as they headed for the kids. "Raoul is not as young, innocent, or as stupid as he appears. He's a player, and a good one." Then, as they got within earshot of the boys, he said, "Put that shit out."

The kids scrambled, ditching joints and sprinting for park exits.

Mendez stepped into the melee, grabbed one of the boys, and pulled him up short. "Not you, Stevie-boy. You and I need to have a conversation."

"Oh, man, I told you not to call me that." The kid jerked free of Mendez's grip. "And what are you doing harassing me in front of my friends?"

"Your friends were smoking weed." Mendez put a hand on the kid's shoulder and shoved him down on the bench. "And I'm willing to bet you sold it to them. I should drag your ass off to jail."

"Oh, man . . ." Steve looked more annoyed than worried.

"But I won't." Mendez straddled the bench beside him. "If you answer a few questions."

The kid rolled his eyes. Obviously, he'd been through this before. Then, nodding toward Alec, he said, "Who's he?"

"A friend," Mendez answered.

Raoul leaned back, both elbows on the table. "I don't talk to no friends." He looked back at Mendez. "Not even yours."

"You'll do what I say, or you'll go to jail. Your choice, Stevie."

The kid turned to Alec. "You a cop?"

"No." Alec crossed his arms.

"Oh, man. You're a fed." Raoul sat straighter, looking ready to bolt. "He's a fed," he said to Mendez. "I ain't talking to no fed."

Mendez clamped a hand on Steve's shoulder again. "Shut up, Stevie. We have some questions, and unless you want me to run you in for possession and distribution of a controlled substance, you'll answer them."

"Oh, man." The kid was a broken record, with a two-word vocabulary. Then, seemingly resigned, he rested his elbows on his knees and shook his head. "Okay, what do you want to know this time?"

"Tell me about Emilio Diaz," Alec said.

Steve frowned. "What's to tell? He comes. He goes."

Mendez strummed his fingers on the hard wooden table behind the boy.

"What? What do you want?" Steve leaned back again. "His address? Who he's fucking? What?"

"What I want . . ." Mendez let out an exaggerated sigh. "Is for you to tell me something we don't already know."

"There's nothing. The guy's a nobody. Some kind of doctor with one of those bleeding heart groups. . . . I don't remember the name. In Cuba."

"Something we *don't* know," Mendez reiterated.

Steve looked from the cop to Alec, a nervous tic below one eye. "Okay, here's something not even the feds know. Diaz was in Miami last February."

Alec straightened, and Mendez glanced back at him. "Last February? In Miami?"

"Yeah, you didn't know that, did ya." Raoul grinned.

According to Diaz's file, it had been over a year since he'd been in Miami. The last time he'd traveled to the States he'd gone to the DFL headquarters in New York. That had been in January sometime. "Why was he here?" Alec asked.

"Well that's the thing, usually he's drumming up support for some antigovernment crap or something. But this time . . ." The kid wiggled his eyebrows. "There was none of that."

"What was he doing, Stevie?" Mendez asked.

"I'm getting to it." The kid was cocky again, sure now that he had something they wanted. "He was here for a meeting."

"What kind of meeting?" Alec asked.

Steve shrugged. "Don't know."

"What do you mean, you don't know?" Mendez's patience was obviously wearing thin.

"I'm telling you. Word on the street was to stay clear. Don't ask no questions, don't go near the meet."

"Are you being straight with me?" Mendez said. "Because if you're not . . ."

"It's the truth," Steve insisted.

A meeting under the radar? Something the FBI had missed? What about the CIA? Were they watching Diaz as well, or someone else? "Who was Diaz meeting?" Alec asked.

"Don't know that, either."

Mendez leaned forward, his hand once again on the boy's shoulder. "Well, you don't know shit, do you, Stevie-boy."

The boy licked his lips, nervously. "I know the meet wasn't in Miami, but up in Palm Beach somewhere." He glanced at Alec again. "Evidently, he didn't want the feds to know he was in town."

Alec took a backward step and ran a hand through his hair. If Steve was telling the truth, then Alec needed to know who Diaz met. It might just be a clue to the CIA's sudden interest in a low-level rabble-rouser and Erin's involvement in all this.

"I need more," Alec said. "I need to know who he met and why."

Steve raised his hands and shook his head. "Can't do it, man. I told you, the word on the street is to keep out."

Alec came forward, forcing the kid to back up against the table again. "And I'm telling you I need that information, and I don't give a shit about what warnings are on the street."

"Hey man, I like breathing."

"How about your freedom?" Alec said. "You like that, Stevie-boy? Because if I don't get that information, what Detective Mendez here will do to you will be nothing to what will happen when I point the Miami feds in your direction. I don't know what you're doing that's illegal, but I have no doubt they'll find something."

"You're fucking blackmailing me."

"The word is negotiating." Alec stepped back, letting his threat sink in. "You do something for me, and I'll do something for you. It's the American way."

The kid hesitated, and for the first time Alec saw the cagey intelligence behind his eyes. As Mendez had mentioned earlier, Steve Raoul wasn't exactly what he appeared.

"Okay," he said finally. "Give me a couple of days."

Alec glanced at his watch. It was almost noon. "You have twelve hours."

"What?"

"Twelve hours." Alec pulled out a blank business card and scribbled his cellphone number on the back. "I need the information before midnight." He handed the kid the card. "Call me."

CHAPTER FOURTEEN

Havana, Cuba

Someone from the DFL camp had sent a driver for Erin. His name was Armando; a tall, wiry man, browned by life in the tropical sun. He was waiting for her outside customs, smiling, waving a sign with the DFL logo, and greeting her like a long-lost relative. Alongside him stood a small, dark woman whom Erin recognized from the DFL files she'd studied before leaving Miami. Plus, they'd been on the same plane.

"Welcome, señorita," he said as he took Erin's bag.

"Have you been waiting long?" she asked, smiling at the other woman while instantly warming to the man.

"No matter." He shrugged. "The customs here," he rolled his eyes, "takes forever. No?"

"Yes. Forever."

Armando clucked sympathetically.

Erin had been through worse customs checks, but none that seemed quite as pointless or bureaucratic. She'd brought only one bag with her, filled with the simple tropical clothing befitting a tourist or a short-term yuppie volunteer. She also carried the Pocket PC translator and a Canon Digital SLR, a semiprofessional camera that looked like something appropriate for a tourist. The two items were the only pieces of equipment she'd brought. She would have felt safer with a gun, but it would have landed her in a Cuban jail cell.

As soon as she could, she planned to make contact with Padilla, the CIA's foreign agent in Santa Clara. Hopefully he'd be able to supply her with a weapon. That is, assuming he hadn't gone underground with Joe Roarke's disappearance.

For now, though, the camera caused enough trouble all on its own. Though nothing special, it garnered a great deal of attention from the customs agent. In addition to examining it in excruciating detail and asking dozens of questions, he issued countless warnings about what she could not photograph while in Cuba: *policía* or military personnel, airports, industrial or military installations, pornography. All of which she already knew.

Fortunately, he hadn't recognized the night lens among the other interchangeable lenses in her case, or she had a feeling things would have gotten a lot worse.

Turning to the woman at Armando's side, Erin held out her hand. "Erin Baker. I take it you're a DFL volunteer as well."

"Sandy Bradley." She shook Erin's hand. "Yes, I'm a nurse."

"Come," Armando said, ushering them toward the exit. "We have a long drive." He escorted them to a battered truck of indeterminate color. "We go to Santa Clara by way of La Habana." His grin broadened. "It will be a treat, no? And make customs seem not so bad."

Erin hadn't expected this. The José Martí Airport was southwest of Havana, and the quickest way to Santa Clara would be due east on the Autopista Motorway. Detouring north into the city, and especially into the old section of La Habana, would take them out of their way. Yet the idea appealed to her.

"I'd like that," Sandy said.

"Me, too," Erin agreed. This may be her only chance to see some of the country, and in Cuba, that meant Havana.

So Armando headed north and within a few minutes was pointing out details of the city unfolding around them.

Erin had read that Havana was a city caught in the 1950s, that it was like traveling to a different time. She didn't agree. It was more like stepping into an alternate universe, an entrancing and alluring universe filled with mystery and contradiction.

They drove past revolutionary billboards proclaiming Cuba's lack of fear of the giant to its north, Victorian churches, ornate and heavy with detail, and decaying buildings, where sections of once brightly colored walls leaked through the grime and neglect.

People filled the streets, their colorful clothes a bracing foil to the faded backdrop of their city. Spanish, Indian, black, and white mingled and merged, all Cuban, all vibrant. Women of all sizes and shapes, in formfitting spandex and tight shirts, carried themselves with a distinct confidence and sexuality. Men in jeans and sleeveless, opened shirts stood alone or in groups on street corners or doorways, flirting and whistling at the passing parade.

It was a city alive, despite all the propaganda to the contrary, despite the lack of twenty-first-century comforts and gadgets that might lead you, at first glance, to believe otherwise.

Of course, Erin had been prepared for the odd mix of cars. The boxy Russian Ladas alongside big-finned Cadillacs, Chevys, and other classic American cars. Due to the U.S. trade embargo, shipment of American cars to Cuba had stopped in 1959. Still, the sight of all these old vehicles, built before she was born, seemed to tilt the world she knew out of focus.

Then they drove into Cubanacán, an area unlike any they'd seen earlier. Stunning estates populated quiet streets, their exquisitely manicured lawns and well-maintained buildings a biting divergence to the surrounding city.

"These are the embassies," Armando explained. And it made sense. Foreign governments would maintain their properties as they would in any other country. They wouldn't be subject to the shortages of money and materials like the rest of the island.

Then the vista changed.

Instead of mansions meticulously tended by foreign governments, one magnificent structure after another

sat des

like they

"Oh m

"Before

rich lived h

glance at the

made a quick w

and now . . ." H

such places?" He

governments."

It saddened Erin to   ions

sinking into ruin, but   ke this. It

shouldn't have bothered   se homes crum-

bling and dying any mo   the faded apartment

buildings they'd passed a few minutes earlier. But some-

how it did. It spoke of waste, of vast inefficiency and

loss.

Armando also showed them the ornate Museo de la

Revolución, the former presidential palace, now dedi-

cated to documenting the revolution. Erin wished she

had time to go through it, to get a sense of what her fa-

ther's family had lived through. They also drove down

Malecón, the heart of La Habana, a wide boulevard

fronting the ocean with a walkway for pedestrians.

It was all too much to assimilate in such a short

period of time. The nurse sitting next to Erin said very

little, her eyes jumping from one unexpected sight to

the next. And even Erin, who'd studied Cuba, seen

countless pictures of the old city, and thought she was

prepared, felt overwhelmed.

Finally they headed out of Havana, east on the Au-

topista Motorway into the Valle de Yumurí, a wide,

low mountains. As
ut around them, Erin re-
of having stepped into a differ-

th the windows down, the hot tropical
g over them. Armando continued his travel-
pointing out places of interest in his heavily accented English: sugarcane fields and small homesteads
dotting the hills, farmers working their land with horse-
drawn plows, an occasional citrus orchard hemming the
road, a massive ceiba tree, broad-trunked and lofty,
spreading branches, dominating an empty field. This
was the other side of Cuba, the beauty she'd seen from
the air.

Every now and then Armando would stumble over a
translation and ask them for the correct English word.
Sandy seemed eager to help him practice in her own
meager Spanish. Erin kept quiet, never knowing what
she might overhear if no one knew she was fluent. After
a while, however, the rhythm of the truck and the heat
lulled their exchanges to a standstill. Sandy had rested
her head against the back of the seat, and Armando
seemed in a daze of his own.

Erin wanted to keep the man talking. As someone
who worked for DFL, he might know what was going
on there. Or at least have suspicions. And though she
didn't expect to get any direct information from him,
you never knew what someone might let slip out in
the course of a conversation.

"This is quite a drive," she said, shifting in the
cracked vinyl seat. "How far is it?"

He seemed surprised by the question, or maybe just

that she was still awake. "Three hundred *kilómetros* to Santa Clara, then another twenty to Casa de la Rosa." He glanced at her, then added, "The DFL camp."

"Do you pick up all the volunteers?"

"*Sí*. Every three months, half come," he waved a hand from one side, then to the other, "and half go."

She let the silence settle again, waiting to see if he'd elaborate. When he didn't, she found another innocuous question to keep him talking. "You seem to know your way around Havana very well. Have you ever lived there?"

Again, that sideways look. This time she realized it wasn't exactly surprise. But maybe annoyance. Cubans had a reputation for being closemouthed when it came to talking about their island and its politics. Maybe that extended to other things as well.

Still he answered politely. "I live in Santa Rosa, a small village near Casa de la Rosa."

"How long have you worked for DFL?"

"Long enough." He shrugged again, effectively ending the conversation, and nodded to a group of people standing alongside the road. She'd read about this, and it didn't surprise her when Armando pulled over.

"Santa Clara," he called through the open window.

Sandy came awake, blinking sleepily and sitting straighter. Then she said, "What?" as a half dozen men, women, and children peeled off from the group and climbed into the back of the truck.

"This is how people in our country get around," Armando explained as he put the truck in gear and started once again down the road. "We have little gas and fewer vehicles. So they must wait on the road for a ride."

After that, they pretty much continued in silence, with only an occasional comment on a passing town or sight. The passengers in the truck bed got out near Santa Clara. Then Armando turned the truck south toward Manicaragua and the foothills of the heavily forested Sierra del Escambray.

As they climbed, afternoon thunderclouds gathered overhead and the temperature dropped. Then the skies opened, forcing them to close the windows as Armando navigated the rain-slick mountain roads. A few minutes later, however, the downpour stopped as quickly as it had started, leaving the air refreshed and cool.

Several miles farther and Armando turned onto a broad drive cutting through a pine forest. Nodding back toward the two-lane road they'd just left, he said, "Santa Rosa is very close. Maybe half a *kilómetro*." Then, just past a small one-story bungalow-type building on their left, the trees opened up to reveal a wide clearing, and Armando stopped the truck.

"Welcome to Casa de la Rosa," he said.

CHAPTER FIFTEEN

Cuba

Joe came awake with a start.

One moment the darkness had soothed and comforted. The next, it was an inky absence of light that suffocated and chilled.

Cold. It permeated his entire body, surrounding him.

Where was he?

Years of training kept him still as memory returned, cloudy at first, then with unmistakable clarity. He'd done some damage back on that street. Put two or three men down before they'd overwhelmed him, before a blow from behind had rendered him unconscious.

Helton.

The name finally came to him. That's why Joe was here. Because of Helton. They'd spent two years in the same squad, fighting in one of the world's premier hellholes. That kind of thing didn't always breed friendship, but you got to know a man. Helton wouldn't have bought Joe's cover as a freelance photographer any more than Joe would have bought such a story from

Helton. There were some soldiers who would always remain soldiers, even if the job title changed.

The only real question was whose orders they took.

Joe allowed himself a moment of self-pity. It would have been better to have died in that street. Fighting. Because if Helton suspected Joe was still in the U.S. military, or worse, working for one of the U.S. intelligence agencies, this could be bad. Very bad.

He pushed the thought aside. He wasn't dead yet. Nor had anyone started inflicting the pain he knew would come. He needed to get out of here.

He started to rise. Stopped. Gasped. Pain knifing through his side. He bit his tongue to muffle his curses. It wouldn't do to let anyone know he was awake. Breathe, he told himself, and forced air into his lungs.

One. Two. The pain would pass. Diminish. Give it a minute.

When he could move again, this time carefully, he traced the binding wrapped around his rib cage. Okay, so they'd done a little damage to him as well. How many ribs had they broken? Two? Three? Whatever number, it was going to make getting out of here, wherever *here* was, that much harder.

Again, with as little movement as possible, he extended his hands to get a feel for his surroundings. He was sitting on a narrow cot, but that was all he could tell. The darkness was nearly complete, and beyond the cot's hard wooden braces he felt nothing but empty air.

Now, he needed to stand.

Damn. It was going to hurt like a bitch. No way around it.

Before he could do more than formulate the thought,

however, the sound of a lock opening snapped at the darkness. Too late. The door banged open and light flooded the room, blinding him.

A large man stood silhouetted in the doorway.

"She said you'd be awake," Helton said. "I guess she knew what she was talking about."

Joe screened his eyes, squinting at the silhouette in the doorway. "Where am I? What do you want?"

"Such a pathetic attempt to maintain your cover." Helton stepped into the room followed by two other men. "Please, don't insult me. We both know good old Uncle Sam sent you. It's just a matter of which agency pulls your strings."

Joe kept his silence, his eyes taking in the room's parameters now that he could see. Small. Damp. He'd guess a basement, except that the floors and walls were cut directly into stone, and the lights were strung from exposed wires. And the two men beside Helton, both carrying automatic weapons.

Shit. They were going to kill him. Only a question of how and when.

"What," Helton said. "Nothing else to say? As I remember, you were always a talker."

"What do you want?" Joe asked, knowing he couldn't give it to them.

"You killed one of my men." Helton crossed his arms, muscles bulging. "I'd like to see you dead."

"Then do it."

"Unfortunately, the Cuban government wants you alive. They like the idea of having a U.S. spy in one of their prisons. Then they could tell the world how the big bad bully to the north is mistreating them." He paused, nodded. "It would be a real coup."

"What a crock."

Helton snorted. "Doesn't matter. I need you to confess your sins. Admit on tape who you work for, and why you're here."

"Not going to happen."

"Well, you see, that's the thing." Helton grinned. "You can talk or you can die. So, I hope your masters trained you really well to keep your mouth shut. Because, personally, I don't care what the Cubans want. I'd rather see you dead."

CHAPTER SIXTEEN

DFL Camp, Cuba

Erin felt like she'd stepped back in time.

In front of her was the large, graceful plantation house of what once must have been a great estate. The house was two stories and square, with wide verandas wrapping around both the upper and lower levels. Its structure was simplicity itself, but rows of intricate tile, blue and gold, framed the windows and doors, and cinched the walls like a woman's belt. Royal palms flanked its corners, and purple bougainvillea wound its way around trellised railings.

"That is the clinic," Armando said, stopping the truck for a moment in front of the house. "Beautiful, yes?"

"Yes," Erin agreed. It was still lovely, even in this time of broken dreams, a reminder of Cuba's former beauty, and future potential.

"Now it belongs to the people." He drove on, and Erin wondered if she'd imagined the touch of sarcasm in his voice.

Behind the house was a cluster of smaller buildings: a stable, several rough-looking wooden cabins, and a large semipermanent gray-green tent on a raised wooden base. Armando parked near the stables, got out, and carried the women's bags to the porch. He explained that the building had been divided into three sections: one for storage, a second for classrooms, and the third for the DFL office.

As he drove away, Sandy went inside the office while Erin hung back, taking a minute to size up her surroundings.

Casa de la Rosa was obviously a working community, with a half dozen men and women moving between the different structures, alone or in pairs, talking, laughing. She let her gaze slide over them, her stomach suddenly a little jumpy as she realized she was looking for her father. She didn't see him. Which was probably a good thing. She wasn't quite ready to confront him.

Two other men, however, caught her attention.

They sat on the rear steps of the clinic, seeming out of place in the tranquil setting. She would have guessed they were PNR, Cuba's Policía Nacional Revolucionaria, except for their lack of uniforms. She also saw no weapons, though that didn't mean they weren't carrying, hidden beneath their lightweight tropical shirts. So, they could be some other, more secret watchdogs of the Castro regime. Or something else entirely.

Whoever they were, she knew they were part of why she was here. Their presence had been the first red flag raised by the agent in Santa Clara. They were the reason Joe Roarke had been sent in. Now they were watching her, making no attempt to disguise their interest. Whatever group or government held their leash had obviously placed them here to keep an eye on this foreign organization and its volunteer staff.

Turning her back on them, she stepped into the dim interior of the camp's office. The screen door snapped shut behind her, and the inside appeared empty except for Sandy.

"Is anyone here?" Erin asked.

"I'll be right out," came an impatient female voice from a back room.

Sandy grinned and rolled her eyes, making Erin smile.

While waiting she looked around, as she had outside. Someone had created a small, neat office at one end of the stable, walled it off, the wood fresh and bare. Two mismatched mahogany desks faced the door, both battered, though the skilled workmanship that must have gone into creating them was still visible. A rotary phone sat on top of one, plus a laptop, though Erin spotted no modem or phone line to indicate an Internet connection. Behind the desk were three antique-looking filing cabinets, also wood, their scarred surfaces a seeming injustice. Like the desks, someone had once cared not only for their utilitarian value, but for their beauty as well.

On the wall near the door hung a bulletin board. In the center hung a large DFL poster. It pictured a man's hand reaching down to grasp a child's. On top, in green lettering, was the first half of the DFL slogan: Doctors For Life. While beneath the hands was the rest: We Believe In It. She'd seen the poster before, hanging in a hallway of UM's medical school. It was part of the organization's campaign to recruit recent medical graduates to their humanitarian efforts.

Also posted on the bulletin board were schedules for teaching assignments and clinic duty, and dozens of pictures of smiling volunteers.

"That's our hall of fame," said a female voice.

Erin turned.

A woman stood in the interior doorway. "Just a way to keep track of our progress," she said, easing into the room and going first to Sandy. "You must be our new nurse."

"Yes, Sandy Bradley."

"Welcome." She turned then to Erin. "That makes you Erin Baker."

Erin offered her hand. "I am."

"I'm Jean Taylor." She was a surprisingly pretty woman, beautiful even. Tall and slender, with no makeup and her hair pulled back, she would still turn heads. It wasn't a face you'd forget, or not notice. And, it hadn't been in the DFL file Erin had studied in Miami.

"Are you a volunteer, too?" Erin asked.

Jean's smile tightened. "I basically help out wherever I'm needed." She moved over to the desk. "Let me close up here, and I'll show the two of you around." She grabbed a set of keys from one of the drawers and started locking up the file cabinets.

"Where did you find this furniture?" Erin asked, wanting to keep the other woman talking. Erin could think of a number of legitimate reasons why this woman's picture hadn't been included in DFL's list of volunteers, but she wasn't going to make any assumptions.

Jean glanced back at her, appraising whether the question was a compliment or criticism. "Gorgeous, isn't it?"

"You'd pay a fortune for this in the States." Erin ran a hand over the desk's marred surface. Claire, with her artist's eye, had taught Erin to appreciate the beauty of old wood. It had come easy to her, since spotting the details in any situation was one of her strengths. "If you could find it at all."

"Something the Cubans have a lot of, is old stuff." Finished with the cabinets, Jean locked the desks. "These came from the house. Excuse me . . . I mean clinic." She rolled her eyes. "DFL rescued them when they took over."

"I have a sister who would give just about anything to get her hands on something like this." Claire would restore its beauty. "Of course, then she'd want to take it home."

Jean laughed. "Wouldn't we all. Ready?" She glanced from Erin to Sandy, who nodded, then led them out of the office.

Outside, the day had started to fade.

"It seems awfully quiet," Sandy said.

Erin had to agree. Except for the two men still hanging around the back of the clinic, smoking and leering, the yard was now deserted.

"Most everyone's at dinner." Jean nodded toward the large tent Erin had noticed earlier. "That's the mess tent. I'm sure it's not what you're used to, but the food is plentiful and decent. The Cubans aren't big on fruits and vegetables, but DFL makes sure we're well supplied."

"How many people are there in the camp?" Erin asked, aware of the two sets of male eyes following them. She'd memorized the DFL numbers and wanted to know if Jean's matched.

"It varies, but we usually have anywhere between twenty and thirty. Some volunteers and some DFL employees."

It was a vague enough answer that Erin couldn't draw any conclusions. "American?"

"Mostly. But we get quite a few Europeans as well." They'd reached the row of small wooden cabins, and Jean opened the door to one in the middle. "Here we are." They stepped inside, and with a sweep of her hand, Jean said, "What do you think?"

Erin glanced around at the dormlike sleeping quarters. A row of eight beds marched down one side, some carefully made, others with the mattress rolled up to keep them fresh. Beside each bed was a shoulder-high cabinet, and at the foot, a storage chest. A bit on the austere side, but clean, with the scent of newly cut wood mixing with pine cleaner.

"It looks like we've just joined the military," Erin said, laughing.

Jean grinned. "I know what you mean. Each cabin sleeps eight, with a communal bathroom at the back." Erin followed Sandy to the other end of the cabin, where a door opened into a large bathroom with rows of showers, sinks, and stalls.

"The cabins are DFL's latest addition," Jean said. "When I first got here, everyone was in tents similar to the mess tent. Let me tell you, this is a world better."

Back in the sleeping area, Erin and Sandy selected their beds, unrolling their mattresses and dropping their bags on top.

"Do you want to get settled first?" Jean asked. "Or head over to the mess tent for dinner?"

"Actually, there's one other thing I need to do before either," Erin said. Like it or not, it was time to establish her cover. "Can you take me to see Dr. Diaz?"

Jean frowned. "I don't know—"

"He's my father."

"Really?" Jean arched an eyebrow, suddenly interested. "He didn't say anything about his daughter showing up."

Erin managed to look embarrassed. "He doesn't know." She glanced at Sandy, who was taking in every word. Within a few hours, it would be all over the camp that Erin was Emilio Diaz's daughter. "I'm afraid I'm going to be a bit of a surprise."

"Well." Jean studied her for a moment. "You will be that." She turned to Sandy. "Why don't you go on to dinner." Then, turning her attention back to Erin, added, "While I take Erin to say hello to her dad."

Erin forced a smile, her sudden set of jitters all too real. "Thank you."

Now that the time to meet her father had finally arrived, she wondered if this was such a great idea. Which was silly, she told herself. He was just a man. Besides, she wasn't here for a father-daughter reunion. She was here to find a friend and bring him home. Meeting Emilio Diaz was just a bonus, who could become a distraction if she wasn't careful.

The three of them went back outside, where Jean once again pointed out the mess tent to Sandy. When Erin and Jean were alone, she said, "Emilio never mentioned he had a daughter."

Erin let out a short laugh. "He wouldn't. We're estranged."

"How estranged?"

Erin's face heated, another unfeigned emotion. "I haven't seen him since I was five."

Jean threw her a sideways glance, her expression curious. "Interesting, your showing up now."

"Well, when I saw DFL's plea for a temporary volunteer, I couldn't pass up the opportunity. I mean," she put a note of longing in her voice, "he is my father."

"Still—"

"Don't worry. He may be why I came," a partial truth, anyway, "but I'm a good teacher and I adore children. I'll do my job."

"I'm sure you will."

As they started toward the clinic, Erin again noticed the out-of-place men. Different ones this time, over by the office. She wondered how many of them there were.

"Just ignore them," Jean said, picking up a part of Erin's thoughts. "As long as you leave them alone, they won't bother you."

"Who are they?" Erin asked.

Jean leaned closer and lowered her voice. "I figure they belong to Castro, though I'm not sure. No one talks about it." She shrugged. "I guess in Cuba, it's best not to ask too many questions."

They climbed an outdoor staircase on the backside of the clinic. Up close, the signs of long neglect were evident in the peeling paint and broken railings. Repairs had been made, but they stood out, functional, marring the graceful lines of the house. The tiles adorning the walls, however, were even lovelier than they'd been from a distance. The royal blue and gold entwined in an intricate filigree pattern that reminded Erin of sun and sea.

"If Dr. Diaz is here this time of day," Jean was saying as they entered the building, "he'll be in his office."

They stopped at an open door near the front corner of the house. Inside was a smallish room with a desk, filing cabinets, and two extra chairs. A man sat, bent over a stack of paperwork.

Jean knocked on the door frame. "Excuse us, Dr. Diaz."

He glanced up, frowning, his eyes barely touching Erin before settling on Jean. "I'm busy."

"I have a bit of a surprise for you." Jean stepped into the room, unintimidated by his brusque manner. "This is Erin, one of our new volunteers."

He frowned at Jean, gave Erin a brief nod, then returned to the papers on his desk.

For a moment Erin just studied him, seeing herself in the man. He was thin, too thin, with straight Latin features, Spanish features.

It shouldn't surprise her that he didn't recognize her,

but it stung, giving rise to another set of nerves. "It's good to meet you, Dr. Diaz," she said. "I've been looking forward to it for some time."

He glanced up again, looking at her more closely, his deepening frown a study in perplexity. "Do I know you?"

"Not really." Her hands fluttered nervously, and she shoved them in her back pockets to keep them still. "But you're the reason I'm here."

Suspicion shadowed his eyes, his gaze darting back to Jean. "What is this about?"

"Actually, we've already met," Erin said, drawing his attention back to her. "A long time ago."

"Young woman." He dropped his pen. "I really don't have time for games. If you have something to say," he folded his hands on the desk in front of him, "I suggest you get on with it."

So be it.

"I'm Elizabeth's daughter." She paused, letting the information sink in, seeing it happen in the widening of his eyes. "And yours."

For a moment he seemed frozen in place: a deer caught in headlights. Then he blinked. "You do not look like her."

She nearly laughed aloud at the absurdity of the comment. He hadn't seen her in over twenty-five years, and his first words were about her lack of resemblance to her mother. "They say I look like you."

Again, he seemed at a loss for words. Finally he stood and came around the desk, awkward and uncertain. He hesitated a second, then moved to embrace her.

Erin stiffened, allowing no more than a brief, perfunctory hug before backing away.

He smiled tightly and nodded, as if understanding her reluctance and accepting it. Gesturing toward one of the chairs, he said, "Do you want to sit down?"

"Sure." Though what Erin wanted to do was run. She realized suddenly she wasn't ready for this, for him. It had been too long since she'd seen him, too many years of hurt.

As he took the chair next to her, he remembered Jean still standing in the doorway and said to her, "I'm sure you have work to do."

She grinned, wiggled her fingers at them, and backed out of the room.

"So you're a volunteer," he said, refocusing on Erin.

"I'm just here for a couple of weeks, filling in for one of your teachers."

"I see," Emilio said, obviously searching for something to say to this daughter he didn't know. Finally he came up with something. "And how is your mother?"

The question surprised her, throwing grief into the mix of her tumultuous thoughts. "She died a couple of years ago."

A dark shadow filled his eyes. "I did not know."

"Of course not." Why would he? Still, it bothered Erin that he hadn't kept up with her even enough to know her mother had died.

"How?"

Though she would have preferred talking about something else, anything else, she answered, "Cancer."

It still hurt, when Erin allowed herself to think about it. It had happened so quickly. She'd been home for

Christmas that year, and her mother had seemed fine. It was just so . . . sudden.

"She was diagnosed in February of last year," she said, the memory catching in her throat. "And she died the following October." Alone. With only her friend Marta by her side. Claire had been in a psychiatric hospital, and Erin, halfway around the world.

The silence stretched between them, long and filled with loss. "I'm sorry," Emilio said finally. "Elizabeth was . . ."

Your wife, Erin thought, searching for her anger. It was easier than dealing with grief, or the emotions she saw in this man's eyes. He'd given up the right to mourn her mother when he deserted them.

"A good woman," he finished.

For several minutes neither spoke. Years of separation and loss wrapped around them in an uncomfortable silence.

"Well, maybe I should go," Erin said, pushing to her feet. "I need to get settled."

"Of course. Don't let me keep you." He stood, stiff and formal. "We'll talk later."

Erin nodded and moved toward the door. With any luck she'd find Joe Roarke and be out of here before that could happen. Coming here had been a mistake. She should have left well enough alone.

"Erin?"

She stopped, turning to look at him again.

"I'm glad you're here."

CHAPTER SEVENTEEN

DFL Camp, Casa de la Rosa, Cuba

As the light faded outside, Emilio sat at his desk, an open bottle of rum for company. With shaky hands, he poured another shot and downed it in one quick swallow. The liquor spread through him like liquid fire, warming him, easing the ache of loss that had settled in his stomach.

Elizabeth. His beautiful, fragile Elizabeth. Dead.

He'd loved her once, and though he hadn't thought about her in years, her loss saddened him in a way that surprised him. He should have checked on her, gone to see her during one of his trips to Miami. Their parting had been bitter, and it would have been good to put that to rest.

Maybe then, things would be different, better with Erin.

He sighed and thought about his daughter. He remembered the infant he'd once sung to sleep, the child he'd told stories to and carried on his shoulders, the little girl it had nearly killed him to leave behind.

The memory seared his gut, the pain he'd thought

he'd put aside, alive once again. Because he *had* left her, just as he had her mother. Now Erin was here, unannounced and fully grown, and angry. So very angry.

Damn.

"Got another glass?"

Emilio looked up.

Jean Taylor stood in the doorway, a testament to Emilio's preoccupation, or maybe the amount of rum he'd already consumed. He hadn't heard her coming, and with the camp gone silent for the night, one could hear every creak and movement in this old house.

"Go away," he said. "I have no time for you tonight."

For a second she didn't move. Then she stepped into the office, closed the door, and crossed to the cabinet where Emilio kept a couple of extra shot glasses. In the seven months he'd known her, he'd never gotten used to her boldness. It threw him off center, disturbing him in a way he didn't quite know how to deal with. She was different than the women he was used to dealing with, an unusual combination of intelligence, beauty, and lack of conscience.

"I take it you're not thrilled with your daughter showing up," she said.

"Go away, Jean," Emilio repeated, hoping she'd take offense at his tone and leave him alone.

"I need to talk to you." Glass in hand, she reached across the desk and claimed the bottle.

Emilio should have snatched it away, but the thought occurred to him too late. Another side effect of the rum. Instead, he watched her pour herself a healthy shot. Then she folded her long, elegant frame into the office's only other chair, sipping at the rum.

"She's a lovely young woman," Jean said.

"It is not your concern."

"Not flashy, mind you." She was staring off in space, as she often did, alone in her own little universe. "But interesting. You can definitely see the family resemblance. Is her mother American?"

"I do not want to talk about this." Emilio barely resisted the urge to growl, and didn't even try to soften his next words. "Especially to you."

Jean refocused, blinked, surprised possibly by the venom in his voice. "Will it be easier to talk to Helton?"

Emilio glared at her.

It was a low blow, or maybe just a reminder of the real power in this camp. Helton would have his questions about Erin, no doubt, and, unlike Jean Taylor, he would have his answers. One way or the other.

The thought sent a shiver of dread down Emilio's spine.

"He doesn't like . . ." She focused on her drink, twirling the rum in her glass. "Surprises."

It was the truth. Though he could be brutal, Helton was a cold, calculating man with a fanatical need for order. His order. The exact opposite of Jean, an impulsive, wildly disorganized, and volatile woman. But brilliant. So very brilliant.

It grated on Emilio that he was stuck with both of them. That he possessed neither Helton's physical prowess nor Jean Taylor's sheer genius. Emilio was a middleman, a facilitator, caught somewhere in between these two despicable creatures.

And sometimes, like tonight, he hated it.

At least he was beginning to feel the rum, the softening of the world's edges that made everything easier. So when Jean reached for the bottle a second time, Emilio no longer considered denying her.

Then, watching her fill her glass, he realized he knew nothing about her beyond her professional credentials. A dual MD and PhD in molecular genetics, she'd gotten both degrees from Harvard. Why she'd deserted her career for Helton's project, Emilio couldn't say. Money, most likely. Or some grudge against the world. Helton would know every boring detail of Jean's life, but Emilio had never cared enough to ask.

"Have you ever been married?" he asked her now.

"Me?" Jean seemed surprised and a bit embarrassed by the question, but she recovered quickly. "My work . . . well, it's always taken precedence. Besides, what man . . ." She didn't finish the statement, surprising him instead by blushing like a young girl. "Men don't take to me very well. It seems I intimidate them."

Emilio didn't doubt that. Her looks alone would scare the average man away. Add to that an IQ that was off the charts along with credentials that would command respect anywhere in the world, and he understood why most men would go running.

Yet, as he sipped at the rum, he wondered if it was the other way around. Maybe it was Jean who did not like men. Or possibly, she was just afraid of them. Though that would be hard to envision, he had to remember she'd been a child prodigy, pushed to scholastic levels beyond her age.

But what did it matter really? Either way . . .

"Maybe you are the lucky one," he said, lifting his shoulders in a small, indifferent shrug. "Marriage is difficult. And children . . ." He shook his head, a liquored melancholy slipping past his usual reticence. "They will break your heart."

Jean pressed her lips together, then finished her drink. "How long since you've seen her? Your daughter?"

Emilio dumped more rum in his glass. "Too long." He hesitated, then set the bottle down near the woman. Maybe a little company on such a night was not a bad thing. "Not long enough." No good would come of Erin being here. Not now, anyway. "She was five when I left Miami."

Jean refilled her glass. "What happened?"

"Hurricanes Frederic and David happened. They hit the island within weeks of each other, and DFL came to the Cuban people's aid."

"And you jumped in to help."

"I could not stay in Miami anymore, not with all this waiting here. These people . . ." He made a vague gesture, sweeping a hand as if to encompass the camp and beyond. "They need me."

"And your wife?" He sensed the disapproval in Jean's voice. "Didn't she need you as well?"

The question saddened him further, and he remembered the days after DFL had approached him about returning to Cuba. He had wanted Elizabeth to come with him, had come close to begging her. Though the truth was, it was not his wife he'd been reluctant to leave. It had been his daughter.

He'd loved Elizabeth, but not enough to keep him in Miami. She must have sensed that, because she had used Erin as leverage, threatening to keep the child from him if he left, striking out at her husband with the only weapon she possessed. In the end, even his fatherly love for the small girl had not been strong enough to keep him from his homeland and the people who desperately needed him.

"Elizabeth was not a strong woman," he said finally. "She did not belong here."

"And you do." It wasn't a question.

"*Sí.* I do."

Jean nodded, the rum showing itself on her face and in the creeping glaze in her eyes. "And now, your daughter shows up." She closed her eyes, her next words slow and lazy. "But she's not like her mother. She'll be okay here."

Jean might be right. During his brief encounter with his daughter, Emilio had detected none of her mother's weakness. Yet how could he be sure? Maybe these things took time to reveal themselves.

"It doesn't matter," Emilio said. "She is here only for a short time. Then, she will be gone again. I can not worry about it."

Jean let out a short laugh, though she still sat, eyes closed. "What a crock. If it didn't worry you, you wouldn't be sitting here in the dark getting smashed." She looked at Emilio then. "You're a lot of things, Diaz, but you're not a drunk."

Sitting forward, Emilio made an effort to clear his rum-fogged brain. What had he been thinking, discussing this matter with her? Was he losing his mind? Reaching over, he capped the rum bottle, then slid it into the bottom desk drawer.

"What are you doing here, Jean? You did not leave your hole to come talk about my daughter."

"No." She sat straighter, making an attempt to sober herself as well. "No, I'm not here for that. I need your help."

Emilio arched an eyebrow. "Your work has gone beyond my skills. You know that."

"No, that's not the kind of help I need." Jean paused, swallowing the last of her rum. For courage, no doubt. "I need help with Helton. He listens to you. I need you to talk to him for me."

"About what?" Emilio heard the suspicion in his own voice.

Jean scooted forward. "You have to convince him to give me more time."

Emilio frowned. "You said the formula was ready."

"Yes, it is, but—"

"But?" Emilio hardened his voice.

"I can't guarantee its stability. I need to run more tests." Jean's voice had turned demanding. "I need more time."

For several long, silent seconds, Emilio watched the half-drunk woman, letting her cling to a hope Emilio had every intention of dashing.

"There is no more time, Dr. Taylor. We have five days, then we must go ahead, whether you have finished your tests or not. That is what Helton expects."

Jean's face drained of color. So the bold doctor did understand fear. At least when it came to Gregory Helton.

"So I suggest," Emilio added, "that you finish your tests quickly. Because, as you said, he does not like surprises."

CHAPTER EIGHTEEN

Casa de la Rosa, Cuba

For the next few hours, Erin had no time alone.

She needed to send off a message to the backup team in Santa Rosa, plus she wanted to explore the camp. In Miami, she'd studied the layout, but that wasn't the same as walking the grounds herself. Besides that, she wanted a better look at the men who'd first brought this place to the CIA's attention.

However, after leaving her father, she'd been intercepted by a couple of veteran volunteers, who'd insisted she join them for dinner. She couldn't refuse without arousing suspicion, so she'd gone along. There was, of course, the added benefit of talking to people who'd been around for a few months. As Bill Jensen had insisted, Erin was on a fact-finding mission, and whether any of the DFL volunteers were involved in Joe's disappearance or not, they might know something that could help her.

After dinner, she joined the other seven women in her cabin, and as the evening wore on, they exchanged idle conversation. She and Sandy were the newbies, and everyone wanted the details on how and why they'd decided to volunteer with DFL. Like Sandy, all had been included in the information Erin had studied in Miami. Which made Erin think again about Jean Taylor's absence from those files.

Since the other woman hadn't made an appearance since leaving Emilio's office, Erin asked, "Is Jean Taylor in the other cabin?"

"Far from it," answered Nancy, one of the volunteers. "The doctors have rooms upstairs in the clinic."

"Doctor?" Wondering if she'd missed something, Erin glanced at Sandy. "I thought Jean worked in the office."

"Me, too," Sandy replied.

Nancy let out an abrupt laugh. "Hardly. She was just covering for me today while I was at dinner. We knew you two were coming in, and someone had to show you around." She shrugged. "Didn't she tell you?"

"Well, you know," Erin pasted a smile on her face, hiding her heightened interest. "I was really tired from traveling." She again glanced at Sandy, who'd already lost interest. After all, what did it matter? Unless, like Erin, you were watching for things out of place. "It probably went right over my head."

Of course, that wasn't it at all. Jean had let them believe she was part of the office staff. Which was odd. She had to know they'd find out she was a doctor, so why not mention it? Especially when Erin had specifically asked if Jean was a volunteer. That, combined with her absence from the DFL files, bothered Erin. Or maybe she was just being paranoid, looking for dark motives where none existed. Either way, she obviously needed to look more closely at Jean Taylor.

The conversation in the cabin, however, had moved past Jean as the women started settling in for the night. Erin joined them, biding her time until everyone was in bed with the lights out. Then she headed for the restroom, her PC device in her pocket. Inside one of the stalls, she turned it on and pressed her thumb to the scanner that would read her fingerprint and change the device's mode of operation. Then she typed.

Have arrived safely. Accommodations good.

In case of intercept, it was purposely innocuous, a prearranged message to let her backup team know she was in place. They'd report to the Command Center in Miami and respond with another preset "All clear." She waited. Several minutes later, seven words scrolled across the tiny screen.

Enjoy your stay. Wish we were there.

Which told her they were nearby and waiting for her next communication tomorrow. Or the emergency signal that would result in her immediate extraction.

She returned to her bed and crawled in, her mind mulling over the possibilities surrounding Jean Taylor and the nameless men who seemed to watch everything and everyone in the camp. She agreed with the agent in Santa Clara, the men's purpose was very unclear. They could, as Erin had thought earlier, be PNR, but she didn't think so. No uniforms. No visible guns. Why pretend to be something they weren't? The Cuban government wasn't shy about using police power to monitor and intimidate its citizenry. It certainly wouldn't hesitate to keep foreigners in line. No, these men were something else. The questions were what, and who held their chains.

As for Jean, Erin knew there could be perfectly reasonable explanations for everything surrounding the other woman. Neither Jean's absence from the DFL files nor her failure to mention she was a doctor meant anything. Under normal circumstances, Erin wouldn't have questioned either. Unfortunately, these weren't normal circumstances. A man was missing. So Erin planned to take nothing at face value, and thus find out all she could about Jean Taylor.

Tonight, though, Erin was going exploring.

She waited, fifteen, twenty minutes to give everyone time to fall sleep. Then she got up quietly and headed for the door.

"Are you okay?" came a whispered voice in the darkness.

Damn. It was Sandy.

"I can't sleep," Erin replied, since obviously this was the other woman's problem. "Too excited and too hot, I guess. I'm just going to go out and get some air."

"Are you sure it's safe? I'll come with you if you want."

"No, go to sleep," Erin said. "I'll be fine."

"Well . . ." Sandy hesitated. "Okay, but don't go far."

"I'll be right out here." Erin stepped outside, hoping Sandy wouldn't decide to follow. Just in case, Erin sat on the small wooden platform fronting the cabin, giving Sandy a few minutes to act, or not.

The night was beautiful, clear and warm, with the sweet scent of tropical flowers floating on the air. A soft breeze rustled the palms, while overhead, feathery clouds skittered across a display of stars that the camp's few lights did little to block. Like the people who worked here, the camp itself seemed to slumber. Outside each of the four cabins, a low-wattage bulb pushed back the shadows. More dim lights outlined the clinic, and from the downstairs windows came the faint glow of night-lights. Other than that, the camp was utterly dark, the mess tent and office a smudge against the dark woods behind them.

Erin found it hard to believe anything sinister could happen in such a place.

After a few minutes, she figured Sandy had either fallen asleep, or at least didn't plan on joining her fellow volunteer outside. So Erin stood, stepping away from the light. Again she waited, listening and watching, for sound or movement that would indicate someone unseen had noticed her. At the count of twenty she slipped deeper into the shadows beside the cabin and made her way to the darkness of the woods beyond. Stopping, she looked back, the inky night around her making the camp seem bright by comparison.

Nothing moved.

Okay. Time to explore. On her own terms.

Picking her way along the edge of the woods, she kept the clinic in sight and worked her way toward the front of the camp. As she rounded the front corner of the building, she saw the men. Going still, she willed herself to blend into the darkness.

Two of them stood, leaning against the railing. She could just make out their dark forms and the glow of their cigarettes. Carefully, she moved a little closer. No words, but the murmur of low voices reached her. Still, she couldn't tell if they were the same men she'd seen earlier in the day and couldn't risk moving any closer. One thing was definitely different.

They were armed.

So, no visible weapons was a daytime thing, no doubt for the benefit of the volunteers. At night, however, automatic weapons were on display. Tonight anyway. But since she picked up no sense of urgency or tension from the guards, she guessed tonight was no different than any other.

She also noticed one other thing: a light upstairs in the front corner room. Her father's office. So, she and the armed men weren't the only ones awake. Interesting. For now, though, she put that thought aside and kept her attention on the guards.

Once confident they hadn't seen her, she fell back, a dozen feet or more into the woods. Now the clinic was barely visible, just a flicker of light through the trees as she again picked her way through the underbrush. This far into the woods, the going was more difficult. Branches pulled and scratched at her legs, roots caught at her feet.

Finally, she reached the road bisecting the woods and connecting the plantation yard to the outside world. Across the open expanse, and several hundred yards closer to the clinic, was her objective: a small one-story house that might have once belonged to the estate's caretaker.

She'd noticed it earlier when she'd first arrived. It had looked empty then, possibly unused, but not now. The wash of light. The raucous male voices drifting on the night air. The shadows moving across the open windows. So Casa de la Rosa's unofficial guards had claimed the bungalow for their own. Not a bad place to keep an eye on all comings and goings.

Erin wanted a closer look.

To do that, however, she needed to cross the road and risk someone spotting her. The only other alternative was to go back and circle the entire camp via the woods, coming at the building from the other side. Unfortunately, that would take time she didn't have. She figured it was already close to midnight, and picking her way through the woods in the dark was a slow process. She needed to get back to her cabin before Sandy, or someone else, noticed her absence.

She'd have to take her chances.

Inching closer to the main road and away from the house, she watched to make sure no one was outside or looking out a window. Then, she sprinted across the road. On the other side, she crouched behind a clump of oleander bushes, listening for any sign she'd been spotted.

She counted to twenty. Twice. Silence.

Only then did she straighten and allow herself to breathe normally. On the move again, she used the brightly lit cottage to pull her through the midnight woods. As she got closer, the voices inside grew louder, almost jovial, masking any sound she might make. At the edge of the tree line, she again hunkered down to think out her next move.

She wanted a look inside.

She didn't know how many men she was dealing with, much less why they were here. If she could at least get a better idea of their numbers, it might indicate the seriousness of the threat. Of course, she wouldn't turn down an overheard word or two that would give her some real information. However, that, she suspected, happened only in the movies.

So, she'd start with the numbers inside the house.

Unfortunately, a wide swath of brush and trees had been cleared around the structure, eliminating the natural cover the woods provided. As she'd done with the road, she gauged her chances of crossing unseen to the window. This was a far riskier proposition. If she was caught here, there would be no explaining her presence.

Before she could decide, however, two men approached the bungalow. Like those on the porch, they carried automatic weapons. Only these two moved with a purpose.

Erin pressed herself to the ground.

They entered the house, and the sounds from inside changed. She still couldn't make out the words, but the laughter stopped, and she detected an element of command in the voices. Chairs scuffled against wood floors, muttered responses, then four men left the cabin and headed off across the camp.

Erin sprang to her feet. Keeping to the woods, she circled the clearing around the cottage, her eyes fixed on the four men. They walked quickly, however, unhindered by the underbrush and darkness that slowed her. Passing the clinic, they seemed headed for the converted stables. Briefly, she saw a flicker of light at their feet. A flashlight. Then, the men vanished. One minute she'd been cursing the growing distance they'd managed to put between themselves and her, the next, they were gone.

"Damn." She didn't want to lose them.

She picked up her pace, despite the chances of tripping on an unseen root or branch. They must have entered the office or another area of the stable. One of the storerooms, perhaps.

The clinic fell away behind her.

It was darker here, without the blur of lights edging the woods to her right. But she must be close. The office was only a few hundred yards behind the main house.

Suddenly she stumbled onto two feet of cleared space.

She stopped abruptly, then backed beneath the shelter of the trees. In the darkness she'd almost missed it: a hard-packed and obviously well-used path. Strange that she hadn't seen it earlier in the day.

So, maybe the men hadn't gone into the stables.

She stood a moment, the path disappearing deeper into the woods pulling at her. She couldn't follow it. She knew that. Not tonight. With no light or weapon, she'd be walking into an unknown, taking a foolish risk. Besides, just because the path existed didn't mean the men had taken it. They could be back at the stables as she'd first thought.

She was tempted, though. So very tempted.

In the end, reason won out. She'd investigate this path, but she'd come back better equipped. For now she followed the edge of packed dirt toward camp, to where it dumped her out behind the office. She realized then why she hadn't seen the path when she'd arrived. It wasn't hidden exactly, but unless you knew the trail was there or happened to circle the old stables, you'd never see it.

Not forgetting the possibility that the men had gone inside, she studied the stables for several minutes. No lights shone in any of the windows, not even a flicker of a flashlight. It wasn't conclusive evidence by a long stretch. Still . . .

She glanced back at the path into the woods. Something told her she'd find answers at its dark end.

Tomorrow.

DAY THREE

CHAPTER NINETEEN

Fort Lauderdale, Florida

The call came ten minutes after midnight.

"Meet me in Fort Lauderdale," Steve Raoul said on the other end of the line. "South Beach. Do you know where it is?"

"I'll find it." Alec shifted his cellphone to the other ear so he could make notes. "When?"

"How soon can you get here?"

Alec glanced at his watch. This time of night, there wouldn't be much traffic. "Give me an hour."

"Okay, there's a beachfront parking lot on A1A, across from the Bahia Mar Marina. Pull in, and I'll find you."

Before Alec could ask anything else, the connection went dead.

For a moment, he considered calling Mendez and telling him about the meet. Steve Raoul was the cop's snitch. As a common courtesy, Alec should let the man know. Under the circumstances, however, Alec didn't feel right dragging Mendez out of bed in the middle of the night. This was far from an official FBI inquiry, and the fewer people Alec involved, the better. Fortunately, Mendez had asked no questions, but Alec didn't want to push his luck. Or that of the Miami detective.

Forty minutes later, Alec turned onto A1A, the road that follows the ocean up and down the Florida coast. He drove the length of Fort Lauderdale beach: a string of bars, hotels, and tourist shops across from the sand and surf. Like its more famous counterpart in Miami, South Beach was at the tail end of the Lauderdale hot spot. Unlike South Beach in Miami, however, it was past the action, just as A1A curved inland to bisect an up-scale residential neighborhood of waterfront homes.

He found Bahia Mar and kept driving south, past the Yankee Clipper, a landmark hotel shaped like the bow of a ship. Then, as the street darkened around sleeping homes, he U-turned and headed back toward the strip. Instead of pulling into the South Beach parking lot, however, he turned into Bahia Mar, flashed his FBI badge at the guard gate, and parked near the marina's restaurant.

Alec wasn't going to sit in the car like a target waiting for Raoul to show. It was one thing to wait in a parked vehicle for a cop in full daylight; it was quite another to wait for a snitch in the middle of the night.

Chances were he'd meet with Stephen Raoul, who'd have some possibly useful information—or not—and that would be the end of it. It would be quick, easy, and uneventful. Then Alec would head back to his hotel room in Miami and decide what to do next. Meanwhile, it never hurt to be cautious. It only took a little extra time and vigilance, whereas the consequences of care-lessness could be fatal.

Retrieving his .38 from the glove compartment, he checked the clip, then slid the weapon into the waistband beneath his shirt. Normally he was more comfortable with a shoulder holster, but wearing a jacket would be like wearing the letters COP, FBI, or some other bull's-eye emblazoned across his back.

Outside the car, a warm breeze stirred the nearby palms and carried the smell of salt and sea. He found the heat disconcerting, like someone forgot to alert the weather gods that night had fallen. Grateful at least that he'd worn light clothes, he walked north, toward the lights.

The Lauderdale strip was still alive, and the crowd young. Music and people spilled from the late-night bars. Cars cruised by, youthful bodies hanging out open windows, catcalling or whistling at pedestrians. Groups melded, opposite and same sex, laughing and flirting, moving together or remaining stationary while the foot traffic flowed around them. It reminded him of Bourbon Street in New Orleans without the nude dancers and their barkers throwing out invitations to the crowd.

Two blocks north, and he crossed over to the beach side of the street with a cluster of twenty-something barhoppers. They headed down toward the water, but he worked his way back south, until the lights and noise of the strip softened once more behind him. Then he veered off into the small picnic area fronting South Beach. He took up a position in the shadows where he could watch the parking lot and anyone approaching on foot from the water's edge.

Even here, there was still activity. The parking lot was about half full, obviously catering to the busy strip. A couple leaned against a car, wrapped in each other's arms, and several groups strolled by on the sidewalk, some heading for vehicles, others walking on toward the Yankee Clipper.

Alec scanned the cars, looking for signs of Raoul waiting behind a steering wheel. He saw no one, but that didn't mean anything. At this distance it would be easy to miss a person hiding within a vehicle's dark interior. Somehow that didn't strike Alec as Stephen Raoul's mode of operation, however. The kid was too antsy, too impatient and cocky to sit quietly inside a car.

So, Alec waited.

Five minutes. Ten. It was now twenty minutes past the time when Alec had said he'd get here, and still no Raoul. Maybe he'd changed his mind or never meant to meet Alec to begin with. Maybe Raoul had just called Alec's bluff.

The parking lot was beginning to thin out. The couple who'd been all over each other had driven away, possibly to take up where they'd left off in a more appropriate location. Several others showed up, walking down from the strip and climbing into cars. Alec couldn't help but wonder how many of them would pass a Breathalyzer if there happened to be a black-and-white waiting down the road.

He glanced at his watch. 1:45. He'd wait another fifteen minutes and call it a night.

Suddenly, Stephen Raoul arrived.

Driving a bright red Jeep, radio blasting, he turned into the lot. He slowed, driving past the parked cars, obviously looking for Alec, then pulled into a space near the middle. First he lit a cigarette, then climbed out, pacing to the front of the vehicle then back again, glancing at the row of empty cars. Like Alec had suspected, Raoul was too full of nervous energy to sit quietly and wait.

Alec let him stew for a bit before stepping out of the shadows.

The kid was quick, spinning toward Alec as soon as he moved. Then, recognizing him, Raoul visibly relaxed.

Alec once again retreated from the light.

Heading toward him, Raoul was halfway up the small sandy rise when a sharp report shattered the night silence. Alec dove to the ground, gun in hand, before putting words to the sound. Rifle fire.

Raoul still stood, shocked, frozen in place.

"Get down," Alec called.

Then he saw the dark stain spreading across the kid's right shoulder. Raoul touched his shirt, and his hand came away wet. He looked at Alec, fear and surprise in his eyes. Then, he dropped.

"Shit." Alec scrambled forward, half dragging Raoul into the shadows beneath the trees.

"Son of a bitch." Raoul cradled his right arm with the other. "That son of a bitch shot me."

Alec pulled out a handkerchief and pressed it against the wound.

Raoul sucked in a breath. "Hey, man, take it easy."

"Sorry." Alec couldn't tell how bad it was, but there was no spurting blood, so the bullet had missed the artery at least. "You'll be okay. Hold this."

Raoul grabbed the blood-soaked cloth, and Alec scanned the area around the parking lot for the shooter. He was still out there, possibly waiting for another shot.

With his free hand, he pulled out his cellphone just as movement from the parking lot caught his eye. A lone figure broke cover and darted across the street toward the marina.

Raoul must have seen it, too. "Don't let him get away."

Alec hesitated, hating to leave the injured man. After all, it was his fault Raoul had been shot.

"Go get him," Raoul growled.

Alec nodded, reporting the shooting to the 911 operator as he started after the fleeing gunman. In the lot, he spotted a couple crouched behind a parked car. "There's an injured man up on the beach," Alec called. "Go stay with him until the paramedics arrive."

Alec hit the street running, dodging around the few cars still on the road, and headed into the darkness of the marina. Ahead of him, he saw the shooter briefly, racing across the docks, before he seemed to vanish. Alec slowed as his feet made contact with the wood, the dark water sloshing beneath him. Gun pointed upward, he worked his way down the main pier, listening with every sense he possessed.

The shooter could be anywhere, on one of the dozen or so narrow wooden docks extending out into the canal, or lying in wait on the deck of a boat. Alec was making himself a target, yet he had no choice. He couldn't go back when there was a chance of catching the gunman. So he kept to the shadows as much as possible, his gun swinging from one sound to the next. The thump of a heavy hull against a piling. The creak of thick rope against wood. And the soft female laughter from a yacht's interior. No sign, however, of the figure Alec had seen fleeing across A1A.

Ahead of him an engine kicked over, a low rumble flaring to life.

Alec sprinted forward, though he figured he was already too late. The gunman hadn't been waiting for Alec; he'd already hit his target and was getting away. Alec came up on the end of the dock seconds after a long cigarette boat opened throttle and leapt across the water toward the open canal.

He raised his .38, aimed, but didn't fire.

He'd be shooting blind at an out-of-range target with no running lights, and no visible name or number. Instead, he pulled out his cellphone, dialed 911, gave his badge number, and reported a suspected shooter heading south on the Intracoastal Waterway.

Back on the beach, three police cruisers crowded the parking lot, the ambulance just arriving, lights flashing and siren howling. Alec showed his badge to the uniform holding back the curious as a couple of paramedics spilled from the emergency vehicle. The cop let him through, and Alec hurried toward the beach ahead of the medical team. He spotted the couple he'd asked to stay with Raoul, and the woman pointed Alec out to one of the cops as he passed.

"How is he?" Alec showed his ID to the cop crouched next to Raoul, propped against the trunk of a palm, his eyes closed.

"He'll be fine," the cop answered. "It looks like the bullet went clear through."

Alec squatted next to Raoul, whose dark complexion had gone pale. "You look like shit, man."

"Yeah, well . . ." Raoul opened his eyes, focusing on Alec. "Whose fault is that?"

Alec winced. "I'm sorry."

"Did you catch him?"

Alec frowned and shook his head. "Not yet." Then, seeing the EMTs heading their way, he said to the cop, "I need to talk to him for a couple of minutes alone before the paramedics take over."

The cop hesitated, then nodded and moved back, just out of earshot.

"What do you have for me?" Alec said, figuring the kid must have stumbled onto something important, something others didn't want Alec to know. Otherwise, why risk taking a shot at Raoul?

"Man, you don't let up." Raoul had closed his eyes again. "I told you this was a danger zone."

"You're right." Alec squelched another flare of guilt, reminding himself this kid was peddling drugs on the streets. "So tell me what you found out. Otherwise the bastard won, and you took a bullet for nothing."

"Spare me the amateur psychology." Raoul licked his lips, suddenly sounding years older than he'd seemed at the park. And Alec remembered Mendez stating that Raoul was not as young as he appeared.

"I've got a name for you," Raoul said, the words seeming to take a lot of effort. "That's it. Nothing more."

Alec leaned closer. "That's good enough."

"Helton," Raoul said. "That's who Diaz met with in February. Gregory Helton."

The name meant nothing to him, but Alec was willing to bet it would mean something to the CIA. "You done good, Steve," Alec said. "Now, I'll make sure you're protected."

"You sure as hell better."

Alec waved over the paramedics, then pulled the cop aside. "Whoever tried to kill him might try again."

"We'll take care of it," the man agreed, and moved off to accompany Raoul to the waiting EMT van.

Alec dragged a hand through his hair. What the hell was he going to do now? Someone had been willing to kill to keep this information quiet, which of itself was enough to make anyone in law enforcement suspicious.

Unfortunately, the next hour was spent with the locals.

As the technicians roped off and examined the crime scene, a couple of detectives arrived. Their questions zeroed in on Alec. He had witnessed an attempted homicide, and not even his FBI badge could get him off the hook. The detectives wanted to know: What was he doing here? Why was he meeting Raoul? What was he working on? Description of the shooter? Dozens of questions, most of which Alec couldn't or wouldn't answer.

He finally extracted himself from their clutches after they'd checked his identity with the local FBI field office. He figured Mathews would have more than a few questions of his own in the morning. Like, what the hell did Alec think he was doing? But for now, with a warning to make himself available for further questioning, the locals let him walk.

As he approached his car, however, he realized the night was far from over. A man leaned against the front hood, looking deceptively casual, relaxed, arms crossed. Alec knew better.

It was Erin's CIA contact. The man Alec had seen on the UM campus.

"I guess I should be surprised to see you here," Alec said.

"No more surprised than I was to find you digging up information about Emilio Diaz."

"Have I been treading on your toes, Officer . . . ?"

The other man grinned at Alec's obvious attempt to get a name and an acknowledgment of his CIA connection. He gave neither. "Yeah, but that doesn't surprise me, either. Considering your history."

Alec sighed. At another time he'd gladly exchange semihostile quips with this guy, or go a few rounds with him even. At the moment, however, he was just too tired.

"Look," he said. "I know you're CIA, and that you sent Erin into Cuba." He dragged a hand through his hair. "So let's skip the bullshit, shall we? It's been a long night, and I—"

"The name's Bill Jensen." He stepped away from the hood and nodded toward the car. "Get in. I need a ride back to Miami. And you and I need to talk."

CHAPTER TWENTY

Miami, Florida

Alec should have been exhausted.

Instead, a strange energy coursed through him, like a low-level adrenaline high. Or too much caffeine. He was often like this during an investigation, when he would push himself beyond the point of fatigue until he was running on pure willpower alone.

Only this time, he reminded himself, he wasn't working a case. This wasn't his investigation, a fact made very clear by the presence of the silent CIA officer riding in the passenger seat of the rental.

As Alec navigated the sleeping streets of Fort Lauderdale, he waited for Jensen to start talking. He'd asked for this meet, so the first move was his.

Alec had spoken the truth at the marina. It didn't surprise him that the CIA knew he was looking into Emilio Diaz, though he'd like to know how they'd found out. And obviously, Jensen thought Alec had discovered something useful. Otherwise, why track him down and demand this little chat? Though, so far, they'd exchanged nothing but silence.

He picked up I-95 off Sunrise Boulevard and headed south toward Miami.

"You know," Jensen said finally. "She'd be pissed off if she knew what you've been up to."

It was true. Erin wouldn't appreciate him researching her father. "Probably."

"Definitely. And she wouldn't be too crazy about the two of us talking, either."

Alec glanced at the other man. "Is that what we're doing? Talking?"

Jensen laughed shortly. "That was the intention."

"How well do you know her?" It was the question Alec had wanted to voice since he'd first spotted Jensen waiting for Erin in the UM parking lot. Asking Erin had been out of the question. Much easier, as they sped down a dark highway in the middle of the night, to ask this stranger.

"Well enough," Jensen replied. "Too well, I think, sometimes."

An unfamiliar roll of jealousy coiled in Alec's gut.

Jensen met Alec's gaze and snorted. "It's not like that, believe me."

Was he that transparent?

"Not my choice," Jensen clarified. "All she'd have to do is nod my way, and I'd give you a run for your money."

Alec didn't know how to respond to that. Erin wasn't exactly sending him come-hither signals.

"Erin's a difficult woman to love," Jensen said.

Alec didn't agree. She was easy to love. The hard part was getting her to admit she was capable of returning it. But talking about his feelings for Erin wasn't something he planned to do. Nor was it why he'd agreed to give Jensen a ride back to Miami.

"If you have something to say," Alec glanced at the CIA officer, "then I suggest you get on with it. Otherwise, let's just skip the bullshit and make this drive as quiet and painless as possible."

For several minutes Jensen said nothing else. Then, "We flagged Diaz's file so that anytime someone accesses it, we're alerted." He shifted on the seat, stretching out his legs and resting his arm against the window's edge. "That's how we found out you were looking into Diaz."

"Since when does the CIA have access to confidential FBI files?"

"Haven't you heard? We're cooperating with each other now." Jensen's voice dripped with sarcasm. "We share."

Alec snorted.

"Tell me about it." Jensen took a deep breath that pretty much summed up the frustration many in the ranks felt about the rhetoric of their respective agencies. All talk and no action, each agency still jealously guarding its own private little fiefdom.

"In this case, however," Jensen said, "we were given access to all the FBI's information on Diaz."

"How long ago?"

"When the situation went critical."

"Which was?"

Jensen hesitated. "I can't tell you that."

"You mean you won't." Alec threw a glance at the CIA officer, who shrugged. "So much for sharing."

Silence again, and Alec realized he'd been wrong earlier. He *was* tired, bone-weary tired. It was time to admit it. He'd just come off an exhausting and ultimately un-resolved case. Now he was chasing down leads for a sit-uation that other, competent officials were already handling. All because Erin Baker was involved.

A smart man would head back to his hotel—Alec could be at his within thirty minutes—and get a good night's sleep. Then tomorrow, he would return to Vir-ginia, where he'd take a couple of days off before letting anyone know he was back.

All he had to do was find out what Jensen wanted, then let go of this insane need to follow up on Erin. He couldn't spend his life protecting her. She'd never allow it and would claim she didn't need it.

"What do you want, Jensen?"

"Isn't it obvious? I want to know what Raoul told you."

Alec let out a short laugh. Of course. He did the work. Raoul took the bullet. And the CIA wanted the informa-tion. "The real question is, why didn't you find Raoul yourself?" He threw the other man a sideways glance. "Or is it that with all your sophisticated gadgetry, the CIA has forgotten the power of human resources?"

The tightening of Jensen's jaw told Alec he'd hit on the truth. "We have no jurisdiction within the States and thus no contacts," Jensen said, obviously having already justified his failure to himself.

"I'm not getting a warm feeling about this." Erin's safety was in this man's and his agency's hands. Yet he'd failed to ferret out an information source that Alec had found in less than twelve hours.

"Look, Donovan." For the first time, Jensen's voice held impatience. "We can argue all night about who has the better investigation techniques. But time is critical here. So why don't you just tell me what Raoul found out?"

"Are you so sure he told me anything? Or if he did, I'd share it with you?"

"He didn't take that bullet for nothing. Someone didn't want him talking." Jensen paused, then added, "As for sharing the information, I'm pretty sure you'd do just about anything to help Erin. Including cooperating with the CIA."

Which was the truth, but Alec had to try once more to get information in return. "Tell me what she's doing in Cuba, and I'll tell you what Raoul told me tonight." It was, of course, a bluff.

Jensen called it. "Are you willing to play Russian roulette with Erin's life? If you have information that will help us bring her out of Cuba safely, then you better let me have it."

Alec frowned, but in the end he couldn't risk jeopardizing Erin's safety. "Okay. Here's what I know. Emilio Diaz was in the States earlier in the year." He threw Jensen a glance to see if this was news to him as well. From the look on the man's face, he was every bit as surprised as Alec had been.

"Go on," Jensen said.

"The FBI has been keeping tabs on Diaz for years. Which you know. Otherwise you wouldn't have wanted access to his files. Right?"

Jensen nodded.

"Then you probably also know that Diaz likes to stir things up in the Cuban American population." Something else suddenly occurred to Alec. "By the way, did you tell Erin about her father's part in all this? Or that you'd been watching him?"

For a second, Jensen didn't answer. When he did, he avoided the question altogether. "What else?"

"I didn't think so." Alec had to clamp down on his anger. Just as they'd done last year, the CIA was using her, playing on her emotions to get what they wanted. They knew she wouldn't be able to resist going into Cuba to meet her estranged father, but they'd failed to tell her he was part of what they were after. The only question was what part.

"Donovan?"

Jensen's voice pulled Alec back. "The FBI has documented Diaz's activities every time he's shown up in the States. This time however, he slipped in and out of the country undetected. I wanted to know how and why, so I sent Raoul to find out."

"And?"

"There wasn't much." Not nearly enough, especially considering the kid had taken a bullet for it. "He gave me the name of the person Diaz met with in February." Alec shrugged. "It doesn't mean anything to me, but I was planning on running it through the system in the morning."

"Give me the name."

Alec hesitated. But when it came right down to it, Jensen had been right. Alec wouldn't play games with Erin's life. "Gregory Helton." He waited for Jensen's reaction. When the other man remained silent, Alec said, "Do you know the name?"

It took a moment for Jensen to answer. "No. But,

whoever he is, we'll find out what he has to do with Diaz."

For some reason, Alec believed him. Or maybe he was just going soft in the head. Because he knew if Jensen had recognized the name, he wouldn't admit it. Not to Alec.

After that, they fell into an uneasy silence.

Ahead, the nearly empty highway snaked out, a dark strip illuminated by overhead lights. At the signs for Miami, Alec turned off the interstate, and Jensen gave him directions to his office. They turned south on A1A, past Alec's hotel. Then Jensen pointed to a dark strip center, and Alec pulled in, driving around to the back per Jensen's instructions. He stopped the car and waited for the CIA officer to get out.

"So, what's it gonna be, Donovan? Are you going to let us do our job and leave this alone?"

Alec thought about Erin, about his certainty that the CIA was using her again. He thought about Stephen Raoul, who was in the hospital because of the questions he'd asked for Alec. And he thought about his own plans to return to Virginia and let Erin handle the CIA. "I can't do that."

Jensen turned to stare out the passenger window. "I was afraid of that."

After a few more seconds of silence, he reached for the handle and opened the door. Then he looked back at Alec. "Well, if you're not going to get out of our way, you may as well come in and help. Because you were right about one thing, we don't have the human resources to track this thing down. But maybe you do."

CHAPTER TWENTY-ONE

Miami, Florida

Alec followed Jensen into the CIA Command Center.

In truth, he didn't know what to make of Jensen's willingness to let him in on the operation. Rumors within the intelligence community claimed the CIA was no longer effective. They relied too heavily on technology and thus had lost the knack for obtaining firsthand information. Possibly Jensen believed Alec could bolster their investigation with his local contacts. Of course, first Jensen would have to admit the Agency had a problem, which seemed unlikely.

So maybe it was as simple as Jensen believing he could control Alec if he kept him close. Either that, or the man had some nefarious plan to use Alec like he was doing Erin.

Whatever. Alec didn't care. As long as he could find out what was going on with Erin and help if possible.

Jensen introduced Alec to the part of his team on duty. The first was Rhonda, a slender black woman with an easy smile, then Al, an even thinner guy, a genuine geek with wire-rimmed glasses and scraggly hair. They weren't much more than kids, which made Alec wonder why the techies always seemed so young.

"We work in rotating shifts, so there's always some-one on the computers," Jensen explained. "We have cots set up in the other room, so hopefully Rob and Zeb are getting some sleep about now." Then turning to his an-alysts, he added, "If you haven't guessed, this is Agent Donovan."

The woman's smile broadened. "Our phantom FBI agent."

"Not anymore," Jensen said. "I've pulled him in to help out."

"Really?" She arched an eyebrow. "I guess you're the boss."

"And don't forget it," Jensen said with a grin. "Now, Donovan's got some information for us." Nodding to Alec, he said, "Tell them what you told me."

So Alec went over everything he'd found out from Steve Raoul once again. The meeting. The location. The shooter and his escape. And the name Raoul had taken a bullet to get.

When he finished, Jensen said, "Okay, find this Hel-ton person. It's probably an alias, so think outside the box. And we need more on that meeting in February. Es-pecially how Diaz got into the country undetected. So get on it."

The two young people turned to their computers.

"One other thing," Alec said, drawing them back around. "I want that shooter. I called in a description of the cigarette boat he used to escape. The locals are pretty vigilant because of the drug runners, and there aren't a lot of boats racing down the Intracoastal in the middle of the night. So check to see if either Fort Lauderdale's Marine Unit or the Coast Guard picked him up."

Rhonda looked to Jensen for confirmation of the order.

"You heard the man," he said. "Make the calls."

Rhonda nodded, and she and Al went back to work.

Jensen led Alec across the room to a conference table. Behind it was a large, freestanding board divided into three sections. The left side contained timelines. On the far right, nearly two dozen photos filled the surface, while the middle board had only one.

Jensen picked up a file from one end of the table and dropped it in front of Alec. "All the details are in there," he said, then headed for a counter littered with coffee paraphernalia.

Alec pulled out a chair, opened the file, and glanced at the first document. It was a communication from a Juan Padilla in Cuba.

"In a nutshell," Jensen said, as he filled two mugs with dark, steaming caffeine. "We had a report from one of our foreign agents in Cuba about some unusual activity in the DFL camp." Then he glanced at Alec, a question on his face.

"Just black," Alec answered.

Jensen nodded and brought the cups. He set one in front of Alec, then sat down across the table. "So we sent in an officer to have a look. He disappeared."

"Just like that?"

"We know he got to Havana," Jensen said. "Other than that, nothing." He spread his hands, palms up. "We don't even know if he reached the camp. Twenty-four hours after he's due to send in his initial report through our agent in Santa Clara, we know something's wrong."

"So you send in Erin to find him." It wasn't a question. "Using her relation to Emilio Diaz as a cover."

"That's about it."

"Isn't that a bit like throwing good money after bad?"

Jensen met Alec's gaze and frowned. "And would you have done anything different? Would *you* have walked away from one of your own, Agent Donovan? Or would you go in to bring him out, or at least find out what happened?"

Alec didn't respond. They both knew the answer. You didn't leave your people behind. And if he was honest, he'd admit that the only reason it bothered him in this case was because Erin was the rescue squad.

"What makes you think she won't fall prey to the same fate as your first officer?" Alec asked.

Jensen ran a hand through his hair. "The first operation was sloppy." He didn't look pleased to admit it. "We didn't take the information seriously."

"But you do now?"

"We make mistakes." A bit of irritation showed in Jensen's voice. "But we try not to repeat them. Erin has backup and a strong cover."

"You mean as Diaz's daughter?"

"No, that's just the icing. Every few months the DFL camp rotates out half its volunteers. This week there will be at least a dozen new faces at the camp. Erin is just one of many."

"And her father?"

"He's been running that facility for over twenty-five

years. He knows everything that happens there. Erin is on a fact-finding mission. So I believe their relationship may help her get information."

"They don't *have* a relationship."

Jensen shrugged. "We'll see. After all, he's still her father."

Alec wrapped his hands around the mug and leaned back in his chair. Taking a sip of the coffee, he thought about Jensen's plan. It might work. "But you think Diaz is involved."

Another shrug. "Either voluntarily or involuntarily. Yeah, I do." He hesitated. "There's one other thing you should know."

His tone caught Alec's attention, who waited for the proverbial shoe to drop.

"DFL is pulling out of Cuba in about three months. They're abandoning their facility in Santa Rosa." Jensen broke eye contact, as if guilty about this last bit of information. "Which makes it even more likely that Diaz is involved. He's put his life into that place and probably feels like—"

"He has nothing to lose." Alec finished the sentence, through a roll of anger. One of the main criteria that could set someone on a dangerous course was desperation, the belief that he'd run out of options and had nothing else to lose.

"We didn't know." Jensen again met Alec's stare. "DFL said nothing about it when we first contacted them. They just admitted it this morning." He shook his head. "You can believe that. Or not."

Alec didn't, but it didn't really change anything, except to make the situation worse. Make Diaz more dangerous. "It could backfire, you know. Their relationship, or lack of one, could hurt or get in the way."

"We considered that." Jensen paused, nodding. "But, in the end, I believe Erin will do the right thing."

Alec snorted, shaking his head. It was an easy thing to say, so much easier than the actual execution. Sometimes, when it came to people you loved, it wasn't always easy to know what was right. It was an argument he couldn't win, though. So he said, "Tell me about her backup."

"We have a team in place within a few miles of the camp. Erin communicates with them daily, and in case of an emergency, they can reach her and pull her out within minutes."

"If she survives that long."

"Erin can handle herself. She's been trained for this, and she understood the risks going in."

"Except the part about her father's involvement."

"She knew it was a possibility."

"But an unlikely one." Alec could almost imagine the hedged conversation between Jensen and Erin, how he'd sucked her into this mission.

"Erin's not stupid," Jensen said.

No, Alec thought, but she was vulnerable. And once again, the CIA had used that vulnerability to manipulate her. He couldn't change that. All he could do was get *his* emotions under control so he could help get her out of Cuba alive.

"You're angry that we sent her in," Jensen said.

This guy's insight was beginning to piss Alec off. "Does it show?"

Before Jensen could reply, Alec stood and went to the

storyboard. One picture in particular, the lone one in the center, drew him. He saw Erin in the man's face, in the fine Latin features and dark, intelligent eyes. He was handsome, and intense. Like his daughter. "She looks like him, doesn't she."

"Yeah."

Alec couldn't help but wonder how she was handling meeting her father after so many years. Erin's emotions were both her strength and her weakness. She fought them, denied them, and struggled to suppress them. Yet they remained close to the surface despite her efforts.

"Have you heard from her yet?" he asked, while keeping his back to the other man.

"Last night. She's in place at the camp." Another hesitation from Jensen, then, "No matter what you think, I want Erin out of there in one piece as much as you. But I have a job to do, as does she."

Alec studied the board and its myriad photographs—all actors in some play they hadn't yet uncovered. He remembered Erin last fall, the way she'd come alive in a fight. She'd chosen this work because it answered a need within her. He knew he'd have to accept this part of her. Or let her go. Then he thought of the possibilities of what could happen to a CIA officer on that island ninety miles south of the Florida coast.

"I need to know if I can count on you, Donovan," Jensen said behind him. "Otherwise, you need to leave. Now."

Alec took a deep breath and turned back around, his decision made. At least about this. He couldn't walk away. Later, he'd have to sort out his feelings about Erin and loving a woman who would spend the rest of her life putting herself in harm's way.

Before he could answer, however, Rhonda hurried over from the computers. "We have news," she said. "The Marine Patrol stopped a cigarette boat near Port Everglades about an hour ago." She glanced at Alec. "They think they have your shooter."

CHAPTER TWENTY-TWO

Casa de la Rosa, Cuba

The hidden path haunted Erin's dreams.

In her sleep, she walked down its dark corridor, whispers reaching her from the trees. She walked faster, not knowing whether she was running toward or away from the voices. Only the path never ended, the woods stretching like a tunnel, its edges becoming stone, tilting down, until she had the sensation of being underground. Cold. And the voices faded to laughter.

She came awake with a start. Eyes open. A lingering sense of menace nudging her thoughts even as the dream images receded. From the windows, early morning light brightened the cabin, stirring the sleeping women and clearing the last gossamer threads of Erin's unease.

She glanced at her watch. Almost 6:00.

After her excursion the night before, she'd managed about five hours' sleep. Not bad. Except for the dream. Even now, though, it disintegrated as she got ready for the day.

Her class didn't start until early afternoon, so that would give her plenty of time to look around the compound in the daylight, particularly the half-hidden path in the woods. Plus, last night she'd seen six men: two on the clinic veranda and the four she'd followed. She wondered if that was all of them. Or would she see more new faces today?

Also, she'd planned on talking to more of the volunteers. At this point she wasn't even certain Joe had made it to the camp, much less that he'd seen something that had caused his disappearance. She couldn't ask direct questions about him, but the better she got to know the others, the more likely she was to hear something that would put her on the right track.

Instead, she spent the morning on paperwork.

She must have read and signed a half dozen release forms for DFL, and at least that many for the Cuban government as well. Then she spent the rest of the morning preparing for her class.

She'd been teaching at the university level for several years, but her only contact with children had been her niece Janie. Most of the time Erin felt like Janie was the teacher, not the other way around. So Erin had a feeling neither experience was going to help her much in a roomful of children.

She hadn't a clue how to begin.

An hour into the class, however, she realized she was

enjoying herself. The previous volunteer had been an experienced teacher who'd created a series of games that made the process of learning and teaching a language more fun than work. All Erin had to do was follow the format. On top of that, the children were remarkable: bright, attentive, and eager to learn. By the end of the afternoon she wished things could be different, that teaching this class was her real purpose for being in Cuba.

Then reality returned in the form of her father.

As the last of the children scurried from the room, he appeared in the doorway. She froze, suddenly unsettled, nervous, searching for something to say, something daughterly. Their meeting yesterday had been cordial enough, if awkward.

Emilio broke her silence by stepping into the room.

"Can I help you?" she asked, both her voice and the question sounding more formal than she'd intended.

He gave her a knowing smile, obviously more at ease than he had been yesterday. "How did your first day go?"

"Okay." She tried to smile, tried to lighten her tone. "Good, actually."

He slipped his hands into his pockets and glanced around the room. "How many? Children, I mean."

A part of her hesitated to answer. She didn't want to deal with him, with the strange, mixed-up emotions he aroused in her. Over the years she'd relied on her anger to keep her feelings about him tightly contained. Now, however, her anger had deserted her, leaving her confused and uncomfortable.

"Eleven," she said.

"Good. That is a good number." He picked up a storybook left by one of the children and flipped through it. "You will have different students each day. Depending on when their parents need them to work."

"Is there something you wanted, Dr. Diaz?"

He winced, possibly at the use of his title. She was, after all, his daughter. "Please, call me Emilio."

"Is that what the other volunteers call you?" It seemed inappropriate to use his first name, and she couldn't bring herself to use a more intimate form of address.

Papi.

The endearment came to her unbidden. It was what she'd called him as a child, a nickname she'd forgotten. Or suppressed.

"You could," he visibly hesitated, "call me Father."

It would be the right thing to do, what everyone would expect. And if nothing else, she had a cover to maintain. "Okay. Father."

He smiled tightly, obviously sensing her discomfort, but left it alone. "Actually, I came to apologize."

"Apologize?" For a moment she thought . . .

"Yesterday, I should not have asked so bluntly about your mother. It was thoughtless, and I am sure it brought up bad memories." He glanced away, shadows once again darkening his eyes. "My only excuse is that I was not expecting you, and I do not deal well with surprises."

Erin couldn't speak.

She didn't understand how he could mourn for a woman he'd left years earlier. Yet, he did. She saw his grief, raw and real in the lines of his face and the set of his mouth. Something inside her melted, just a bit, at the thought.

"It's okay," she said finally. "You had no way of knowing."

He met her gaze, gratitude and something else replacing the grief. "Thank you." He glanced away again, cleared his throat, and said, "I also came to ask you to have dinner with me. I could show you my clinic afterward, if you like. And, we can talk."

Again, he'd caught her off guard. Though this, she suspected, shouldn't have surprised her. He was here, looking for something from her. Forgiveness maybe? Or, possibly, he was just going through the motions his peers here at the camp expected.

"I'd like that," she answered, and, strangely enough, it was true. Though she didn't want to think too hard about that now. She would rather believe that it had more to do with her mission. The more she knew about this place, the greater her chances of finding Joe. If she had a certain amount of curiosity about her father, well, that was natural.

Besides, she still had a question to ask him. Why?

A few minutes later, as they made their way across the compound, Emilio glanced at her left hand. "Are you alone then? No husband?"

She thought of Alec. Smiled. Though that really wasn't a road she wanted to travel at the moment. "No, I'm not married, but I have Claire and Janie."

Her father looked at her, a question in his eyes.

"Mother remarried after you left," Erin answered. "Claire is my half sister, and Janie is her daughter."

"Yes." He nodded, his expression grim. "I remember now that Elizabeth remarried. But she had another daughter. . . . That, I didn't know."

It suddenly came to Erin that this was as hard for him as for her. Making casual conversation with his estranged daughter, trying to bridge the twenty-seven-year gap in their relationship, didn't come easily to him. Nor to her. Maybe they shouldn't even try.

The silence continued as they arrived at the dining tent, got their food, and found a quiet table in the back. Several volunteers greeted him as they passed, and Sandy gave Erin a quick thumbs-up. She knew they were being watched and figured their awkward relationship was the main source of current camp gossip.

"So, tell me about yourself," her father said, once they'd taken their seats. "What do you teach at the university?"

She thought about the senior seminar she'd just finished on U.S.-Cuban relations. "International Studies. I earned my doctorate at UNC Chapel Hill, then went to Cairo for two years."

"Cairo?" He hadn't touched the contents of his food tray except to sip at his coffee. "A dangerous place. And a long way from home."

She made a point to eat, taking her time before answering him. "My focus of study is Mideast cultures. So when the opportunity to go to Cairo came up, I couldn't turn it down."

"Why not study a people closer to home?"

She sensed a touch of censor in his voice. "Like Cuba?"

"It *is* your heritage."

"I've never had much interest in Cuba." Though that wasn't exactly true. She'd been drawn, or more accurately, she'd been torn by her curiosity about her father's country.

"And yet, you are here." Another shadow darkened his eyes. "Why is that, Erin?"

She couldn't answer. He'd caught her with her own words. Instead, she continued with her biography.

"When Mom died," she said, "I came home to be near Claire and Janie." She couldn't tell him how she'd been in Cairo when her mother died, that by the time she knew her mother was seriously ill, it had been too late. "I was lucky enough to get a position at Georgetown," she added.

She saw the curiosity behind his polite smile. Why was Claire, a woman old enough to have her own child, and her daughter, living with Erin?

It was one more thing she wasn't going to explain: Claire's kidnapping and how it had torn their family apart, marking them all. Especially Claire. How Claire couldn't be left alone for fear she'd hurt herself. That was private, family business, and although he was her father, he'd made it clear long ago that he was no longer family.

Or maybe she imagined his curiosity, because he didn't voice it. Instead, he said, "Georgetown is an excellent school."

"I didn't like living in the Washington area. None of us did. It's expensive, and the winters were too long and cold."

He nodded, obviously an explanation a native of this tropical island could well understand.

"So, when a position opened at UM, I applied and got it."

He sipped at his coffee. "You have done well for yourself. I am proud of you."

The compliment pleased her. Though why she should care what he thought of her was another question she didn't want to explore. She nearly laughed aloud at the thought. Wouldn't a psychiatrist have a field day with her mixed-up crazy feelings about her father? All she'd have to do was add her interaction with the CIA to the mix, and they'd probably lock her away in a padded cell.

CHAPTER TWENTY-THREE

Miami, Florida

Frustration. It was an emotion Alec understood well.

All law enforcement people lived with it on a regular basis, but some days were just worse than others. Today had been one of those. After eight hours at the Fort Lauderdale police station, interviewing two suspects in the previous night's shooting, Alec knew very little more than he'd known at the start of the day.

Now it was late afternoon, and he figured he'd take one more crack at making the day yield information. He turned his car toward Holy Cross Hospital, where the paramedics had taken Steve Raoul. Alec hoped the kid could tell him something about Gregory Helton, or at least where he'd heard the name. However, when Alec arrived at the hospital, Raoul was gone. He'd checked himself out hours earlier, claiming he couldn't trust the cops to keep him safe.

Strike two.

Though Alec could hardly blame the kid. Someone had taken a shot at him over a single name, and there was no reason to believe they wouldn't try again.

So Alec headed back to Miami. Forty minutes later, as he came through the door of the CIA Command Center, Jensen waved him over to the conference table.

"Talk to me," Jensen said.

"Not much to tell." Alec ran a tired hand through his hair and dropped into a chair. He needed a few hours' sleep. "The Marine Patrol pulled over a cigarette boat with two men, near Port Everglades, about forty-five minutes after the shooting. The boat matched the description I'd called in from Bahia Mar."

Jensen nodded. Alec had told him that much over the phone, along with the men's names.

"They were headed out the cut," Alec said. "Full throttle. No running lights. So, even without my call, they might have been stopped."

"Weapons?"

Alec shook his head. "Nothing. The Marine Patrol tore the boat apart."

"They probably dumped the rifle."

"No doubt, and we could spend the next year dragging the Intracoastal and never find it. Also, no way did it take them forty-five minutes to get from Bahia Mar to Port Everglades."

"How long?"

"The way they were moving? Ten, fifteen minutes tops." Alec hesitated. "What if they dumped more than a rifle? Say, they dropped off the shooter as well."

"A third man? Possible." Jensen picked up a pencil, twirling it absently in his hand. "What's our boater's story?"

"They claim they were out for a midnight cruise."

Jensen snorted. "Yeah, right."

"They know I can identify the boat, and the locals threatened to charge them with a half dozen crimes each, including attempted murder of a federal officer." Alec came forward in his chair, leaning his arms on the table. "They were sweating, but neither of them talked." He paused. "Whoever they're protecting, they're more afraid of him than us."

"Tony Calabria."

Alec waited for an explanation.

"We talked to DEA. Calabria is a local crime boss. DEA claims your boaters are low-level dealers on his payroll. DEA's had their eyes on them for some time, but they want Calabria."

"Of course." Why take down the soldiers when you can get the general?

"Also, according to DEA, neither of the boaters has anything in his background that would lead us to believe he could have fired that shot." Jensen dropped the pencil. "Of course that doesn't mean too much. Hell, they could be out shooting cans in the Everglades." Though they both knew that was unlikely, at least with the kind of high-powered rifle necessary to make the shot that had wounded Raoul.

Alec pushed back in his chair again, rubbing his hands over his face. Then he said, "So, we have a possible drug connection. Diaz sneaks into the States and sets up something with this Helton character and one of the local drug lords. Diaz has the facility and the medical expertise."

"And he needs money to keep his clinic up and running," added Jensen.

"Let's not forget the Cuban government."

"Big money in drugs." Jensen nodded. "So Castro's government agrees to look the other way. They might have even pressured Diaz to go along."

"It all seems to fit." Alec hedged. "Except . . ."

"You're not buying it?"

Alec shrugged. "If this is about drugs, what are we doing here? And why isn't DEA all over this?"

"Calabria's people could be just setting things up," Jensen suggested. "Until someone intercepts a shipment into the States or a new source of drugs hits the streets, it's not even a blip on DEA's radar."

"So the CIA just stumbles onto it?"

"Sometimes we get lucky."

Alec shook his head. "Tell that to your missing officer." Or to Erin, who was putting her life on the line looking for him.

Jensen came forward in his chair, his expression suddenly intense, almost angry. "And that's why I'm not turning this over to DEA or anyone else. Even if this is about drugs. I have one officer missing and one in play.

Until they're both off that damn island, this is still *my* operation."

It was something they had in common, Alec realized. Loyalty. As Jensen had pointed out yesterday, you didn't leave your people behind or trust someone else to keep them safe. Alec couldn't help admiring the man's determination, and it gave him a bit of insight about why he was here. Why Jensen had allowed Alec to stay. Jensen understood that as long as Erin was inside Cuba, Alec *couldn't* walk away.

After a moment Jensen regained control, and the cool CIA officer resurfaced. "Anyway, we'll know more after we find Helton."

Which brought them back to Erin, to the reason she'd been sent into Cuba. Whether Alec liked it or not, she was the key. Without her, and the human information only a person on the ground could provide, they were taking potshots in the dark. "And when we hear something from Erin."

Jensen met his gaze. "That too."

CHAPTER TWENTY-FOUR

Casa de la Rosa, Cuba

After finishing their meal, Erin followed her father back out into the early evening. The sun had fallen behind the western trees, changing the harsh tropical light to a soft pearlescent glow.

"Let me show you the clinic," he said. "And you can see for yourself the good we are doing here."

He took her through the front screen door of the plantation house. The expansive entrance hall had been turned into a typical doctor's waiting room. Except, like everything else in the compound, they'd made do with whatever furniture they could find. A couple of once-elegant chairs and an old, threadbare couch lined one wall, while on the other, someone had built a long wooden bench out of spare lumber. Opposite the entryway, a reception table sat in front of a pair of French doors. Beyond that, she caught a glimpse of the central courtyard, alive with color.

"Cuba has made great strides since the revolution," Emilio said. "All her citizens have access to free medical care."

"Then why the need for DFL?"

He shrugged and slipped his hands into his pockets. "Because drugs and medical supplies are not so easy to get." He started toward an interior door on their right. "The U.S. trade embargo has made sure of that."

She might have argued with him if she'd sensed any accusation or outrage in the statement. As it was, he'd spoken as calmly as if he'd claimed the sky was blue. So she followed him into the right wing of the house without comment. After all, she wasn't here to discuss politics.

"This is the heart of the clinic," he said. "As you can see, we took down the interior walls."

The wide-open room was divided into six logical sections, each consisting of an examination table, workstation, and retractable curtain. Unlike the waiting area, the equipment here looked new and in good shape.

"Nothing like this exists in Santa Rosa," he said, as if reading her thoughts. "DFL equips its facilities well, and that is why they are needed here."

It made sense. Free medical care solved only half the problem. Equipment and medications were the missing pieces an international aid organization could furnish that the postrevolutionary Cuban government could not, or—depending on your point of view—would not, supply.

She caught a glimpse of Emilio Diaz that she hadn't expected. "That's why you work for them, isn't it?"

"The Cuban people need what DFL offers." There was a strength, a conviction in his voice she hadn't heard before. "But it is not easy dealing with this government, with their interference. Other organizations have already pulled out. But, this is my country, *my* people, I understand how things work. If I can help by working for DFL, if I can keep them here, how could I do any less?"

She couldn't respond.

This was a side of her father she had never considered: a man fighting for a principle, dedicating his life to a bleeding people. The thought bothered her, fighting the image she'd built in her mind of him over twenty-seven long, lonely years. She had more questions, but the answers might solidify this new view of a man she didn't want to admire. She wasn't certain she was ready for that.

Emilio broke into her thoughts, bringing her back to the mundane, the world as she knew it. "We have two examining rooms in the back for when we require privacy, and," he motioned toward a side door to the veranda, "direct access outside for when we have people waiting for inoculations or vaccinations. Sometimes the lines are very long."

Her reality slid back into place, though it seemed a bit off now, not quite right, as did her perception of the man at her side. "Does that happen often?"

He shrugged. "Now and then." He paused, studying her for a moment, then added, "Tomorrow we start to vaccinate for dengue. All the volunteers, and as many villagers as we can get to come in."

"I thought that was under control." Dengue and dengue hemorrhagic fever were mosquito-borne viruses usually found in the tropics. Eradication of the disease was one of the touted success stories of the revolution.

"So the government would like you to believe." Her

father shrugged, and again, she detected no judgment on his part. He was just stating facts as he knew them. "The last doctor who reported a case was jailed. So, we do it here. Quietly. Since we are not part of the state system, no one questions us." He paused, sighed, and added, "We all do what we have to do."

He led her toward the back of the house, past the two private examination rooms. Then they stepped out into the central courtyard, onto a covered breezeway that framed all four inside walls.

"This is lovely," Erin said.

The exterior of the house may have been patched together in haphazard fashion with functionality as its goal, but this garden had been tended with an eye for beauty. Water danced sweetly in a small central fountain. Meandering stone paths led from the house through clusters of pink oleander, red hibiscus, and frothy palms. And several stone benches sat strategically beneath a sprawling ficus tree.

"It is an indulgence." Her father smiled, a bit self-consciously. "Several of the women from Santa Rosa tend it. It gives them work and needed dollars. Besides, it is good for the patients and staff to have such a place."

Erin didn't know what to say. It was another jarring note, another unwanted side to this stranger that shoved her thoughts down unfamiliar paths.

"Come," he said. "I have one last thing to show you." He headed across the garden and through a door leading to the far wing of the house. "This is our hospital wing."

The left side of the house was divided into two sections, one for men and one for women, each containing eight beds.

"There is a state hospital in Santa Rosa," her father said. "But the patients must supply their own sheets and soap. So, in some cases, it's better when they come here."

A bit dazed, she followed him as he stopped and talked to each patient, asking a question, giving an answer here, offering a word of reassurance there. She desperately sought to take a mental step back to the anger she'd always felt when she thought about her father, or even to the grudging sympathy and curiosity of a few hours ago. She couldn't do either. Not faced with the people in these beds, sick and hurting, and the kind man who tended them.

Finally they were outside again, where Erin felt she could breathe.

"So what do you think?" he asked.

What could she say? "You're doing good work here." Beyond that, she needed time to think over what she'd learned about him, about the man who was her father, and put it into perspective.

"We could use your help."

She looked at him, suddenly wary. "Besides teaching?"

"Your classes are only in the afternoon, yes?"

She nodded.

"As I told you, we start vaccinating for dengue tomorrow. We are short volunteers and could use an extra pair of hands."

She stepped back and crossed her arms. "I'm not a nurse." Plus, her mission required uncommitted time when she wasn't expected in any particular place. Already DFL's bureaucracy had cost her the morning hours when she could have gotten a better look at the path she'd seen the previous night.

"No, but the things you could do would free up the nurses we have." Then, before she could respond, he added, "Think about it. Now come, I will walk you back to your room."

As they started toward the cabins, however, a truck turned off the road and pulled into the yard, stopping between the stables and house. It was the first vehicle she'd seen since Armando had dropped her off the day before.

"Finally," Emilio said beside her. "They are weeks late."

"What is it?"

He started toward the truck. "Drugs, medical supplies, equipment."

Erin followed him.

Armando and another man climbed out of the truck's cab, chattering in rapid Spanish as they raised the rear door and prepared to unload. Two of the aimless men she'd come to think of as guards walked over to the truck, though neither offered to help. Instead, they laughed and poked fun at the Cubans' expense.

"Hey, amigos," one guard taunted. "If those boxes are too heavy, we can get one of the girls to help you."

Armando and his partner ignored them, hauling boxes off the back of the truck and piling them high on handcarts. Then, with one of the guards in the lead, the three of them headed toward the back of the converted stable.

"Where are they going?" Erin had expected them to take everything into the clinic, but it looked like they were headed toward the path she'd stumbled on last night.

Emilio glanced at her, his expression distracted. "We have a locked storage facility in the woods."

A place armed men visited in the middle of the night?

"Isn't that risky?" Cuba's population was poor, and drugs difficult to get. A thief could demand and get a high price for them on the black market.

He brushed her question aside with a wave of his hand, all his attention focused on the truck. "It is very well protected. Plus, there is no road. You can not drive a truck back there and load. It would make it difficult to steal much."

Erin nodded.

On the surface it made a certain amount of sense, but she didn't buy it. Even the best security systems could be breached with the right equipment, and if the place you wanted to rob was off the beaten path, it would be that much easier. There had to be another reason for the storage shed's location.

Before she could question her father further, however, the three men returned with their empty handcarts. As they'd done before, Armando stayed on the ground while the other workman climbed into the truck bed and handed down cartons. One box after the other, they unloaded, until, while wrestling a particularly large one, Armando lost his grip. The box dropped and split open, spilling and shattering glass at the men's feet.

The guard sneered, laughed. "Clumsy idiot."

His face tight, Armando crouched to pick up the box

and its contents. Erin glanced at her father, whose expression was as unreadable as the man's on the ground. Though, she noticed his fists, tightly clenched at his sides. The man in the truck climbed down, evidently to help, but stopped as the second guard waved him aside.

"Hey, you," said the guard, nudging Armando with a booted foot. "Aren't you going to apologize to the good doctor here? You broke some of his precious supplies."

Emilio took a step toward the guard. "Leave it."

Ignoring him, the guard said to Armando, "I'm talking to you." He again used his foot, this time hard enough to knock Armando off his haunches. "Apologize."

Laughing as Armando scrambled to his feet, the guard turned to Emilio. "Where do you find these monkeys?"

Armando brushed off his clothes, muttering. *"Hijo de puto."*

The guard spun around, his smile gone, and grabbed Armando's arm. "What did you just call me?"

Armando shook off the man's hand. "I said you are a son of a whore." Then he backed up and spit on the man's boots. "And I spit on you."

Face flushed with anger, the guard moved with dangerous speed, slamming the other man against the truck and pressing a thick-muscled arm across his neck while a 9mm Soviet Makarov appeared in his hand, jammed beneath Armando's chin. "You want to say that again?"

CHAPTER TWENTY-FIVE

Casa de la Rosa, Cuba

Emilio moved quickly toward the two men, looking for a way to insert himself between the gun and its target. "Put that away."

The gunman kept his eyes on Armando, a man Emilio had known since first coming here in the late seventies. "This is not your business, Doctor."

"Whose business is it then?" Emilio knew only too well the kind of men Helton hired. This man was more than capable of killing without remorse. "Armando works for me. The cost of the supplies will be deducted from his wages."

"This isn't about your precious supplies anymore," the gunman sneered, his sarcasm ripe and vicious. "It's about this monkey learning to keep his mouth shut."

"Let him go." Emilio put more bravado in his voice than he felt. When it came right down to it, he could do nothing if this man decided to pull the trigger. And as much as he'd like to believe otherwise, there would be no repercussions. Helton would do nothing. "And put the gun away."

Suddenly, the weapon swung toward Emilio. "Do you like this better, Doctor?"

Without warning Erin moved up beside him. Emilio threw out an arm to stop her. She went very still, but he sensed her tension. It didn't feel like fear.

"Don't be an idiot," she said, though he had no idea whether she was speaking to him or to the man with the gun. What did she think she was doing?

"Get out of here." Emilio was afraid to take his eyes off the man holding their lives in his hands. Then to the gunman he repeated his earlier command. "Put the gun away. Otherwise, you *will* be replaced."

In his peripheral vision he saw that a small group of volunteers had gathered. *Damn*. So much for keeping these deliveries low-profile. "Unless you plan to kill everyone here."

For a few long, interminable moments, the gunman didn't flinch. He stood, eye to eye with Emilio. Strangely, he found himself thinking that if the man pulled the trigger, it would almost be a relief. This insanity would cease. Except this thug might then turn his weapon on Erin, and that, Emilio could not accept.

The gunman's eyes flickered briefly to Erin.

"You are out of line," Emilio said, bracing himself to throw himself at the man if necessary. "There will be consequences."

Another long stretch of silence.

Then, slowly, the fury faded from the other's eyes. As if in slow motion, he lowered the gun, then slid it into the waistband of his jeans and pulled his shirttail down to cover it.

"You better watch yourself, Doc." He took a step

back, throwing a disgusted look at Armando still cringing against the truck's bumper. "Someday you'll go too far."

"No doubt." Emilio took a deep breath, though he kept his eyes on the gunman as he slunk away. To Armando and his partner, he said, "Go. We do not need you anymore tonight. Get some food and rest." Then, though he had no intention of letting this cargo sit out in the open overnight, he added, "You can finish in the morning." Emilio would unload the damn truck himself if necessary.

The men didn't need to be told twice. They both took off in the direction of the village.

Then Emilio turned, annoyed beyond reason at the gaping volunteers who'd gathered. Were they disappointed that no blood had been spilled? "Everything is finished here. There is nothing else to see. Please, go back to your cabins."

As they started to disperse, he remembered Erin. She still stood next to him, still tense. Jean had been right. There was nothing weak about his daughter. Foolish. But not weak. Nothing of her mother.

"What did you think you were doing?" he asked, his fear sliding dangerously close to anger. "That man could have killed you, *would* have, without a second thought."

She met his anger with steady eyes. "The gun was pointed at your head, not mine."

"You think he would have stopped after killing me?" Could she possibly be so naïve?

"I think," she said, "that men with guns don't belong in a medical compound full of volunteers." She crossed her arms, her voice unreasonably calm, maddening. "So, what are they doing here, Father?"

"They are for protection." A lie he barely got past his lips.

"Protection?" She obviously didn't believe him, and why should she? She would have to be stupid.

"Castro has eyes and ears everywhere on this island."

"So, are they Castro's men then?" He could see she didn't believe that, either. "PNR? Military perhaps? That guard didn't sound Cuban to me."

"Go to bed, Erin." He shook his head and backed away from her. "You'll learn that in Cuba it's not a very good idea to ask too many questions."

CHAPTER TWENTY-SIX

Casa de la Rosa, Cuba

For hours, Erin lay awake.

She relived every moment of the scene by the truck. The gunman's rash actions, a bully throwing his weight around. Armando, frightened to the point of panic. The 9mm Makarov pointed at her father's head. And her own stupidity as she'd reacted to the threat instead of hanging back.

It all circled in her mind, a cyclone of vivid, dizzying images.

If it weren't for Joe's disappearance, she might have dismissed the whole incident as nothing more than the usual paranoia of Castro's regime. The gunman could have been just another lowlife, the type tyrannical governments bred like cockroaches. Under the circumstances, however, she had no doubt he was something more, that he was part of why Joe had disappeared.

Also, there was the storage facility in the woods. She didn't buy her father's explanation for its location. It didn't feel right. So, she needed to get a look at it. Soon.

The piece that really bothered her, however, was that she'd almost blown her cover. Or at the very least, put a large dent in it. When the gunman had aimed his 9mm at her father, she'd reacted without thinking.

If Emilio hadn't stopped her, she would have put the gun-toting lunatic on the ground. Which would have been a disaster. Some of the volunteers might have bought her martial arts training as an explanation, but anyone with any experience—military, mercenary, or law enforcement—would see right through her. Sparring in a ring was one thing, taking down an armed man in a real-world situation was something else again.

She had to stay focused.

Her purpose here was to find out what happened to Joe Roarke, so the CIA could bring him out of Cuba. Alive, if that was still possible. She couldn't let anything, not even her father and her unresolved feelings about him, distract her.

DAY
FOUR

CHAPTER TWENTY-SEVEN

Casa de la Rosa, Cuba

The rain woke her.

A light morning shower that seemed to be the standard in these mountains. It temporarily refreshed and cooled the air, even now at the height of summer. By the time she'd finished showering and dressing, the sun had pushed through the clouds, promising another warm day.

She ate breakfast with Sandy, Nancy, and a couple other volunteers. She didn't see her father, but Jean showed up, taking a table by herself across the room.

Erin hadn't seen Jean the day before, which was surprising considering the size of the compound. Of course, there could be a perfectly logical explanation, but Erin couldn't afford to take anything at face value. Plus, she wanted to know why Jean hadn't mentioned being a doctor.

"Shouldn't we ask Jean to join us?" Erin said to the group at her table.

One of the women snorted. "Don't bother. Miss High-and-Mighty doesn't mingle with the peons."

"That's not fair." Nancy frowned. "Dr. Taylor is just very busy."

"Doing what?" asked the first woman. "You don't work in the clinic, Nancy, so you don't know. She's hardly ever there."

"She works the night shift," Nancy clarified. "That's why you don't see her. And I *do* know, because I make the schedule."

The first woman rolled her eyes. "Whatever you say."

The hostility surprised Erin, and she wondered if it was Jean's looks or her medical degree that was the source. Or was she really as off-putting as this one woman claimed? Jean had seemed nice enough when she'd shown Erin and Sandy around. It could be simple jealousy. A woman who possessed both beauty and brains was a lethal combination, intimidating.

"What are you planning to do this morning?" Nancy asked, deftly moving the conversation away from Jean Taylor.

Erin pushed her plate aside. "I promised my father I'd help out in the clinic." Not exactly the truth, but close enough.

Sometime during the sleep-tossed night, she'd come up with a plan. Her priority today was getting a look at the dispensary in the woods. She was convinced the armed men weren't here for the staff's safety. Instead, their function was to protect something else from prying eyes.

Erin's first guess would be drugs.

With the medical equipment and expertise available in the camp, setting up a coke kitchen or meth lab would be a simple matter. Hell, housewives could do it in their homes. And the money from transporting drugs back to the States would be substantial, enough that the Cuban government might turn a blind eye.

So she wanted a look at that cabin in the woods. It was as good a place to start as any.

Other than that, she'd fall back on her initial strategy. Which was to get better acquainted with the medical staff and volunteers, including her father. Sooner or later, someone would reveal something.

With that in mind, she couldn't pass up the opportunity to work in the clinic on a limited basis. And although she told herself it had nothing to do with spending time with her father, she wasn't fooling herself. Emilio Diaz had captured her interest yesterday, if not in the clinic, then certainly when he'd risked his life for Armando.

"Erin?" Nancy waved a hand in front of Erin's face. "Still with us?"

Erin realized she'd been staring and turned her attention back to the other women. "Sorry. Just daydreaming."

Nancy grinned and jabbed the woman next to her with an elbow. "So he's making you work double duty?"

Erin looked from Nancy to the woman next to her. "He said he's short a couple of volunteers."

"Well, that's true enough." Nancy started to gather up her tray. "But everyone," she threw a pointed look at the woman who'd made the negative comments about Jean, "figured he'd go easy on you. It looks to me, however, like it's the other way around."

The woman beside Nancy flushed.

Maybe she's a troublemaker, Erin thought, and Jean

was just an easy target. "He's probably overcompensating," Erin said. "He doesn't want to show preferential treatment to his daughter."

"Well, just don't let him work you too hard. You are, after all, a volunteer." Nancy picked up her tray, then stood. "And tomorrow, we're taking a day trip to Santa Clara. We probably won't go again while you're here, so plan on coming with us."

"Okay, I'd like that." It was time she made contact with Padilla, the CIA agent in Santa Clara. After she got a look at the dispensary, hopefully she'd have some information to pass on to Miami.

For now, though, she wanted to talk to Jean.

As Nancy walked away, Erin stood as well, saying to the others, "Excuse me."

After dropping off her tray, she refilled her coffee cup and headed across the tent. "Mind if I join you?"

Jean looked up from the paper she'd been reading and smiled. "Erin. Sure." She motioned toward the empty seat across from her. "How was your first day?"

"Great." Erin pulled out the chair and sat down. "Legalese is my favorite bedtime reading material."

Jean laughed. "It's a bitch, isn't it? All those forms, half of which have been translated from Spanish, which only makes them worse."

"And no one warns you before you show up."

"That's bureaucracy for you." Jean smiled. "And your class?"

"Fine. No problem."

Then Jean leaned forward, a sudden gleam in her eyes. "So, how did your reunion with Emilio go?"

"We're . . . " Erin hesitated, not wanting the conversation to go in this direction. Nor did she like the other woman's blatant curiosity. "We're getting to know each other."

"Well." Jean settled back in her chair, seeming disappointed. Had she expected Erin to share some juicy tidbit? "That's something at least."

Erin laughed lightly, suddenly feeling a bit uneasy.

She was beginning to understand why the others weren't crazy about Jean. On the surface she was friendly and funny, but there was something about her, something just a little off. But the question was, did it have any relevance to Joe's disappearance? Tomorrow Erin would send Jean's name to Miami via the agent in Santa Clara and see what they came up with.

"So, where were you yesterday?" Erin asked, probing gently. "I was looking for you before lunch."

"Were you?"

"Yeah, I thought we could eat together."

Erin could almost feel the other woman withdraw as she smiled tightly. "I was busy yesterday."

Doing what?

Though Erin couldn't ask the question, she waited a few seconds for Jean to volunteer the answer. When she didn't, Erin said, "Well, I expect you heard about our little encounter with those weird men last night."

"Yes, I did." As surely as she'd slammed a window, something shuttered Jean's eyes, completing her withdrawal. "Look, Erin," she motioned to the paper she'd been reading, "I really need to finish this."

Dismissed, Erin backed off. "Oh." She put just a shade of hurt into her voice and grabbed her coffee. It seemed she'd just touched too closely to a forbidden topic. "Not a problem." She stood. "I'll catch you later."

"Sure."

Erin started to turn away, then stopped. "Jean, why didn't you tell me you were a doctor?"

Jean blinked. "I'm sure I did."

"No, I don't think so."

"Well." Jean pressed her lips together and shrugged. "I guess it never came up."

Erin pasted on a smile. "You're probably right. It's no big deal. See you later." Again, she started to turn away, only this time Jean was the one who stopped her.

"Erin?"

She paused to look at the other woman.

"You know," Jean said, her voice clipped and brittle. "Be careful. It's not a good idea to ask too many questions in Cuba. It can be very dangerous." There was no mistaking the threat behind the words.

Erin smiled, tightly. "So I've been told."

As she left the tent, Erin's thoughts shuffled through the enigma of Jean Taylor. Something was up with her. Whether it could lead to information about Joe, Erin couldn't say, but she hadn't imagined the sudden chill in the other woman's voice, nor the menace in her last statement. The sooner she could get Jean's name to the Command Center in Miami, the better.

For now she headed toward her father's office, wanting to tell him herself that she'd help out in the clinic on a limited basis. Plus, maybe if she asked the right questions, he'd reveal something about Jean, or even Joe.

Erin entered the clinic through the rear stairway. Then, halfway down the hall, she came to an abrupt stop. From her father's office came an unfamiliar male voice.

"What's going on, Emilio?" The stranger kept his voice low, though it contained undertones of anger. "I've been gone less than forty-eight hours, and I come back to chaos."

Erin pressed herself against the wall.

Emilio let out an abrupt laugh, followed by clipped words. "You are exaggerating."

"I *heard* about the delivery problem last night."

"Did you?" Emilio's tone turned angry. "And whose fault is that? Those men are a danger to this camp and everyone in it. I have told you this many times."

"Now who is exaggerating?"

"And what will you say when they kill someone?" Something hard slammed against the desk. "When one of the villagers or volunteers gets in their way and pays with his life? Will I be exaggerating then?"

"Enough, Emilio. I didn't come here to talk about my men. We've had that discussion before, and the subject is closed." There was a finality to his tone, that of a man accustomed to giving orders and having them obeyed. "The men stay."

There was a slight pause, a tension Erin could sense even through the walls. Then Emilio said, "What do you want from me then?"

"I want to know what *she's* doing here?"

Erin frowned, wondering who they were talking about. Jean Taylor, possibly?

"We have many new people coming in over the next week," Emilio was saying. "But we needed someone short-term to take over the English classes until the regular volunteer arrives."

Erin's breath caught in her throat. Not Jean. They were talking about her.

"The classes could have waited," said that harsh stranger voice. "Why bring in someone new now?"

"You said everything should continue as normal. The normal procedure is for the office staff to fill vacant spots when necessary." A chair squeaked, as if one of the men had finally sat down. "That is what happened. This is not something I control."

"Do you run this facility or not?"

"I can not know every detail." Erin heard the touch of sarcasm in her father's voice, a minor triumph. "That is why DFL provides me with a staff."

Either the other man didn't hear, or chose to ignore, Emilio's condescension. "A bit coincidental that your daughter shows up now, don't you think?"

"She came to see me." It was a flat, unemotional statement. "This is not coincidence."

"But now, Emilio? Why now?"

"Who can say?" Her father's voice was almost too casual, too nonchalant. Was he enjoying pulling the tiger's tail, or did he know something he wasn't sharing with his obviously unpleasant visitor?

"I don't like this," the stranger said. "And I'm holding you responsible. Make sure she doesn't get in the way."

"I've already taken steps to keep an eye on her."

"Make sure that you do." Wood scraped against wood, like a chair being shoved back. "I won't stand for any more screw-ups, Emilio."

Erin had heard enough. She backed up.

Then, heavy footsteps on the old wood floor told her she'd never make it down the stairs without him seeing her. And he didn't sound like the kind of man who'd take kindly to an eavesdropper. She slipped into the closest room, wedging herself behind the open door. Hopefully, the empty office didn't belong to the man already coming down the hall.

She held her breath as he passed, watching through the slit between the door and its frame. She couldn't see much, just the shape of a large man heading for the outside door.

Then he stopped.

He stood there, unmoving. Listening? Had she made a sound, giving herself away? Or maybe he sensed something? Someone watching him? She could only guess. But if he turned, he would see her shadow behind the door. Of that, she had no doubt.

One second. Two. Three. Four.

She willed herself to absolute stillness, while her brain raced through the possibilities. If he saw her, she wouldn't hesitate. There would be no explaining herself. She would have to fight her way out of this. Get past him. Get out of camp. Send the signal to the backup team to pull her out. She could do all that if necessary— maybe even survive it. Then the search for Joe Roarke would begin again. The CIA would send someone else, with each passing day decreasing the likelihood they'd find him alive.

Go, she commanded silently. *Just open the door and leave.*

Then, as if hearing her, he obeyed. He stepped outside, letting the screen door slam behind him, his heavy boots echoing through the house as he descended the stairs.

Erin closed her eyes, relieved. For an instant, she'd thought her time at the DFL camp had come to an end. Now, she just needed a way to get outside without anyone seeing her.

CHAPTER TWENTY-EIGHT

Casa de la Rosa, Cuba

Getting out of the clinic proved easier than Erin had expected. Following the hallway, she found the inside stairway and took it to the first floor. She came out in the back corridor between the hospital wings, but she didn't want to leave through that door, either. So she cut through the clinic, where Sandy was on duty.

Acting as if she belonged, Erin said, "Sandy, have you seen my father?"

"Sorry." She looked up from a workstation where she was arranging rows of vials and needles. "He hasn't come down yet. Are you here to help out? They tell me to expect an onslaught of locals for these vaccinations today."

"Not yet. I'll be back in a couple of hours. I feel like a slug, so I'm going for a run." The story would buy her some time when no one would be looking for her. "Then I have to prep for my class. After that, I'm all yours."

"I'll take what I can get."

"Would you tell my father for me?"

Sandy waved her on. "Sure. See you in a couple."

"Thanks." Erin grinned, then headed out through the reception area.

On the wide veranda, she stood for a few minutes, her eyes sweeping the area. The yard was empty. However, near the caretaker's cottage sat an unfamiliar jeep, which she guessed belonged to the stranger in her father's office.

She thought about the conversation she'd just overheard.

DFL listed her father as camp administrator, but he'd obviously lost control. The other man, whoever he was, had placed armed men in the camp, rendering Emilio nothing more than a figurehead. And although she hadn't seen the man, she suspected his face wasn't among those she had studied in the DFL files.

The questions were still: What were any of them doing here? And what had happened to Joe Roarke?

Something else had struck her about the man as well. From his accent, she would bet he wasn't Cuban. He sounded American.

Besides that, one other thing had become blatantly clear. Whatever was going on here, her father knew about it. The knowledge sent a pang of regret through her. She hadn't realized until this moment how much she'd wanted Emilio to be completely innocent.

Taking a deep breath, she descended the steps.

She had a job to do. Gather information. Find Joe Roarke. If her search implicated her father, then so be it. She wouldn't let her emotions interfere.

Now, it was time she had a look at that dispensary.

She'd decided the best way to access the path without being seen was through her classroom's storage area, a small walk-in closet with shelves and a back window. The camp guards wouldn't appreciate her sudden interest in the dispensary, and she couldn't count on getting past them in the open. However, the makeshift school was part of the converted barn and only a few yards from the woods.

So the window was her best bet.

As she crossed the camp, she watched for an unfamiliar face. She didn't see him, though a couple of his men were near the back of the clinic. Besides that, she passed and waved to several of the staff. Then she was inside her classroom.

After checking to see that she was alone, she slipped out the back window as planned, pressing herself against the building once her feet touched the ground. If anyone saw her now, things could get dicey. How would she explain crawling out a window or sneaking into the woods? So for a moment, she stood very still, listening for the sounds of approaching feet.

Nothing.

With one final glance to make sure no one was watching, she crossed to the woods. The temperature dropped immediately. The canopy of trees blocked the sun and cooled the air, the undergrowth still damp from the early morning rain shower. And as she moved deeper into the forest, the world seemed to fade behind her.

The dispensary couldn't be far. She guessed it had taken the three men about fifteen minutes round-trip to transport and unload their boxes. Yet it felt like she'd entered a different world, miles away from the safety of the DFL camp.

Around her, the trees closed in, mainly pine, but cedar, and other exotic species she didn't recognize, as well. Underneath, bracken ferns covered the ground, and a parasitic vine with bright red berries wound its way up host trunks. The scent of pine and the musk of vegetative decay permeated the air. Along with the silence. Except for the trill and call of birds, she heard only her own footsteps, emphasizing the stillness of the place.

Suddenly, an uneasy tingle crawled up the back of her neck.

She kept her pace while resisting the urge to glance behind her. Fortunately, the path was well worn and easy to follow, as her heightened senses focused outward. Behind her. Not on the trail but off to the side.

Someone was following her.

He was good, someone your average volunteer wouldn't detect. So she kept moving, pretending not to notice while bracing herself for an attack. Meanwhile, she couldn't help thinking of Joe. Had he explored this worn path and the place at its end? Had it caused his disappearance? She hoped, and feared, she might soon find out.

Finally, the trees opened up.

In the center of the clearing sat the dispensary. She took a deep breath to steady her nerves, no longer detecting her stalker. She knew she hadn't imagined it, nor did she believe the person was gone. Her tracker was simply beyond her range of awareness. Nothing she could do about it now, except play the part of the innocent volunteer exploring the extended camp.

She moved out of the shelter of the trees.

The first thing that struck her about the building was its size. It was small, too small for a drug laboratory. Other than that, it was sturdily built but plain, and sealed up tightly. The windows were covered with plywood, and the heavy door looked strong enough to withstand a battering ram. She didn't see any cameras. However, a keypad next to the door indicated an alarm system. On the surface, it could be exactly what her father had claimed, a secured building for housing medical supplies and equipment.

Or possibly, something else was kept here.

If this *was* about drugs, maybe they weren't producing them here, but just storing them. Possible. Though it blew a big hole in her theory about the medical environment being a perfect manufacturing site. Unless, of course, the lab was somewhere else in the camp.

Either way, she wanted to get a look inside.

Unfortunately, she couldn't do it now without bringing the men with their 9mm Makarovs running. With the right equipment she could bypass the alarm, but she had nothing like that with her. She never would have gotten it by Cuban customs. Tomorrow, on her trip to Santa Rosa, she'd meet Padilla, the local CIA contact, and see if he could supply her with a handheld computer capable of bypassing the security system.

Then, as she circled around to get a look at the rear,

something at the tree line caught her eye. One section of bushes looked different than the rest, the shade of green flatter. As she got closer, she realized it was a foliage blind, like the ones used by hunters. It hid a break in the woods, just good enough to fool the casual observer. She squeezed behind it and found a dirt road.

Well, well, she thought. So much for no vehicle access.

Just then, the sensation of being watched returned. It hit her suddenly and hard, and she barely kept herself from reacting. She left the shelter of the trees, making her way toward the cabin, heading for the front. Still the curious American volunteer, she let herself practically run into a bulk of a man.

She jumped back, a hand fluttering to her chest, her startled reaction not entirely feigned. "Damn," she said. "You scared me to death." He was a large man, tall and heavily muscled. "Where did you come from?"

"I could ask you the same question."

She recognized his voice from her father's office and realized a part of her knew he'd been the one following her. "I came from the DFL camp." She edged backward a bit and motioned toward the path. "You?"

"Why are you here?"

She crossed her arms and put a hint of indignation in her voice. "What business is it of yours?" Then, pulling herself to her full height, the act of a haughty American woman, she added, "Who are you, anyway?"

He eyed her for a moment, as if not quite sure what to make of her. Then he said, "I'm Gregory Helton, the DFL administrator."

"Really?" Erin visibly relaxed and held out her hand, not believing for a minute that this man had anything to do with administration—though she didn't doubt he ran the camp with an iron fist. There was a menace about him, an aura of danger in the way he handled himself that screamed soldier. "We haven't met yet. I'm a new volunteer. Erin Baker."

"I know who you are, Ms. Baker." He crossed his thick arms, letting her hand dangle in midair. "What I don't know is why you're here."

"Well," she shrugged and grinned. "I'm exploring. I heard that the dispensary was back here, so I thought I'd come have a look around."

Again he studied her, disbelief in his eyes. Trust wasn't something this man knew much about. "You may as well go back to camp, because there's nothing here to see."

She glanced behind him and pushed him a bit further. "Can I see inside?" She saw the cable, snaking up from the ground to the cabin.

"It's locked."

"I can see that." She pasted on a vapid smile. Was the cable for a phone line? Electricity? Alarm? Or all three? And could it be her way to bypass the alarm to get inside? "I'm just curious why it's way out in the middle of nowhere."

"That, Ms. Baker," he took her arm and started her toward the path, "is none of your business."

She pulled away from his grip and looked back at the cabin. "Is there some reason I shouldn't be here?"

"You don't belong."

"But—"

When he grabbed her arm again, his grip had

changed. She wasn't going to simply slip his hold a second time.

"I suggest you curb your curiosity," he said. "This is Cuba, remember. And these woods can be very dangerous. Especially for a woman alone."

CHAPTER TWENTY-NINE

Casa de la Rosa, Cuba

Erin didn't like being manhandled.

Yet Helton kept a firm grip on her arm as he led her back toward the camp. That alone was enough to make her want to strike out and put him on the ground. An action that would be unbelievably stupid.

Not only would it blow her cover and destroy her chances of finding Joe, it might get her killed. She wasn't sure she could take him down. He outweighed her by a good hundred pounds of muscle, and she had a feeling he knew how to handle all that weight.

When she gave martial arts classes at the CIA farm, someone would always ask what happened when you met an opponent twice your size with just as much skill. Erin's answer had always been that it came down to heart and the desire to survive. That was true, but only to a point. Because sometimes, in reality, you just lost.

She had a feeling Helton would crush her.

So, she kept the urge to strike out firmly in check and continued her façade of the overly curious volunteer. Halfway down the path he finally released her, and she let out a relieved breath.

Then as they cleared the woods, he stopped and studied her. "You look like him, you know."

Erin lifted her chin, refusing to answer while rubbing her arm where he'd held it.

"Let's just hope you're not as stupid." With that, Helton turned away and strode off across the yard toward the clinic.

Erin watched him go. A big, dangerous man. It might just be worth the risk to make him bleed a little. Too bad she couldn't indulge herself.

Then, as she headed for the makeshift schoolroom, she noticed Nancy watching from the office door. With a quick look over her shoulder to make sure Helton was no longer in sight, Erin switched directions and headed into the office.

Nancy looked at Erin sympathetically. "I see you've met our charismatic administrator, Mr. Helton."

"You mean, Mr. Charming?" Erin rolled her eyes. "Oh, yeah. I came across him in the woods, and you would have thought I'd committed a felony."

"He's a piece of work, isn't he?"

"That's an understatement." Erin wondered if Nancy had any idea just how much of one. "What's a man like that doing here, anyway?"

"Well, I suspect DFL sent him to smooth the transition."

"Transition?" Erin crossed her arms. "What do you mean?"

"Well, I'm sure the Cuban government isn't happy about DFL pulling out, and they—"

"Wait." Erin held up a hand to stop her. "DFL is leaving Cuba?"

"You didn't know?" Nancy looked surprised.

"No." It would have been a nice detail for Jensen to share. "I had no idea."

"In about three months. The incoming group of volunteers will be the last." Nancy shrugged. "I guess DFL decided they've had enough of the Cuban bureaucracy."

She thought of Emilio's pride as he'd shown her around the clinic last night. He'd spent his life building this place, and now DFL planned to take it away. "What about my father?"

"Well, I really don't know for sure, but the rumor is that he fought the decision and lost." She frowned. "But I think he's planning to stay."

He would. This was his home. As he'd said, these were his people. Which might explain his involvement with someone like Helton. Emilio was desperate. "So, you think Helton is here . . . why?"

"Well, again, I'm not sure, but I think he's here to protect DFL's interests. All the medical supplies and drugs belong to them, and maybe DFL thought Dr. Diaz . . ." She hesitated. "Your father wasn't the best person to keep their assets safe." She looked embarrassed. "Seeing as he fought the decision and is planning to stay and all."

"So, Helton showed up after DFL announced they were leaving?"

"Pretty much. But I'm really just guessing about the reason. All I do is handle the scheduling and help coordinate the volunteers. I don't do anything for the paid staff."

"So who else besides my father is on DFL's payroll?" According to the DFL files, Emilio was the only staff member at the camp. Everyone else was a volunteer.

"Just Mr. Helton and Dr. Taylor."

Of course. The two missing pieces in the DFL records. Erin took another guess. "So, you don't ever communicate with DFL directly?"

"Oh no, never. Dr. Diaz, or maybe Mr. Helton now, handles all the interface with the New York office."

How convenient. Especially if you want to pass off someone like Helton as DFL staff. And Jean Taylor? Erin wondered if the other woman was even a doctor.

"What about the armed men?" Erin asked, interested to hear Nancy's take on them as well.

Nancy settled onto the corner of her desk. "Yeah, that was quite a spectacle last night."

That's not exactly how Erin would have described it, but it would do. "It was pretty scary there for a few minutes."

"They're not supposed to carry guns," Nancy said, lowering her voice. "At least that's what your father told me a couple of months ago, when they first showed up."

"Are they from DFL, too, working for Helton?"

She shook her head. "No, they're either Cuban police or military, I don't know which. But we see them all the time when we go into Santa Clara. Sometimes they even ride with us into town."

"So what are they doing here?"

"They're keeping their eyes on *Cuban* property."

Except Emilio had called them Helton's men, so if Nancy's assessment was correct, Helton was here with the Cuban government's knowledge and consent. Instead of voicing that concern, however, Erin said, "So, we have Helton on one side, and a group of supposedly unarmed Cuban police or military on the other."

"A rather volatile situation."

"I guess."

Nancy's perspective was an interesting mix of half truths and speculation, which Erin suspected Helton or Emilio had initiated. Why? What were they hiding? And again, she came back to drugs. It wouldn't be the first time the Castro regime had turned a blind eye to drug runners on its soil. If the money was substantial, and with drugs it always was, who knew?

"Anyway," Nancy said, recapturing Erin's attention. "I saw you with Helton and thought I should warn you."

"Thanks. I'll keep clear of him."

"Personally," Nancy added, "I'm glad I'm leaving at the end of the week. Things are just getting too weird around here."

Erin couldn't argue with that. Only she doubted Nancy had any idea of just how weird, or how dangerous.

CHAPTER THIRTY

Casa de la Rosa, Cuba

Emilio had never seen Helton angry.

The man kept himself firmly under control at all times and expected others to do the same. When they didn't, his response was quick and often violent, but not angry. He simply meted out his own form of discipline. Watching him these last few months, Emilio had come to realize that for the first time in his life, he truly understood the term cold-blooded killer.

Right now, however, Helton was as close to anger as Emilio had ever seen him. His eyes sparked with a dangerous fire, his mouth set in a grim line. He'd come into the clinic, where Emilio had been checking over some charts. Fortunately, no one else was within earshot.

"We need to talk." It wasn't a question or request, but a command meant to be obeyed.

"Let us go up to my office," Emilio suggested.

"Let's."

Helton followed him upstairs, shutting the door behind him. Not slamming it, but consciously closing it with a finality that sent a chill down Emilio's spine.

"What is wrong?" Emilio asked.

Helton's back was still turned, and he stayed that way a moment longer. Regaining control? Emilio could only guess, and nothing he came up with boded well. When Helton finally turned, however, the coldness was back in his eyes. The iron control Emilio had come to expect from the other man was firmly back in place.

Somehow, it didn't make Emilio feel better.

Without preamble, Helton said, "I found your daughter in the woods this afternoon. Near the dispensary."

"Erin?" Emilio blinked, unsure how to react, or what he could say that wouldn't make the situation worse. The dispensary was strictly off-limits. Everyone in the camp knew this. It was part of the orientation all staff members underwent when they first arrived. Except, he remembered, since most of the new volunteers wouldn't be arriving for a few days, it had been put off until the end of the week. "What was she doing there?"

"That, Dr. Diaz," still standing, Helton leaned forward, resting his massive hands on the desk, "is what I want to know."

Emilio slowly lowered himself into his chair, forcing his body to reflect a calm he didn't feel. This was dangerous ground. Very dangerous. "Well, what did she say?"

"She said . . ." Helton paused, for effect no doubt. "That she was exploring."

"And you don't believe her." Of course Helton wouldn't believe her, or anyone. The man didn't understand the meaning of trust. Or honesty.

"Do you?"

Emilio shrugged. "What else could it be?" In truth, he

didn't know what he believed, but he couldn't stand by and let Helton decide Erin was a threat, either. It would be her death sentence.

"She was with me last night when we unloaded the truck," Emilio explained. "And she asked about the dispensary's location. So maybe that is exactly what she was doing today. Exploring."

"Bullshit."

Emilio stood his ground. "You are being paranoid."

"Paranoid men live longer."

But those around them don't. "I'll talk to her and find out what's going on."

"I want her out of here." Helton pushed off the desk to his full height, a big man filling up a small space. "The sooner the better. Send her back to Miami, or wherever she comes from. Tomorrow."

"And how do you suggest I do this?" Emilio folded his hands. "I still answer to DFL as well."

"Not for much longer. Besides, what do you care what they think? They threw you and this facility away."

Emilio flinched. Helton had struck too close to the truth. "It will look suspicious and there will be questions if we send her away for no reason."

"Do you want her to live?"

Emilio sucked in a breath. The idea of Erin in this maniac's hands frightened him. "Okay, if you insist."

"I do."

"I will send her home with the group that is leaving the day after tomorrow. I'll say a long-term volunteer has surfaced to handle the classes." He paused, again holding back any signs of his fear. "Will that be soon enough?"

Helton hesitated, his eyes narrowing as if trying to see the trap in Emilio's words.

"It will make a lot more sense to everyone," Emilio insisted. "And no one will suspect anything."

Helton eased off a bit. "Day after tomorrow?"

Emilio took a deep breath. "Yes, with the others."

"Take care of it, Doctor." Helton waited a moment, then said, "We are too close to the end here for any more mishaps. Do you understand?"

"Yes, yes of course. I'll send her home."

"Until then, keep her under control. . . ." Helton caught and held Emilio's gaze. "Or I will."

DAY
FIVE

CHAPTER THIRTY-ONE

Casa de la Rosa, Cuba

Erin waited.

It seemed to take forever for the camp to settle down for the night. She lay on her back, listening to the sounds around her.

The other women in the cabin talked about their day. Several were heading back to the States soon, and their chatter revealed both reluctance to leave and eagerness to return home. They exchanged confidences and contact information and reminisced about the time they'd spent in this sultry jungle.

At times like these, Erin acutely felt the distance between herself and these other volunteers. She was a fake, here for reasons these women wouldn't want to know.

Even without the CIA, though, she wouldn't fit. She was a temporary fill-in, and she was Emilio Diaz's daughter. An outsider on both counts. And it saddened her in a way she didn't fully understand. She'd never been a joiner, so why this sudden need to belong? It was a question she couldn't answer.

So she turned her attention to the music drifting through the open windows.

Always in Cuba, you heard music. It was a fascinating dichotomy that, despite the country's extreme poverty, the Cuban people found reasons to celebrate. Tonight, a trio had come in from town, setting up in the mess tent. They'd played a mix of son, salsa, and timba, while the locals showed the volunteers how to dance to the energetic music. The group had quit around ten. After all, mornings came early at the clinic, and patients in the hospital wing needed their sleep. But a lone guitarist still played; soft, melancholy songs that drifted on the night air, soothing and sweet.

Even that ended, though. And finally, the camp slept.

Still, Erin didn't move, the light snoring of her roommates the only sounds interrupting the chittering of insects and occasional nocturnal animal calls from the woods. Tonight it was critical that no one see her leave. So she waited. Then, after what seemed hours, she used a penlight to check her watch. Nearly 1:00. Just a little longer, in case any stragglers still wandered into the sleeping facility.

Another fifteen minutes. Still silence.

Then she quietly rose, grabbing the small backpack from under her bed and heading for the bathroom. Earlier, she'd filled the bag with things she might need: dark clothing, her camera, a penlight, and a knife. Plus a voltage meter she'd taken from the storage shed after dinner. She thought again about a gun, but only briefly. It was pointless to waste energy wishing for something she couldn't have.

First off, she sent a short message to her backup team.

Everything good. Visiting Santa Clara tomorrow. Wish you were here.

As she'd done the previous two nights, she waited for their reply. It came quickly. *Enjoy Santa Clara.* They'd notify the Command Center to watch for something from Padilla, the agent she intended to contact. *Wish we were there, too.* Again, the phrase that told her they were on standby, ready to pull her out at a moment's notice.

The nightly message sent, she pulled on the dark clothing, rechecked the contents of her backpack, then climbed out one of the rear windows. Like all the DFL buildings, the back of the cabin faced the woods. As she'd done earlier in the day, she pressed herself against the wall and listened to the sleeping camp.

She was going back to the cabin to take a look at that cable. It was just possible she could bypass the alarm system with nothing more than a voltage meter and a set of batteries. If she was right, it was old technology, something called a McCullar Loop, and fairly easy to detect and fool.

Ten seconds. Twenty.

Above, a full moon painted the night with shadows. On one hand it helped, because she could avoid using the penlight. Yet a dark night would better hide her movements. She couldn't pick her night, however, nor afford to wait for the moon to travel its course across the sky. With Helton's appearance at the camp and his obvious distrust of her, she figured she didn't have a lot of time.

Thirty seconds. Sixty. It was now or never.

She moved to the edge of the cabin and peeked

around the corner. She couldn't see the guards, though she knew they were around. They were always around. This time, hopefully in front, half asleep on the clinic's front porch and not patrolling the camp or woods. She darted across the open space to the shadows behind the next cabin.

Then again she waited, listening for approaching feet.

Only silence. So she repeated the process, again working her way around the perimeter of the camp, using the silent buildings as cover. Until she reached the converted barn and the trail leading into the woods.

There she stopped, her senses open to the surrounding night. Now she could hear them. Two male voices, speaking softly across the yard. She edged her way to the corner of the barn, her back flat against its rough wood walls, then peered toward the house.

They sat in the clinic's shadow, the red glow of cigarettes marking their location. One of them laughed while the other spoke rapidly, though Erin couldn't make out the words. Just a couple of guards, entertaining themselves as they worked a late and uneventful night shift.

She moved back from the corner and glanced toward the tree line. It was a quick five seconds across open ground. From where the guards sat, they'd have to really look to see her, and then they'd never recognize her at this distance. It was too dark. Still, she hesitated, her eyes fixed on the blackness of the woods.

Erin had never been afraid of the dark, always fearing the deeds of men more than things that go bump in the night. This darkness, however, was so intense, so absolute. She was a city girl, accustomed to at least faint light on even the blackest nights. And there was the jungle itself, an unknown, foreign element, a world unlike her own. Here, she was the intruder, the interloper.

Then she remembered something Joe had said on their first mission together. She'd been a neophyte officer, and scared. Joe must have seen it. Actually, looking back, she suspected anyone with even half an eye for such things would have seen it, and Joe was very observant.

"Don't ever be ashamed of your fear," he'd said. "Because without it, you're dead. Face it. Claim it. Then use it. And you'll be one of the survivors."

She smiled at the memory. They'd made it through that mission and two years' worth of others without mishap, and she never forgot his advice. Nor would she forget *him* now. With a deep breath, she swiftly crossed the open space to the shelter of trees near the trail.

Darkness instantly enveloped her.

Glancing back, she saw the spill of moonlight in the open yard, but with her back to the camp, she could hardly see the next tree in her path. Bracing herself, she flicked on the penlight and pointed it toward the ground. Then, keeping just off the well-trod surface, she started forward.

It was tough going, nothing like earlier in the day.

The woods were thick with underbrush, which caught at her clothes and hampered her forward progress. Plus, since she couldn't see more than a few feet in front of her, she had to trust the hard-packed dirt of the path as her guide. Every now and then she stopped and listened, moving on only after determining she was still alone.

Finally, she sensed a lessening of the darkness ahead. She was near the clearing. Shutting off the penlight, she let the natural light guide her forward until she spotted the small wooden structure.

At night it was even less impressive than during the day. It looked long-deserted, a place for vagabonds or mountain men to squat. Erin knew better. According to Emilio, the cabin was used for drug storage; an out-of-the-way place that wouldn't tempt a thief. Plus she'd seen the road and security in the daylight, including the cable promising technology of some kind. So it was definitely more than it seemed in the moonlight, and more than he'd admitted.

Suddenly she sensed a shift in the night.

A slight sound froze her in place. An animal? Then, after a moment, she realized it was voices, moving toward her.

Had the guards seen her after all?

Quickly, she slipped deeper into the woods. She considered running, but knew she couldn't get back to her cabin without being seen—even if she could keep her bearings in the woods. So her only option was to use that darkness. Lowering herself to the ground, she hid within the underbrush she'd been cursing only a few moments earlier.

Now she could hear the shuffle of feet on the path and the voices growing closer. She listened intently for tone and timbre, words, if she could make them out, or a recognizable voice. She couldn't distinguish either, but she also heard no urgency, no sense of a search or alarm.

Maybe they had no idea she was here.

She had to take a chance. Inching forward on her belly, she positioned herself at the edge of the trees where she could see the meeting point of trail and clearing. If the guards weren't in the woods looking for her, they had to be heading toward the cabin.

After a few minutes she saw a light playing along the bushes bordering the path. She sank a little lower, willing herself to become a part of the surrounding greenery.

Then the light spilled into the clearing with two dark shadows: one large, broad-shouldered, moving with the grace of a soldier. Erin couldn't see his face clearly but knew it was Helton. The second figure was smaller, though still tall and slender. A woman? Then the moonlight caught them.

Jean Taylor.

In truth, Erin had known the woman was somehow mixed up with Helton, but she'd wanted to be wrong. She'd hoped she was just being paranoid and that there was some rational explanation for Jean's absence from DFL's records. Now, with Jean and Helton chatting like old friends, Erin had to admit the truth. Jean was not an innocent bystander.

Erin pulled out her camera, careful not to stir the bushes around her. She'd send pictures back to Langley and see what they could come up with. Maybe one or both had some kind of record that would help her figure out what they were doing here.

As the couple crossed the clearing, Erin snapped one picture after another, the whiz and whir following them to the door. A moment later they disappeared into the dark interior, and Erin waited for the lights to come on inside. Even with the windows boarded up, some sliver of brightness should leak through the edges. The cabin remained dark.

She shifted on the damp ground, working through the possibilities.

If the cabin was larger, she'd have guessed there was an internal room of some sort. However, the building was too small. Which left only three possibilities: Jean and Helton didn't need lights for their purpose here, the windows were blacked out from the inside, or, maybe, there was a basement.

The last option had the most promise, especially since no one would suspect anything under such an insignificant structure. Still, it was only a guess, and no better than the other two. Unless she could get a look inside.

That, however, wasn't going to happen tonight. Not with Helton around. Her plan had been to take a look at the cable in back to see if she could bypass the alarm. Except now, poking around outside was out of the question. Explaining her presence during the day was one thing. Helton might not believe her, but he couldn't call her an outright liar, either. If he found her here in the middle of the night, however, the situation would go critical real quick.

So, she'd wait. Maybe they'd leave soon.

Fifteen minutes later there was still no sign of either Helton or Jean. Erin set down the camera and shifted her weight, trying to find a comfortable position. The dampness seeped through her clothes, and she didn't even want to think about what could be crawling beneath her.

She yawned, rubbing at her tired eyes.

This was her fourth night of little sleep, and it was starting to wear on her. So when the door finally reopened, she almost missed it. No light seeped out for the moments it took Helton to step outside and close the door behind him. He was alone. And a few seconds later, he disappeared back down the path in the direction of the camp.

Where was Jean?

Had Helton harmed her? It was certainly possible. Erin suspected Helton was capable of just about anything. Jean, however, hadn't seemed frightened. Nor did Erin sense any animosity between them. Instead, they'd looked like they were both here of their own accord.

Erin also had to consider other reasons Jean had remained behind, though she could think of none that were innocent. She wished she could just walk up and knock on the door, or break it down if necessary. Neither was an option, of course, any more than facing off with Helton this afternoon had been a rational idea. At all costs, she must maintain her cover and attempt to find Joe Roarke. All other considerations were secondary.

Eventually, if Jean was unharmed, she'd leave the cabin. Erin wanted to be here when she did. So she settled in to wait.

Hours later, however, as the night crept toward morning, she wondered if she'd made a mistake by not knocking on the door. The hell with the alarm. A woman could be hurt and dying inside. Or already dead. Again, she suppressed the irrational urge that could get her killed. She was cold and wet and tired. Now was not the time to make rash decisions.

Erin glanced at her watch.

She had about thirty more minutes. Then she needed to head back to her cabin whether Jean showed or not. As it was, Erin would be cutting it close. The camp would soon start to wake, and someone would notice Erin wasn't in her bed. Still, she waited out the time until the darkness eased with the first signs of morning. Then she rose on cramped legs and made her way back toward the clinic.

As she neared the edge of the woods, a light rain began to fall. Chilled and wet, Erin fought off the feeling that she'd just wasted a night. She longed for a hot shower and sleep. The shower she'd get, but the sleep would have to wait. In a few hours she'd be going into Santa Clara with the other volunteers. And if nothing else, she had the pictures. She'd get them back to Jensen via Padilla, the CIA's foreign agent in Santa Clara. Maybe Langley could make something of them.

Or, more specifically, of Gregory Helton and Jean Taylor.

CHAPTER THIRTY-TWO

Santa Clara, Cuba

Despite her night with no sleep, Erin needed to make the trip to Santa Clara.

If nothing else, it would get her away from the camp for a few hours, away from the constant surveillance.

More than that, however, she needed to make contact with the outside world. She'd meet with Padilla and give him Helton's and Jean's names, along with the pictures she'd taken the night before. He'd pass on the information to Jensen in Miami and hopefully give her a better idea of who she was dealing with.

Also, she wanted a weapon. Something to fall back on in case everything went to hell.

So at breakfast, she joined Nancy and her group and checked on their departure time, letting them know she'd be joining them. Nancy seemed pleased.

"Have you seen Dr. Taylor this morning?" Erin asked, sipping her coffee. She'd been watching for Jean, wondering if she was going to show for breakfast.

"No, why?"

Erin shrugged, still worried that she'd left a dead or dying woman alone in that cabin. Though she expected if that were the case, the alarm would sound soon enough. "I thought I'd see if she'd like to come along."

"No chance of that," said one of the other women.

"She works the late night shift," Nancy explained. "I doubt she'd want to come."

Erin believed that was the case, but she hoped Jean would at least make an appearance. In the end, however, there was nothing Erin could do except make sure she was ready to leave when the truck set out. Jean was on her own.

The drive through the pine-covered foothills of the Sierra del Escambray was beautiful, a world dominated by a dozen shades of green, from the deep carpetlike moss covering the ground to the lighter lichen spreading up tree trunks. The earlier rain shower had freshened the forest, leaving it bright and shimmering in the mid-morning sun.

The group of volunteers was in good spirits, like excited children on a field trip. For many of them, this would be their last excursion before returning home at the end of the week. So they'd piled into the back of Armando's truck, laughing and singing the entire way. Erin would have preferred sitting in the cab, talking to Armando again. He obviously had no love for the men occupying the DFL camp, and she was willing to bet he had information that could help her. Though she doubted it would be as simple as asking him.

They arrived a little before 10:00.

Santa Clara had been founded in the late 1600s by residents of Remedios, who'd fled inland from the northern coast to get away from pirate raids. It also played a significant role in Cuba's war for independence against Spain, and again in the late 1950s, when Che Guevara and Fidel Castro's rebel army fought to overthrow Batista. Now it was an old and beautiful colonial city, important for its many historical landmarks as well as its central location.

Armando dropped them off near the Hotel Santa Clara Libre on Parque Vidal. It was a large square at the heart of the city, with sprawling guasima trees, royal palms, poinciana, and scores of squawking blackbirds overhead. In the center stood a picturesque white-and-salmon-colored gazebo.

"Too bad it's Tuesday," Nancy said, nodding toward the charming structure. "On the weekends, they hold concerts in the bandstand."

Erin smiled, experiencing a touch of the same regret

she'd felt the night before. She wished she was here under different circumstances. "Yeah. Too bad. Maybe next time." Though of course, for her, there wouldn't be a next time.

"Come with us, Erin," Nancy said, interrupting her thoughts. "We're going to explore the Museo de Artes Decorativos. It's supposed to have some really great antique and furniture displays."

Erin took a backward step. "Thanks, but I have some shopping to do. I'll catch up with you later."

Nancy hesitated, obviously reluctant to let Erin go off alone. "Are you sure? We're all going."

"I'll be fine, really," Erin said. "Now, go on. I need to buy a couple of presents to take back to Miami. And who knows if I'll get another chance?"

"Well, okay then. After the museum, we're going to walk up to Independence Boulevard for lunch at a place called Pizzería Pullman." She looked hopeful. "Will you join us then at least?"

Erin laughed. The idea of coming to Cuba and eating pizza seemed a little absurd.

"Yeah, I know," Nancy said with a grin. "Some of us have been here a long time and are really ready for some non-Cuban food."

"Sounds nice." Erin figured it wouldn't take her more than an hour to meet with her contact, but she wanted to give herself a buffer in case she ran into unexpected trouble. "How about if I meet you there around noon?"

"That'll work." Nancy pointed toward the other end of the square. "The boulevard is a block north, and the restaurant is on your left."

"I'll be there."

Waving at the others, Erin started off on her own.

The shop she was looking for was supposedly a couple of blocks off the square. It was owned and operated by Juan Padilla, a Cuban American who'd returned to Cuba over ten years ago. She'd studied pictures of him and knew what he looked like. Plus, he would expect someone to come in after Joe Roarke. Other than that, she'd have to rely on a CIA script to let him know they were on the same side.

She actually walked past the shop once and had to ask for directions before finding it tucked away in an alley off one of the main roads. From outside it didn't look like much, a dark, seedy little place with a variety of mostly used household items in the windows. Yet in her briefing, Bill Jensen had instructed her to buy jewelry.

Above the door, a tiny bell chimed as she entered.

A pleasant-looking middle-aged man greeted her. Juan Padilla. *"Buenos días, señorita."*

"Buenos días," Erin answered, keeping her Spanish stilted and very American. *"Entiende el ingles?"*

"Sí," he said. "Though my English is not so good. We do not get many tourists here."

"Actually, I'm not exactly a tourist."

"No?"

"I'm teaching outside of Santa Rosa," she said, giving him the first hint of her identity. "At the Doctors For Life facility."

"You are a *norteamericano*?" he asked, eyebrows arched with curiosity while his eyes held caution.

"I'm from Miami." Erin grinned. "Some people may consider it part of the States, but those of us who live there know we're just a suburb of Havana."

He laughed. "Whichever is the case, you are welcome here. Now, what can I show you?"

"I'm looking for a gift for my sister." She glanced around the cramped store. "Jewelry perhaps. I'm told you have wonderful silver pieces."

"You have come to the right place." He moved behind the glass counter. "Anything in particular?"

They'd fallen into the rhythm of questions and answers scripted by the CIA and drilled into her before she'd left Miami.

"Something unique," she said while following him over to the display case. "Something I can get only in Santa Clara. Perhaps a locket?"

"I have many lockets." He pulled out a black velvet tray filled with silver jewelry. "Do you see anything you like?"

She looked over the display of silver-plated costume jewelry, not unlike what you'd find in any department store in the States. Black market, she suspected, since the embargo would block such items from legal channels.

"Very nice," she said. "But friends of mine told me this is a place where I can get something really special." It was the final signal that would let him know her true purpose here. "They told me about backroom merchandise." If he answered correctly, she could go on. If not, she'd have to leave. Quickly.

He smiled broadly. "Your friends have good taste."

"Yes." She breathed a sigh of relief. "They are very picky. And determined to have only the best."

"Just a minute." He disappeared behind a bright orange curtain into a back room, returning a few minutes later with a carved wooden box. Setting it on the counter, he opened it with a flourish. "These are for my very best customers."

Inside was an array of truly lovely silver pieces, all beautifully filigreed. Erin picked up a locket inlaid with black coral.

"I expected you sooner," he said quietly, though no one else was in the shop.

She held the necklace up to the light. "I got here as soon as I could."

"Have you found Roarke?"

"All I have is a couple of names and some pictures I need developed." Still holding the pretty silver piece, she slid her right hand into her bag, pulled out the disk, and, keeping it flat beneath her palm, placed it on the counter. "Can you take care of that for me?"

"*Sí.*" The disk disappeared below the counter as quickly as it had appeared. "They will go out this afternoon."

"I'm not sure about this black coral," Erin said, talking again about the necklace. "Aren't they a protected species?"

He shrugged. "I have several others if you prefer." He picked up a plain silver chain. "Perhaps this?"

"I need to know something about the man and woman in those pictures. They're using the names Gregory Helton and Jean Taylor, though those might be aliases. Also, see if anyone can tell me something about the building. It's supposed to be a medical storage facility, but I have my doubts about what they're storing. See if you can find out anything locally that will help. Someone had to build the place, and someone had to install an alarm system."

"I'll see what I can do."

"And I need a weapon," she said. "As you know, the place is crawling with armed guards." She took the second necklace from him. "This is nice."

"How soon can you get back to Santa Clara?"

"I'm not sure I can." Erin put down the chain and picked up the locket again. Claire would love it. "If I try to come back without the rest of the volunteers, it will raise suspicions. And this man Helton is already watching me."

"It is a lovely piece, yes?"

"Yes, but . . ."

"I have more that I can show you," he offered. "But not here."

She met his gaze, waiting.

"You are teaching in Santa Rosa, no?"

She nodded.

"Well, you are in luck." He gave her a broad smile. "I travel from town to town on occasion, since the tourist trade is not so good here. I have rented a booth in the market at Santa Rosa the day after tomorrow. Perhaps you could make it?"

She wished it could be sooner. With Helton watching her, she had an uncomfortable feeling that she didn't have a lot of time.

"I can't get there sooner," he said, as if reading her thoughts.

"Day after tomorrow will be great."

"I'm sure I'll have something that will interest you." His words referred to merchandise while his eyes told her something else entirely. He'd bring her Miami's response to her pictures, and maybe more. "But it is good to come before noon, or all the good merchandise will be gone."

"I'll be there."

"Meanwhile, let me wrap this for you." He reclaimed the locket. "Think about it. If you change your mind, you can return it to me when we meet in Santa Rosa."

"That's very kind of you."

He returned to the back room with his store of silver trinkets. When he came out again, he carried a slim jewelry box wrapped in plain brown paper and something else wrapped in an off-white cloth. A gun?

"For your drive back to Santa Clara." He slipped the bundle into her bag. "It is not much, but it is all I have."

"*Gracias.*"

He smiled, and she picked up her bag and camera, then headed for the door. His words, spoken almost too softly to hear, in a tone that sent a sliver of unease down her spine, caught her just before she went through. "Be careful."

CHAPTER THIRTY-THREE

Santa Clara, Cuba

Erin stood for a moment, just outside the dingy shop.

The late-morning sun seemed brighter than it had earlier, and she waited for it to dispel the fear behind Padilla's words. After all, she'd just made contact with the outside world, and in a couple of days, hopefully, she'd have some answers from Miami about Jean and Helton. Plus, there was the extra weight in her bag that gave her a little more security.

Erin glanced at her watch.

She still had over an hour before she had to meet the other volunteers for lunch. She could explore the town or join them at the museum, but she'd lost her taste for playing tourist. Instead, she headed for the restaurant. She'd wait for the others there while considering what to do next.

A few minutes later, she took an outside table at the Pizzería Pullman.

In truth, she couldn't wait forty-eight hours for information from Miami. After she got back to camp, she'd get a few hours sleep, then go back out to the woods.

She'd go earlier this time. First, she'd check out the road behind the cabin, then, depending on what she found, she'd decide about tampering with the cabin's security system. If her guess was right, she'd be able to bypass it and get a look inside. Hopefully, she'd find some answers. And if not, there was always Padilla the day after tomorrow, who would have whatever information Langley had on Jean and Helton.

Resting her head against the wall behind her, Erin closed her eyes, feeling the warmth of the sun against her face. Sleep. She needed just a few hours. Given half a chance, she could nod off right here.

Sudden, raucous laughter brought her back.

She opened her eyes behind her sunglasses. A few tables away, three men were just sitting down. She recognized them immediately. After all, they'd been watching her and everyone else at the DFL camp since she arrived. Plus, she'd seen one of them shove a gun into a frightened man's face and threaten to kill him.

Helton's men.

Nancy had said she often saw them in Santa Clara. Erin hadn't thought much about it at the time, but now she wondered. Today's trip was no secret, and Nancy had also said the volunteers ate at this same restaurant every time they came to town. So, were these men watching the volunteers even here? Or was it just coincidence? And did they know she was here?

Either way, Erin intended to find out.

After dropping a couple of bills on the table, she left the restaurant and headed up the boulevard. She hoped the men hadn't noticed her, or this wasn't going to work. She'd spotted only one place where she could watch them discreetly: a *diplotienda,* or dollar-only outlet. It was one storefront up and across the street from the pizzeria, but she had to get over there without them seeing her.

She walked several blocks before crossing the street and doubling back. It was a fairly busy area with a lot of foot traffic, tourists and natives. She kept her pace leisurely, stopping to look in windows and blend with groups as she worked her way back to the *diplotienda.*

Of course, once inside the store, she had no idea whether the men had seen her or not. All she could hope for was that they were more bluster than brains, and that their egos wouldn't allow her to slip past them without their acknowledging her.

For the next fifteen minutes she browsed the store, checking the window often to make sure they were still at their table. The dollar-only stores were like small department stores with a variety of Western goods for sale, and as the name implied, they accepted only dollars. Though at one time these stores were open only to foreigners, now they welcomed anyone with U.S. currency.

She saw Nancy and the other volunteers show up. If they noticed the three men, they made no sign, laughing and talking among themselves while taking a table at one end of the seating area. She saw Nancy glance at her watch, then look up and down the street. Erin hated worrying her.

"May I help you?"

Erin turned. A smiling salesclerk had come up behind her, and Erin realized she'd have to buy something if she was going to hang out in this store much longer.

"Yes," she said. "I need a couple of things I forgot to bring with me."

The woman just smiled, waiting.

With a final glance out the window, Erin led the clerk back into the heart of the store. She bought batteries for her camera and backup disks, then claimed she wanted to browse a bit more. Which, now that Erin had spent some money, the woman was more than willing to allow.

Erin worked her way back over to the window, picking up a Nike T-shirt as if considering it. The men were still at the table, though it looked like they'd finally finished eating.

"Come on," she silently commanded them. "Let's go."

As if they'd heard her words, one of the men stood, digging money from his pocket and tossing it on the table.

"It's about time," Erin said, moving a little away from the window, but not so far that she couldn't see the other two join the first man as they deserted their table.

A moment later they were out of sight, heading away from the restaurant. Erin set down the T-shirt and stepped outside. She was going to follow along and just see where they went.

CHAPTER THIRTY-FOUR

Miami, Florida

"Agent Donovan?"

Alec came instantly awake. "What's wrong?"

It was the girl, Rhonda. "We've heard from Officer Baker. She—"

He was off the cot and through the door before she could finish speaking.

Except for his unsuccessful trip to Lauderdale, he'd lived at the CIA Command Center for the past forty-eight hours. All the time waiting to hear something significant from Erin.

He'd worked beside Jensen's team on the computers, eating in their small kitchen, and occasionally catching some sleep on one of the cots. The hours had merged together, sometimes seeming interminable, like he'd been here for weeks or even months. At other times it felt like he'd just arrived.

Still, they knew little more than they had two days ago.

He'd gone through miles of security video from airports across Florida and finally discovered Diaz had flown into Orlando in February. Alec had then pulled customs records for that day, matching names to the faces on the video feed. It was a long, arduous process, but he'd come up with the name on the passport Diaz had used to enter the country. Which gave them only a piece of the how, and nothing of the what or the why.

While he'd concentrated on the February meeting, Jensen's technical team had tried to identify Gregory Helton. It was like looking for one particular grain of sand on some wide-open beach. They'd found thousands of people with variations of the name, but no one flagged in any of the Justice Department computer systems.

"It has to be an alias," Jensen said. "One he's never used before. Otherwise, something would have surfaced."

"Maybe he's a civilian," Alec offered. "Someone not in the system."

Jensen had frowned, unhappy with the possibility. It would mean that any one of those thousand people they'd ruled out could be their man. So they'd gone back to square one, cross-referencing Gregory Helton, Emilio Diaz, and Cuba. The process would take days, and the chances of success were limited. Until Erin uncovered something, however, they didn't have much else to go on.

They'd heard from her twice more through the backup team, but both communications had been brief and uninformative. At least they knew she was okay. For the moment. What they needed from her, however, was information.

Meanwhile, Alec had continued his struggle to distance himself from the woman and think of her as a CIA officer on a mission. He hadn't succeeded, but at least he'd learned to keep his views on the subject to himself. And Jensen seemed to accept that and the help Alec offered.

Now, as he approached the group huddled around one of the computers, he said, "What have you got?"

Without taking his eyes off the screen, Jensen said, "Erin made contact with Padilla in Santa Clara." He stepped aside to let Alec get a look. "She sent pictures of the camp."

Alec studied the slide show of dark, grainy images, all with a green cast.

"She's using a night lens," explained Rob, the techie wielding the keyboard. "I'm going to clean it up, then maybe we'll have something to go on." .

"She also passed on two names," Jensen said, a spark of hope in his voice. "Neither of whom show up in the DFL files."

"Gregory Helton?"

Jensen grinned. "You got it."

"The other?"

"A woman. Jean Taylor."

"Just give me a minute," said Rob. "And I'll have pictures to go with those names. Then maybe we can find this joker in the system."

They all watched as the young man worked his magic. Still, the image that emerged, though better, was hazy and without discernible features.

"Hold on," Rob said, as if reading their minds. "I'm not done yet."

"This must be our guy." Jensen pointed to a large, hulky man beside the smaller, slender form of a woman.

"Don't need much cleanup to see that. And that building," he glanced at Alec, "Erin says it's a storage facility in the woods. Only she doesn't buy their explanation about its use."

Alec kept his eyes on the screen. "Drugs?"

"As I said," Jensen agreed. "It fits."

"I've almost got it," Rob said, and everyone went quiet. "If I can just clear up these faces. . . ."

Slowly, with each burst of keystrokes, the two people came into focus on the computer screen. Helton was a big man, tall and large-boned, raw-looking, with jagged, hard-edged features.

"Looks like a great guy," Alec said.

Jensen snorted.

The woman, on the other hand, was a completely different story. Jean Taylor was tall and slender, with even features, high cheekbones, and a generous mouth.

Rob sat gape-mouthed, obviously taken with the woman. "Wow."

"She's a looker," agreed Rhonda. "Someone's honey, perhaps?"

"Okay," Jensen said. "We've got images. Maybe *now* we can find these people. Run their faces against passports and driver license photos across the country. I want to know everything about them."

Alec backed away as the techies scrambled to their respective computers.

"Officer Baker is meeting Padilla again tomorrow morning," Jensen was saying. "Let's get her some answers."

Alec had barely glanced at the woman. All his attention was on the man. To the size and hard lines of him.

To the thought of Erin and her damn stubborn nature. She wouldn't like this man, and *that* scared Alec.

CHAPTER THIRTY-FIVE

Santa Clara, Cuba

Erin had no trouble following the men from the restaurant. They were cocky. Full of themselves. Men with guns, certain no one would dare challenge them or get in their way. And if someone did, it would be a mistake.

They headed away from the square, away from the streets filled with tourists, into the residential heart of the city. The roads narrowed and the buildings grew seedier and closer together. Erin kept well behind the three men, snapping pictures of the surrounding buildings, just another *norteamericano*, feigning an interest in Santa Clara's unique colonial architecture.

At one point she wondered if she'd ever find her way back to Parque Vidal, but she didn't consider turning around. If she could verify that these men were either PNR or Cuban military, it would help Langley understand what they were up against.

Finally the buildings opened up again onto a smallish square, less commercial and picturesque than the Parque

Vidal. It was older and more functional for the area residents, with an open-air market selling knockoff clothing, one of the state-run grocery stores, called *puestos*, and a small café with outdoor seating. Overlooking it all, like an old soldier, sat an aging stone garrison, which looked to have been converted for some bureaucratic or official use.

The three men headed straight for the building.

Erin fell back, taking pictures of the surrounding structures, the market, and several children playing in the street. Next she swung around and took another just as the men entered the garrison. Then, letting her camera hang loose around her neck, she looked for some sign naming the building. When she didn't see any, she approached a woman sitting on one of the stoops.

"*Discúlpeme.*" Erin nodded toward the garrison. "*Que edificio?*"

The woman looked at her with wary eyes, stood, and went inside without answering.

Okay, Erin thought.

Now she knew it was a government facility. The woman's frightened response confirmed it. Now Erin needed to know what kind. So she snapped another picture and crossed to the café, sitting at one of the outside tables. When the waiter came over, she ordered an espresso in stilted Spanish, wanting to keep her fluency hidden. When he brought it a few minutes later, she made sure he spoke English, then tried to get more information about the old garrison.

"That building over there." This time she didn't make the mistake of pointing or even looking toward the structure. "What is it?"

He glanced around nervously before saying, "That is for the Policía Nacional Revolucionaria. It is not a place for you." Then he hurried off.

He was right. She wanted nothing to do with the PNR.

The Policía Nacional Revolucionaria, or PNR, was a branch of the much feared and hated Ministry of Interior (MINIT). Most PNR officers were uniformed and served the same function as policemen in the U.S. and Europe, though without the legal restraints that kept their foreign counterparts in check. The system was rife with corruption, bribery being its currency of choice.

However, within the intelligence community it was known that there were other, less visible sects within the PNR. A secret police that reported directly to Castro himself. These groups operated with impunity and were not subject to anyone's laws except their own.

So, if the guards at the DFL camp were PNR, it was highly likely that they were not regular officers, but members of Castro's secret *policía*. Again, she considered the possibility that the Cuban government had sanctioned drug trafficking into the States. It would explain a lot. Except why this was a CIA operation and not DEA.

Glancing at her watch, she realized she had only thirty minutes before Armando picked up the volunteers. She'd have to hustle to get back in time. Now the question was, could she find her way back through the maze of streets she'd taken to get here?

"Discúlpeme," she said to the waiter again. "Can you tell me how to get back to Parque Vidal?"

The waiter started to answer, then his eyes widened at something behind her.

Erin turned.

Two armed and uniformed *policía* approached her. "Come with us, Señorita."

Erin went very still inside while donning the attitude of an American tourist. "Where? And what for?"

The man nodded toward the garrison. "Come now, Señorita."

"I will do no such thing." Erin picked up her bag and camera, slinging them over her shoulder. "I'm an American citizen, and I've done nothing wrong."

One of the men relieved her of the camera.

She knew protesting would get her nowhere. However, they'd expect a tirade from an American, so she gave it to them. "Wait, you can't take that. It's an expensive—"

The second man, stoned-faced and mean-looking, grabbed her arm. "Watch your mouth."

It flashed through her mind that she could probably shake these two. They wouldn't be expecting her to fight, and they certainly wouldn't be expecting the kind of fight she could deliver. She might even disable them long enough to get away before they could pull their guns. But what then? An American tourist capable of felling two armed policemen? If they caught her after that, she'd have a hard time explaining herself.

So, it was better to go with them now and see what they wanted. Though she expected she already knew. She'd been snapping pictures of an official building. A definite taboo, but also something a tourist might do without thinking. Hopefully, that was all there was to it.

"Okay," she said, shaking off the man's hand. "There's no need to manhandle me. I'll come. But you're going to be sorry." An idle threat, but again appropriate for an American tourist. Besides, it made her feel better.

As they escorted her to the garrison, Erin's mind jumped to the gun in her bag. She needed to get rid of it. If they went through her things, which they no doubt would, she wouldn't be able to explain the weapon. Somehow she didn't think a woman claiming the need for self-defense would get her very far with the local PNR.

Inside, the garrison felt even older.

The stone, thick walls and worn floors, gave her a sense of stepping back centuries before the revolution. The Spanish had built this place and had unwittingly captured their time within its enclosed space. Not even the familiar, modern layout of a police headquarters helped. The long counter, manned by a uniformed PNR; the string of wooden benches, half-filled with scared or harried civilians; the doors, leading off to warrens of offices and cells: all of it seemed temporary. Just one more incarnation of men and government within these old, haunted walls. When Castro's revolution died, another regime of men would occupy this space.

"Officer, I need to use the ladies' room." It was the only way she could think of to get rid of the weapon in her bag.

He looked at her blankly.

"*Dónde esta . . . baño?*" Again, she kept her Spanish stilted and hesitant.

He shook his head. "No," he said, starting to grab her arm.

Erin again pulled away and put a tremor in her voice. *"Baño,"* she said, loud enough for others in the room to hear. "I need to use the ladies' room."

The man glanced around, embarrassed.

A large, middle-aged woman nearby rebuked him in rapid Spanish. "What is wrong with you? Where is your decency?"

Another woman, obviously emboldened by the first, chimed in. "What have we come to in this country that our officials deny us such basic needs?"

Within seconds there was a chorus of unhappy people chastising the man, like a barrage of stinging insects. Erin almost felt bad for him. Almost.

Finally he gave in. Holding his hands up, palms out, he said, *"Sí, Sí.* Okay." Taking her arm in a firm grip, he led Erin down a long corridor, past offices to a closed door at the end.

Nodding toward it, he said, "Quickly."

"I will." Erin opened the door. *"Muchas gracias."*

Inside, her hopes of getting rid of the gun faded fast.

It was a small, bare room, with a single commode and sink. She'd been counting on a place to stow the gun, like a full trash can or an old cabinet or closet for storing cleaning supplies. There was nothing like that. In fact, there were no paper towels or toilet paper, both of which she'd forgotten were rare in Cuba's public facilities. It was just four stone walls, with a painted window, barred and cut into the rock, about seven feet high.

That was her only option.

She pulled the gun from her purse and climbed up onto the commode. With the weapon still wrapped, she slid it through the bars as far as it would go, until it touched the window. From the floor, she stepped back. If you were looking for it, you could see just the edge of the off-white fabric. Otherwise, it could go a long time before anyone noticed. As far as hiding places went, it wasn't very good, but it was all she had. And all she needed was a few hours.

Someone knocked loudly on the door. "Señorita?"

"*Un momento,*" she called, turning on the water tap.

A moment later she was back out in the corridor with the frowning officer. "*Gracias,*" she said again. "Now what?"

He grunted, then ushered her back down the corridor and into a small office. Without saying anything more, he left her in the room alone, closing and locking the door behind her.

"What's going on?" she called, hitting the hard wooden door with her fist.

But there was no answer.

Erin sighed and looked around. It was a plain office, empty except for a desk and two chairs. She circled the desk and opened one of the drawers. Empty. So she went through the others. They were all bare. Evidently this wasn't a working office, but just a place to store unruly Americans.

With another sigh, she sank into one of the chairs.

There was no telling how long they'd make her wait. Minutes? She laughed abruptly. More likely it would be hours.

They still had her camera, with the pictures of the guards from camp. Would they be called in? That thought made her shiver. She thought she could bluff her way past the regular PNR, but she didn't relish the idea of explaining herself to Helton or his men. At least she'd gotten the pictures of the dispensary off to Miami.

She glanced at her watch. It was nearly 3:00. About now, Armando and the other volunteers would be getting ready to head back to Santa Rosa. How long would they wait? Would they look for her? It seemed unlikely since they wouldn't know where to start. And what about Emilio? What would he think when she didn't return with the others? Would he be worried? Or glad to be rid of her?

"Damn." What a mess.

She should have been more discreet about taking pictures of this place. Though she knew that hadn't really been an option; better to be a careless tourist than a spy. She wondered if someone had reported her, or if one of the PNR officers had seen her himself. Whichever, it was going to cost her. The question was, how much? Would they hold her for a few hours and let her go, or would things get nasty? From everything she'd read, Cuban officials were unpredictable.

Maybe she should have run.

CHAPTER THIRTY-SIX

Casa de la Rosa, Cuba

Emilio had been thinking about Erin all day.

He remembered her as a little girl, bright and inquisitive, full of life and spunk. He'd always been particularly proud of how she'd stood up for herself with the other children, even those older and larger than she.

The memory made him smile.

Was it any wonder that she'd turned into such a headstrong woman? It was the biggest regret of his life that he hadn't seen the transformation, hadn't watched his daughter grow to maturity. Maybe now things would be different. Though he could never recapture the time he'd lost, more years stretched in front of them. They could start again. Father and daughter.

Then he thought of Helton's threat, and his smile faded.

He needed to talk to Erin and warn her to stay away from Helton, his men, *and* the dispensary. Plus, he wanted to be the one to tell her he was sending her home tomorrow. He had a feeling she wasn't going to like it, and he was not certain how to make her understand the urgency of the situation. She was too curious, too stubborn, and he couldn't allow either trait to spark Helton's anger again. It would get her killed.

Emilio had just finished inoculating the last of the villagers for the day when he heard a truck pull into the yard. That brought the smile back to his face. He'd been listening for the volunteers' return for the past hour. They were late.

He nearly laughed aloud at the thought.

He had not seen his daughter for twenty-seven years, and now he missed her after just a few hours. It was pathetic. Yet there it was. He was looking forward to having dinner with the beautiful and intelligent young woman who'd taken the place of his big-eyed child.

Suddenly the door burst open and Armando strode in. "Señor Diaz, your daughter did not come back with us."

Confused, Emilio frowned. "What do you mean? Where is she?"

"She is still in Santa Clara. . . ."

He broke off as the door opened once again and a tall, large-set woman strode through. Emilio searched his memory for her name. She worked in the office.

"It's not Armando's fault," Nancy said. "Erin wanted to do some shopping on her own, but she was supposed to meet us for lunch. Only she never showed."

Armando looked miserable. "We waited for an hour at the hotel where I pick them up, then we reported her missing to the local *policía*."

"He wanted to stay and search," Nancy said. "But I made him bring the others back."

"I'm sorry. . . ."

"It will be okay." Emilio placed a shaky hand on the

other man's shoulder. *Erin missing?* It was enough to bring him to his knees. "You did the right thing." He had to think. And fast. "But we need to go back to Santa Clara and start a search ourselves. You know the authorities will do nothing."

"I'll go with you," Nancy offered.

"No. There's nothing you can do there. You need to stay here in case my daughter returns." Turning again to Armando, he asked, "Does anyone else from the village know their way around Santa Clara?"

"*Sí*, my brother."

"Good. We will bring him." Emilio gave the other man's shoulder a reassuring squeeze. "Get the truck ready, and I will be there in a minute." To Nancy he added, "Let Dr. Taylor know she is on call in case of an emergency."

Suddenly Helton showed up. "What's going on here?"

"Erin is missing," Emilio said. "She didn't come back from Santa Clara with the others."

Helton frowned.

Emilio ignored him, turning to gather a few things and stuff them into his medical bag. He prayed he would not need them, but he was a practical man. And if Erin was hurt, he didn't want to rely on the medical care or supplies available in Santa Clara.

"Where do you think you're going?" Helton demanded.

"To look for my daughter."

Helton grabbed Emilio's arm. "Forget it. I'll send a couple of my men with Armando."

Emilio jerked his arm from Helton's grasp and met the man's fierce glare. "I am going, and you can not stop me."

Of course, Helton *could* stop him. He'd kill Emilio in a minute under different circumstances. For now, though, Helton still needed him. Or so Emilio hoped.

"If you want to help," Emilio said, as if not teetering on the edge of his own murder, "get Jean Taylor to cover the clinic." Then he headed toward the door.

"Diaz!"

Emilio kept walking. Outside, dark clouds gathered on the western horizon, promising another late afternoon of showers. It suited his mood. Climbing into the passenger side of Armando's truck, he said, "Go."

Armando put the truck in gear, the tires spitting gravel and dirt as he hit the accelerator. As they drove out of the yard, fear dug its claws into Emilio's gut.

After twenty-seven years, he had found the one thing he had lost when he left Miami. His daughter. His Erin.

He could not lose her again.

CHAPTER THIRTY-SEVEN

Santa Clara, Cuba

It was after 5:00 by the time they got around to her.

They'd kept her waiting over two hours, and she'd actually started to nod off when the rattling of the lock snapped her back awake. Two men entered: one of those who'd approached her in the café and another, older man she hadn't seen before. The second was short and round, but carried himself with authority. He also had her camera.

"It's about time," Erin said. "What is going on? Why are you keeping me here?"

Ignoring her questions, the older man took the chair behind the desk. Then he nodded to his obvious subordinate, who reached down and took Erin's bag from her.

"Hey . . ." She made a grab for it but stopped at the man's glare. Even the most outraged American would back down after being held by a foreign police force for over two hours.

He handed her bag to the older man, who said, "I am Captain Garcia. And I will ask the questions."

He dumped the contents of her bag on the desk. Wallet. Passport. The items from the dollar store. Her Pocket PC. And the wrapped box of jewelry she'd bought from Padilla.

Garcia picked up the passport first and flipped it open, glancing from the picture to Erin several times. Then he checked the customs stamps. "Is this you, Señorita Baker?"

"Of course."

He nodded, swapping the passport for her wallet.

She bit her lip as he rifled through its contents, looking closely at her University of Miami faculty ID and her Florida driver's license. Then he opened the box and took out the locket, turning and holding it up to the light.

"Where did you get this?" he asked.

A tendril of real fear curled in her stomach. Not for herself, but for Juan Padilla. "In a little shop near the Plaza de la Revolución." It was the farthest landmark she could think of from the Parque Vidal and Padilla's shop.

"What is the name of this shop?"

Erin shrugged. "I don't remember. I'm not even sure it had a name."

He eyed her for a moment, unbelieving, then picked up the PC. "What is this?"

Again, Erin had to resist the urge to snatch it from him. Though she knew the communication's mode could be accessed only with her thumbprint, she didn't like having the device in someone else's hands. It was her only link to the backup team in Santa Rosa. "An electronic translator." She reached across the table. "Here, let me show you."

"Just tell me what it does."

"Well," Erin sat back reluctantly, "you key in a word, phrase, or sentence in English, and it translates it into Spanish for you." She shrugged. "It's an electronic version of an English-to-Spanish dictionary."

He pressed the "on" button, then typed a word. Waited. Typed again. "Humph. Interesting. You Americans and your gadgets." He shut it off and turned his attention back to her. "Why are you here, Señorita Baker?"

For a second she watched his hands, still holding her communication device. Then she met his gaze head on. "Because your men brought me here." She tried to put some bravado in her voice, the last hurrah of a frightened but outraged foreigner.

"I mean," he clarified, surprisingly patient, "why have you come to Cuba?"

"Oh." She gave him a shaky smile, as if she hadn't understood him the first time. "I'm a volunteer at a medical aid organization called Doctors For Life." She settled into the chair, forcing herself to relax, crossing and uncrossing her legs as if unsure what to do with her own appendages. It wasn't all for show. "It's near Santa Rosa."

He nodded. "I know of this place. What do you do there? Are you a doctor?"

"Oh no." She laughed, a little nervously. "Well, not a medical doctor anyway. I do have a PhD, but I don't suppose that matters. I'm teaching the village children English. I'm a substitute teacher really, the regular—"

He interrupted, obviously irritated with her rambling. "Why are you in Santa Clara?"

"I came with a group from the camp, from DFL, all volunteers." This time she let a bit of impatience show in her voice. She couldn't allow him to think she was too cowed. "We came to spend the day and see your city." She glanced at her watch. "They were expecting me over two hours ago. Now I have no idea how I'm going to get back to Santa Rosa."

"Where were you supposed to meet them?"

She hesitated, not wanting to lead him anywhere near Juan Padilla's shop. But she couldn't lie about information he could easily check, either. "At the Hotel Santa Clara Libre on Parque Vidal."

"You are a long way from there." He folded his hands on the desk in front of him. "Can you explain this?"

"Well, I was—"

He lifted her camera. "Taking pictures?"

"Yes." She crossed her arms. "I like the colonial architecture."

"It is forbidden to take pictures of official buildings."

"Really?" She acted surprised. "Well, I didn't know that. I just thought . . ." She glanced around at the ceiling. "This old garrison is fascinating. I just wanted my friends at home to see it."

He kept his eyes on her, a suspicious and intelligent man. A dangerous combination. She wondered how much of her act he was buying. If any of it. Then he stood abruptly. "We will check your story. You must wait."

"But I need to get back. They'll be—"

He was out the door with her passport and his uniformed subordinate before she could finish her sentence.

"—worried."

She sank into the chair once again.

The next two hours passed in slow motion. She was hungry and tired and way beyond guessing how long they were going to keep her. She figured they'd let her go eventually. If they'd planned to put her in jail, they would have done so already. That didn't help with the tedium.

First she paced the small room, counting the steps from one end to the other. Fifteen. Then back again. She stretched and worked her cramped muscles, determined to be ready for anything. Once, she pounded on the door, demanding something to eat. It was as pointless as a child's temper tantrum. No one on the other side of the solid chunk of wood even acknowledged her.

So by the time Captain Garcia returned, she was beyond acting like an angry American and ready to fight her way out of the room if necessary.

"How much longer are you going to keep me here?" she demanded. "For taking a few stupid pictures?"

Her anger rolled right off him. "We were able to confirm your story, Señorita Baker."

"I'm happy for you," she snapped. "Can I go now?"

"Certainly." He handed over her passport. "One of my men will drive you back to Santa Rosa."

"Thank you, but I'll find my own way. I've had just about enough of your hospitality." She grabbed her bag, very conscious that he'd never returned the Pocket PC, and hiked it over her shoulder. "I'll rent a car, or call DFL. I'm sure they'll send someone for me."

"I'm afraid that would not be wise. A woman alone on the streets of Santa Clara is not safe after dark." He motioned to the uniformed officer behind her. "Drive Señorita Baker to the DFL facility near Santa Rosa."

"That's not—"

"I insist."

Something told her he wasn't offering out of the goodness of his heart, but he wasn't taking no for an answer, either.

Ten minutes later she was in the passenger seat of a four-wheel-drive Jeep. Evidently the embargo applied only to citizens who needed drugs or medical supplies, not to the officials in uniform who wanted to drive the newest in American cross-country vehicles.

She didn't say anything as they headed out of the city, going south into the mountains. The driver didn't seem inclined to speak, either. It was for the better, she decided. She hadn't quite gotten over her anger at being held for over four hours, and she needed this time to settle down before getting back to the camp.

The drive took on an air of surrealism as the darkness deepened, and they began their climb into the Sierra del Escambray. The sliver of road seemed foreign and intimidating, the giant trees crowding in on both sides. Overhead, the moon had not yet risen, and a wash of stars painted the sky. Too far off to add any light and too foreign for a city dweller, they only added to the aura of otherworldliness.

It only got worse when they turned off the main highway onto a smaller road, heading for the mountain village of Santa Rosa. With the dense vegetation even closer now, the headlights swept the brush, illuminating small sections before returning it to the night.

Erin shivered, wondering when she'd grown such an aversion to darkness.

Suddenly the driver slammed on the brakes, bringing the Jeep to a screeching halt. In front of them, angled across the road, sat a rusted-out truck. Two men stood in front of it, arms crossed.

For a moment no one moved, or even seemed to breathe.

"What is this?" said the driver, evidently angry.

One of the men stepped forward, coming toward them, a hand raised in greeting. As he crossed the headlights, however, Erin tensed and reached for the door handle.

She knew his face: cruel and unyielding in the glare of harsh lights. He was the same man who'd shoved a gun to Armando's head. The same one she'd seen earlier in Santa Clara.

"Something's wrong," she whispered to the driver in perfect Spanish. "Be careful."

He glanced at her, surprised, the scent of fear replacing his earlier bravado. He made a grab for his weapon. Too late. A single shot blasted through the open window, ripping into flesh and bone, rocking him sideways in his seat.

Erin tasted blood, acrid and bitter, her own and his, as she flung herself out the door. Another blast sounded behind her, and she dove for the ground, the stench of death heavy and close in her nostrils. Regaining her feet, she saw the second man, hand reaching for his gun, coming toward her.

Too slow. Too damn cocky.

Anger, lethal and blinding, blurred her reason. She rushed him, relishing his startled expression. She kicked the gun from his hand with enough force to break his fingers, then swung around and planted a second strike to his face. His scream and the crunch of bone beneath her foot sent a thrill of satisfaction through her system.

Behind her, a roar. And it brought her back.

"You fucking bitch." It came from the man who'd shot the driver. "I'm going to kill you."

She sprinted for the woods, the darkness beyond suddenly a safe haven. Beckoning. But so far. Another howl of anger from behind her, and the spit of gunfire shredded the leaves of nearby bushes.

Faster. If she could reach the trees, she might make it.

Then, pain ripped through her side, shocking, debilitating. She stumbled. Fought for balance. She pressed a hand against the sudden burning. Then pulled it away, sticky with her own blood.

CHAPTER THIRTY-EIGHT

Santa Clara, Cuba

Erin raced blindly into the woods.

Her side screamed with pain, but she ignored it, still fueled by anger and adrenaline. She would pay for that later. With the burst of speed spent, the comedown of adrenaline would be brutal.

There was no help for it.

She heard them behind her, the curses of the one whose nose she'd broken, the fury of his partner. These first few minutes were critical. She needed to put distance between them, and the darkness gave her hope. It would hide her as much as hinder her flight.

She headed downhill, away from Santa Rosa and the DFL camp. For now, the camp was unsafe. Even if she could get by the two men hunting her, she had no idea what would be waiting for her there.

No, that wasn't true.

She knew exactly *who* would be awaiting her. Gregory Helton. These men worked for him, and they'd just tried to kill her. Whether *she* had been the target, or the PNR driver, didn't matter. She was now a liability.

It started to rain, and she cursed the heavens for adding another obstacle to her survival. She wore only a pair of shorts and a T-shirt, appropriate attire for a day of touring a tropical city, but hardly a defense against the chilly and wet mountain night.

She needed shelter, someplace out of the elements.

Meanwhile, she ran. Movement her only chance. The years spent on miles of trails and beaches, her legs pumping, fueled her headlong flight, helped her focus. The ground, however, uneven and rain-slicked, betrayed her.

She slipped once, or maybe more than that. She couldn't say. Except the fall ripped at her, sending shards of fire through her middle and restarting the bleeding that had begun to slow. She pulled herself to her feet, forced herself to keep moving.

Once. Twice. She lost count.

Things were getting fuzzy. The aftereffects of adrenaline starting to take their toll. Weakening with each step now, she pushed on, sensing death nipping at her heels.

Then she stumbled, sliding down a gravel slope.

For what seemed an eternity she lay there, out of breath and out of strength, the cold rain pounding her. She was going to die here. Loss of blood and the elements would kill her.

A stupid way to die.

The thought made her laugh. Hysterical. Railing at fate. Then, something else surfaced. Defiance. She couldn't stop, not while she still breathed. She'd always been stubborn, as her mother had claimed. That thought, too, made her want to laugh hysterically.

Rolling over, she pushed herself to her knees, fought

the dizziness threatening to flatten her again. Then she saw it: a small opening, tucked into the side of the mountain. Not far. Maybe a few feet, maybe yards. She could make it. Unless she was already hallucinating.

She struggled to her feet, swayed, then staggered forward, her will bent on reaching what she hoped was a cave. She reached it, again with no sense of time or distance, grateful though for having found it.

Crawling in, she told herself the rain would end soon. A few minutes. It was all she needed to catch her breath and regain her strength. She hadn't heard the voices in a while. But the truth was, the longer she stayed here, the more her strength ebbed.

She couldn't tell how badly she was hurt.

She suspected that if the bullet had struck a major organ, she wouldn't have made it this far. She was, however, losing a lot of blood. If it had been daylight, the two gunmen could follow a crimson trail to her.

She needed to move.

If she didn't, they'd find her and finish what they'd started back on the road.

Instead, curling into a ball, she tried to stem off the chill. She longed for a fire, just something small to help ease the shivers that racked her body. Her thoughts drifted, dulled, started to fade, but she pulled them back. Concentrating on her anger, her will to survive.

Had Helton ordered her murder?

Did he suspect she was CIA? Or was she just an annoyance he wanted to get rid of? Either way, why would he risk it? Why call more attention to himself and his operation? And what about Emilio? Despite everything, she couldn't believe he would have any part in Helton's attempt on her life.

Her mind drifted again, and she fought it. She couldn't allow herself to sleep. It would be the end. And she couldn't bear the indignity of surviving Helton's men and their bullets only to die of hypothermia in this squalid cave.

She turned her thoughts to Emilio and smiled, remembering not the man but the father.

She'd called him *Papi*. And he'd often spoken to her in Spanish, calling her *"Mi hija."* My daughter.

How could she have forgotten . . .

Or his laugh. She heard his beautiful voice, singing silly childhood rhymes. And she wrapped herself in his smile. He'd carried her around the house on his shoulders, until they both were weak with laughter.

Her mother was there.

Not the sad, broken woman who'd lost her youngest daughter first to a madman, then to madness itself. But the young beautiful Elizabeth who'd dressed Erin in the frilly dresses that the Little Havana community favored.

She smiled at Erin, a cloud of White Shoulders reaching across time and death to soothe her daughter.

"Mama?"

"Hold on, Sweetie. He's coming for you." She started to fade, drifting away from Erin's outstretched hand.

Erin's eyes stung as they welled with tears. "Mama." She reached out, wanting just one more touch. "Don't leave me. I need you."

"He's coming." Elizabeth drifted away . . . and Erin felt her heart break, yet again.

With a start, she snapped awake. Shivered. "Mama," she whispered, grasping to regain the dream.

Then she heard them. They'd found her.

"This way." It was a male voice, seemingly far away. Yet how far could he be if she could still hear him through the stone walls?

She pulled herself to her feet, determined to flee. It might be too late, but she wouldn't let them find her in this hole and shoot her like a cornered animal. She would fight. Or flee. But she wouldn't die here.

Using the wall as support, she tumbled from the cave.

A blinding light hit her, and she automatically raised a hand to her eyes.

"There she is."

She willed herself to run, to make her legs move. One step. Two. Where was her strength? Her feet felt like lead. She'd claimed to have the survival drive, that edge that gave her the advantage over death.

"It's not a matter of winning or losing," she'd once told a class of CIA recruits. "It's matter of survival and who is willing to get meaner quicker. Who is willing to pull out all the stops."

Erin stumbled, realizing she'd been a fool. And so damn cocky. Then everything went dark.

DAY SIX

CHAPTER THIRTY-NINE

Miami, Florida

Alec found the woman.

Jean Marie Taylor, MD, PhD, born 1973 in Cambridge, Massachusetts. She was the only child of Drs. Daniel and Marie Taylor. Daniel, a neurologist, had been on the faculty of Harvard Medical School until his death in the early nineties. While Marie still maintained a lucrative private practice in downtown Boston. Her specialty was internal medicine.

From an early age, Jean had been an outstanding student, getting her undergraduate degree in biology at Stanford before she was twenty. Afterward, she returned to the East Coast to get her medical degree at Harvard, then went on to get her PhD in molecular genetics and virology. On graduation she went to work for WHO—the World Health Organization.

That's when things got scary.

Her work for WHO was in vaccine development, which set off warning bells in Alec's head. Her star seemed on the rise until about a year ago, when she suddenly left WHO under mysterious circumstances. Alec could find no reason for her sudden departure from the organization, except a note in her file that the cancellation of her contract had been by mutual agreement.

Alec suspected there was more to it than that.

From all accounts Jean Taylor was a brilliant woman. Someone like that didn't just up and walk away from her career. Nor would WHO be inclined to let her break her contract, unless they had a good reason. Add to that the small matter that no one had seen her since she'd left her job, and you had a puzzle.

He took the information to Jensen and waited impatiently as the CIA officer read over the fact sheet. Once Jensen had finished, Alec said, "So?"

Jensen looked up, a worried expression on his face. "I don't like it."

"Me neither."

Jensen snorted and dropped the paper he'd not let go of since Alec had brought it in to him. "She seems a little overqualified to be running a coke kitchen."

"My thoughts exactly." Alec sank into the chair in front of the other man's desk and ran a shaky hand through his hair.

"Still, the money's good in the drug trade," Jensen said, obviously mulling over the possibilities. "A hell of a lot better than what she'd make at WHO."

"Except," Alec offered, "the DEA doesn't know anything about drugs coming out of Cuba."

"They could be wrong." Jensen picked up the fact sheet again, looking it over. "It wouldn't be the first time."

Alec considered that possibility. It might be as simple as a beautiful woman wanting the good life. A life that vast amounts of money could supply. Or it could be something else. Something . . .

"Let's not jump to any conclusions," he said. Had they all become paranoid lunatics since 9/11, jumping at every bump? "We need the real story behind why she left WHO. And where she was between leaving her job and turning up in some backwater clinic in Cuba."

Jensen hesitated, eyeing Alec for a moment, then nodded. "You're right. Come on."

Alec followed Jensen back out to the central room. He made three copies of the fact sheet, then handed them over to his team. To Rhonda he said, "How's the hunt for Helton coming?"

The young woman glanced at her computer as it searched the Justice Department files to match the face to a name. "It shouldn't be much longer."

"Good. We need that information. Meanwhile, Donovan's identified our mystery lady."

Rhonda read the information about Jean Taylor quickly, then looked up. "Interesting woman."

"Yeah," Alec said. "A little too interesting."

Rhonda arched an eyebrow. "I didn't know there was any such thing."

"Interesting or not," Jensen said. "We need her information converted to code and included in the package for Officer Baker tonight." He glanced at his watch. "You've got three hours."

"I'll get right on it."

"Al," Jensen said. "I want you to find out what happened at WHO. The real story why she left." He shook his head. "Not the coverup crap they put in her personnel file. Get on a plane and go there if you have to."

Al nodded.

"Rob, figure out where she was between the time she left WHO and when she turned up in Cuba." Jensen paused, catching his breath. "And Zeb, you keep on the West Palm Beach meeting. Find out what it was about. Someone has to know something."

With the four young people busy at work, Alec walked with Jensen back to his office. "How do you communicate with your agent in Santa Clara?"

Jensen settled into his chair. "That's Rhonda's brainchild. After putting all our messages into a prearranged code, she uses various online chat rooms. Padilla logs on between 3:00 and 6:00 a.m. every night, and they chat away."

"Clever."

"It's not foolproof, but we change the code regularly and move around from chat room to chat room. So far," he shrugged, "it's worked. We'll get this information out tonight, along with anything we find about Helton, and by tomorrow morning Erin will know what she's dealing with."

It sounded like a solid plan, though Alec still felt uneasy. Jean Taylor's bio bothered him, and all they had was speculation and guesses about what she was doing in Cuba. His mind circled the question, finding nothing concrete to grab on to.

He needed a few hours' sleep.

He'd been awake since they'd received the message from Erin, nearly twelve hours ago. And he could no longer think straight.

It seemed like he'd just laid down, however, when a commotion woke him. In the central room, he found the entire team clustered once again around a single computer terminal. This time it was Rhonda at the keyboard, looking harried and exhausted.

"What's wrong?" he asked.

Jensen led him over to a computer away from the others. Indicating the image on the screen, he said, "Meet Lawrence Helton, aka Gregory Helton."

Alec studied the face on the screen. Helton was a homely man with hard features and nearly black eyes. "I liked him better from a distance."

"Military Intelligence has been after him for years." Jensen propped a hip on the table. "Ever since he went AWOL from his Special Forces unit in the early nineties. He was being held, facing assault charges and a court-martial, and escaped, killing a couple of MPs in the process." He glanced at the screen again. "He's one highly trained, mean S.O.B., who works for the highest bidder."

"A mercenary."

"One of the best."

"And now he's in Cuba?" With Erin. Just the thought sent a chill down Alec's spine. "Doing what?"

"Well, that is the question. But it looks like your instincts were right. Between what we know about Helton and the additional information we've gotten about Taylor, I'd say the chances this is about drugs are pretty slim." He hesitated. "I'm pulling Erin out and turning this over to Military Intelligence. Helton, and whoever he's working for, is their problem now."

Alec waited, reading something else on Jensen's face. Fear.

"What's wrong?"

Jensen hesitated. "We've lost contact with her."

Alec went cold inside, bitterly cold.

"She should have reported in through her backup team last night," Jensen said, "after returning from Santa Clara. But they haven't heard from her. It could be nothing, but . . ."

"Send them in after her."

"I can't." Jensen glanced away, his expression pained, before again meeting Alec's gaze. "Not without knowing the situation. We don't know there's anything wrong, and if I send them in, they could put her in danger. Or, they could be walking into a trap." Again that hesitation that told Alec things were only going to get worse. "Our only hope is her meeting with Padilla tomorrow morning."

"Except?" Alec's voice, his words, sounded distant, even to his own ears.

"We haven't been able to make contact with him, either." The fear on Jensen's face was clearly visible. "Rhonda's been in the chat rooms since three, hunting for him. He's always there. Every night, like clockwork." Jensen's voice held a note of desperation. "Padilla's never missed. But tonight, he's just not there."

CHAPTER FORTY

Santa Clara, Cuba

Emilio sprang forward as Erin tumbled to the ground.

Armando reached her first, peeling off his jacket and covering her still form and shielding her from the rain.

At her side, Emilio reached for the medical detachment which would still his trembling hands. He couldn't lose her now. He wouldn't.

"Hold this." He handed Armando his flashlight. "Keep it out of her eyes."

He checked her pulse and breathing. Both were weak, but still there. Hypothermia. He grabbed the flashlight once again and ran the light over her body. Blood covered her hands and left side.

He returned the flashlight to Armando. "I need to get a look at this. Hold it steady."

As he peeled away the tattered fabric of her T-shirt, he saw where the bullet had torn through her side. For a moment, fear rendered him unable to proceed.

"*Mi hija.*" It came out in an agonizing whisper.

"Señor Diaz? You must help her."

Armando's voice brought Emilio back.

"There's not much I can do here," he said. Though he reached into his bag and pulled out a stack of sterile gauze pads. "This will slow the bleeding." He pressed them to her side and saw her wince even through the veil of her unconsciousness. He taped the makeshift bandages in place, then said, "Let's get her back to the clinic."

As he moved to lift her, Armando said, "Señor, let me."

Emilio ignored him and pulled Erin into his arms, lifting her and standing with a strength he didn't know he still possessed. Though he didn't question it, either. She was *his* daughter, and *he* would carry her.

Armando led him back to the road, keeping the light trained on the ground in front of Emilio's feet. Then Emilio climbed into the cab, his child still in his arms, and Armando draped a blanket across her.

She woke once in the time it took to get back to Villa de Rosa, her eyes opening and finding his. "Papi?"

"Sshh. It is okay now. I have you. You will be fine. Sleep."

She smiled, a tight, pain-fogged smile. "She told me you'd come for me."

"Who, *hija*?" He brushed damp tendrils of hair from her cheek. "Who told you?"

"Mama." Her eyes lost focus, her lids drifting shut.

Emilio's heart clenched, and he bent to kiss her forehead. "Sleep, little one. I will take care of you."

They were all waiting when Armando and Emilio pulled into the yard in front of the clinic: a score of anxious volunteers and staff. Jean Taylor. And Helton. No one said a word as Emilio climbed from the truck, and they parted from his path as he carried Erin inside.

"Keep them out," he said, knowing that Armando could die obeying his command. Emilio no longer cared.

Inside, he cleaned and dressed her wound. Nothing more than a flesh wound, he tried to reassure himself. The bullet had ripped a chunk of her flesh as it traveled to places unknown.

Still, someone had tried to take her life, and the reality of that started to boil within him.

Suddenly she was awake.

"Where am I?" Her eyes cleared and focused as she swiveled her head to see her surroundings. Gone were the soft tones and half-crazed words of the child in the truck. This was a strong-willed woman, who had managed to survive the mountains with a bullet wound in her side.

"You are safe," he assured her.

"This is the clinic." Fear stretched her voice, and she struggled to rise.

"You must not move." He pressed her back into the bed, felt a strength she shouldn't possess fighting him. "I have stitched up your side, but you have already lost too much blood. You must rest."

"I'm in the clinic," she said again, gripping his arm.

"Yes." He reached for the needle he'd prepared earlier. "I brought you here."

"I can't stay."

"You must." He pressed the needle into her arm. "There is no place else."

He felt her tense, fighting the drug that would put her

to sleep. Breathing deep. Her eyes determined. She was strong, so incredibly strong. Nothing like her mother.

As her grip relaxed, her eyes caught his, still starkly aware. "He's trying to kill me, Papi."

He leaned closer. "He will not try again." Emilio would make certain of it.

She licked her lips and nodded. "It was his men. Helton. They killed the driver. I . . ." Again, she visibly fought the tendrils of unconsciousness that reached for her. "I broke one of their faces. . . ."

"It is over now." He touched her head, smoothing the furrows of her brow. "You are safe."

She grabbed his hand, the drug close to winning. "You believe me, don't you?"

"Yes, *mi hija.*" He did. "Now go to sleep. I will protect you."

She closed her eyes. Slowly her breathing relaxed, steadied, as she lost the battle to stay awake. Finally her body surrendered to healing sleep. Only then did Emilio let the anger within him take hold.

Helton would pay.

He found both Armando and his brother standing guard at the clinic door. They had rifles. Something Emilio would never have guessed of the two simple men.

Armando sent him a questioning look.

"She is sleeping." Emilio took a deep breath to steady his own hands. "Stay with her. Inside. If anyone comes near her, kill them."

"And you, Señor Diaz?" Armando asked.

"I have some business to take care of."

He found Helton in the cabin he'd requisitioned for

his own use as both office and sleeping quarters. Jean Taylor was with him.

"Get out," Emilio said to her.

She looked ready to object until Helton nodded toward the door. Emilio would have laughed, if he'd still been capable of such a thing. The brilliant Jean Taylor taking orders from a murderer.

When she had gone, Helton settled into the chair behind his desk. "I see you found your daughter."

Emilio barely kept his anger under control. "Did you do it?"

Helton yawned. "Do what?

"Did you order your men to kill her?"

"Now who's being paranoid?"

Emilio closed the distance between them and slammed his hands flat on the desk. "Answer me."

Helton stood, his size alone intimidating, but the coldness in his voice was truly frightening. "I don't answer to you, Dr. Diaz. But I will tell you that your stupidity is wearing on my patience. I have word from Florida that the authorities are asking about your last visit."

"That's ridiculous." Emilio straightened, meeting those frigid eyes. "No one knows I was there."

"Evidently, someone does."

"Even if that's true, it has nothing to do with Erin."

"Maybe. Maybe not. But that, and our little visit from Mr. Roarke . . . Well, I would say I have good reason to be a bit paranoid."

Emilio was beyond caution. If he'd had a weapon, he would have pulled the trigger until the man fell riddled with bullets. He'd never experienced such hate, such need to cause harm to another human being.

"You will not touch her again." He emphasized each word. "Do you understand?"

"Don't threaten me, Emilio." Helton's hands clenched into fists. "I could kill you with my bare hands."

"No doubt. But you will not. Not yet, anyway. You still need me, or this project will come crashing down around your ears." He felt the power, the certainty of his words. "And if that happens, I expect those who hold your leash will not be happy. What they will do to you." He snorted. "I do not expect it will be pleasant."

He saw the reality of his threat in Helton's eyes. And the fury.

"Leave her alone," Emilio said again. "She is no threat to you. I will have her on the plane back to the States with the others. As we agreed. And your plan will go forward."

Helton had gone rigid, obviously struggling for the control he so honored.

"When she is safe," Emilio said. "Then you can do with me as you please."

"You can count on that."

CHAPTER FORTY-ONE

Miami, Florida

Alec couldn't sit and do nothing any longer.

It had been two hours since Jensen had delivered the bad news about Helton, Erin, and Padilla. Now it was after 6:00 in the morning, and the chances of Padilla showing up in one of the chat rooms had dropped to nearly zero. Alec had turned the information over in his head, looking at it from all angles. And he knew what he had to do.

He'd been holed up in this Command Center for nearly three days now, playing by Jensen's rules. Alec had watched airport video feed and scanned computer files for pieces of information. It wasn't what he was use to, how he found the children he often sought. He was a man of action, who did what had to be done. And right now, that didn't mean staying in Miami.

He knocked once on Jensen's door, then opened it and entered without waiting for a reply.

"I'm going in," Alec said without preamble. "To Cuba."

Jensen didn't even glance up from his computer screen or act surprised. "It's out of the question."

Alec rested his hands on Jensen's desk and leaned forward. "Someone has to pull her out."

Jensen finally looked at him. The man who'd let his emotions show a couple of hours ago was gone. In his place was the quintessential agency officer. Calm. Cool. Remote. "Weren't you the one warning me about throwing good money after bad?"

"I was wrong, and we both know it."

"Maybe, but—"

"Erin knows and trusts me." Alec straightened, planting his hands on his hips. "Who else are you going to find in the next twenty-four hours who meets that criteria?"

"Forget it, Donovan. Padilla still has another window to log into the chat rooms. He'll be out there tonight."

"What if he's not?" Padilla was dead. Or gone to ground. Alec had seen that in Jensen's eyes earlier. "What are you going to do if he's not online tonight? It will be too late then to send someone in to rendezvous with Erin."

Jensen shook his head and went back to the computer. "We don't even know if Erin's still alive."

Alec didn't believe that, couldn't even consider it, and he wouldn't be deterred. "I'll go in as a Canadian businessman and be there by this afternoon. I'll attempt to contact Padilla myself, but if I can't, I'll keep his meeting tomorrow morning with Erin and bring her out. Clean and simple."

"Nothing's ever that clean." Jensen looked up then, a trace of sadness in his eyes. "Or that simple."

"I want to do this, Jensen." Alec *would* do it, but it would be so much easier with Jensen's support. "You don't have anyone else."

"I've already broken protocol by bringing you into this."

"Then why change now? Besides, I was already in it." Alec crossed his arms. "All you did was pull me under your net so you could keep an eye on me."

He could see Jensen hesitating. He knew it was a good idea. Hell, it was the only idea that made sense. Then he said, "Forget it. I'll never get it approved."

"Then don't ask for approval," Alec said. "Just do it. Or I'll go on my own."

Jensen sighed and gave up on the computer. Pushing back in his chair, he eyed Alec. "You're going in whether I give you the okay or not, aren't you?"

Alec had won. "Wouldn't you?"

CHAPTER FORTY-TWO

Casa de la Rosa, Cuba

Erin opened her eyes.

Bright sunshine filled her vision, as did her father's face.

He was leaning over her, checking the place where the bullet had torn through her side. He looked so serious, so concerned. Yet she knew she was in no danger from the injury. Not anymore.

Now that her mind had cleared, she realized the bullet must have simply grazed her. Otherwise, she would have died on that mountain. It was the hypothermia brought on by the rain and chill that would have eventually killed her. Not the bullet.

"Will I live?" she asked, putting a grin in her voice.

He looked up and smiled. "You are awake."

"And feeling like I've been run over by a Mack truck."

He frowned, concern etched into his features.

"Just kidding," she said. "I feel so much better. Almost like new."

His expression relaxed. "That is good." He replaced the bandage. "This is not much more than a flesh wound." Then, a dark shadow flickered across his eyes. "You were very lucky."

"Yes." She started to rise, and he helped her into a sitting position. "The PNR driver, however . . ."

"We found no one else."

"Really?" Although it shouldn't surprise her. Even Helton wouldn't want the attention a dead member of the PNR would draw. But there would still be questions about the missing man, wouldn't there? Unless Helton's sway with the Cuban government extended to murdering one of their own.

"Oh, good," a female voice said from the doorway. "You're up."

Erin forced a smile for Jean Taylor as she waltzed into

the room with an armload of flowers. "You worried us to death."

"I'm sorry," Erin said.

Her father frowned at the woman. "Dr. Taylor, my daughter is not yet up for visitors."

"Nonsense. She looks fine to me." Jean sat on the corner of Erin's bed. "What ever happened to you yesterday?"

"Jean . . ." Emilio's voice held a warning.

"Stop hovering, Emilio. Here." Jean shoved the flowers at him. "Get one of your nurses to put these in water."

Emilio's face flushed with anger.

"It's okay," Erin reassured him, willing him with her eyes to trust her. She could handle Jean Taylor. "I can talk to her for a few minutes."

He hesitated, but finally backed away.

Jean lifted Erin's chart from the table near the bed and flipped through it. "Just checking to make sure good old Dad is treating you right. After all, he was a little shaken last night."

Erin didn't reply, no longer trusting this woman. Or even liking her. And she could tell by the look on her father's face when he reentered the room minus the flowers that he felt the same.

"Well," Jean said. "I don't see any glaring mistakes here."

Again, Erin caught the anger on her father's face. "That's good to know."

"So, what *did* happen to you yesterday?" Jean said again, giving the chart a final once-over before returning it to the table. "Nancy said you were supposed to meet them for lunch, then never showed."

Erin's eyes flicked to her father, then steadied on Jean. "I was arrested."

"Arrested?" Surprise, then delight lit Jean's face, and she threw back her head and laughed. "I love it. For what? Tell me you were caught shoplifting. Or wait, better yet, spouting anti-Castro rhetoric. They take that kind of thing *very* seriously here."

"Neither," Erin admitted. "I was taking pictures of the wrong building."

Jean's mouth shaped into a silent O. "They didn't warn you about that when you went through customs?" She shook her head, humor still lighting her eyes. "No pictures of official buildings or uniformed personnel, please."

Erin again smiled, playing along. "They did."

"And you ignored the warning?" Jean raised her eyebrows in mock horror. "I'm surprised at you."

"Just call it my silent protest of Castro and his government."

Jean laughed again. "I like that. I'll have to try it sometime."

Erin took a deep breath. "Actually, I wouldn't suggest it. The experience was less than pleasant."

"Hmm." Jean pressed her lips together and nodded. "I guess it did end pretty badly."

"Yes. It did." Erin put a slight quiver in her voice.

"Emilio said you were stopped by bandits."

Surprised, Erin looked to her father again, and Jean followed her gaze. Then to cover the mistake, Erin said,

"I guess that wasn't a dream last night. I really did talk to you."

Her father picked up her ruse and came back to her side. "You told me a little anyway, about how you were run off the road and robbed."

"Really?" Jean said. "That must have been scary. Did you see their faces?"

Erin shook her head. "It was dark, and I was too frightened."

"Of course." Jean smiled tightly, her expression calculating. For some reason Erin didn't think the other woman believed her. So the mistrust was mutual.

"Well," she said finally. "You get better. I hear you're going back to the States in the morning."

Erin glanced at her father. "Am I?"

"I hadn't gotten around to telling her yet," Emilio answered, giving Jean yet another disapproving frown. Then to Erin he said, "I think it is for the best. The medical facilities in Miami are better equipped to take care of you."

She'd have to think about this. For the moment, though, she'd let them believe they'd won. "Well, I guess I better rest up for the trip then. Thanks for stopping by, Jean."

The other woman seemed a bit taken back by the sharp dismissal, but then shrugged. "I'll stop in again later."

Once she was gone, her father moved again to Erin's side. "I thought it best that no one knew what you saw last night. It could be dangerous."

"You're probably right." Then after a pause, she said, "Am I safe here?"

"Until tomorrow. But just in case, Armando and his brother have been taking turns outside the door. They are very determined to keep you safe and will not let anyone in who would harm you."

"The question is, would they know the difference?"

Emilio frowned, obviously unsure how to answer that, or even what to make of his strange daughter.

"Tell me, did any of the . . ." She thought a moment, then reworded her question. "Did you have to treat any broken noses last night?"

His frown deepened. "It is time for you to stop asking questions, Erin. This is Cuba. Rest now. I have other patients to take care of."

As he started to move away from the bed, she grabbed his hand. "Thank you. . . ." She hesitated. "Papi."

He smiled, though she could have sworn there was sadness in it. "Get some rest."

Once he'd gone, she closed her eyes. He was right. She needed to rest, to regain her strength. Because tomorrow morning she wasn't going back to Miami. Not yet anyway. Instead, she was going into Santa Rosa to meet with Juan Padilla.

CHAPTER FORTY-THREE

Santa Clara, Cuba

It amazed Alec how quickly the CIA moved when necessary.

By 3:00 that afternoon, just nine hours after he'd charged into Bill Jensen's office demanding to go to Cuba, Alec landed at José Martí Airport, southwest of Havana. His CIA-arranged Canadian passport got him through customs without a hitch. He then rented a car and headed for Santa Clara.

It was almost too easy.

As he drove east, he made note of the surrounding countryside. It was beautiful; rolling green hills of sugarcane and citrus beneath a cloudless, tropical blue sky. Then about an hour into the drive, the air-conditioning in his rental car gave out. The heat closed in, and he would have gladly traded the scenery for cooler temperatures.

His focus, however, was on getting to Erin.

He'd spent hours with Jensen's techies, memorizing the details of making contact with the CIA's agent in Santa Clara. He knew how to find Juan Padilla's shop and what phrases to exchange to let the man know Alec had been sent by the CIA.

Alec feared it had been for nothing, though, since he didn't expect to find Padilla. Alec had no proof, and he hoped he was wrong, but his gut told him that if the man had been alive and free, he would have made contact in the chat rooms the previous night. Jensen, at some level, must have agreed with that assessment. Otherwise Alec would have had to find his own way into Cuba.

The rest of his briefing had been on getting to Santa Rosa and Erin. There would be an open-air market, where she was supposed to meet with Padilla. As a tourist, traveling through the length of Cuba, Alec would be looking for souvenirs. And her.

He knew Erin wouldn't be happy about his showing up here, even with the CIA's backing. He couldn't blame her really. From the very beginning he'd interfered in this situation, forced his way into an operation he had no business touching. He'd discovered a side of himself he'd not known existed and wasn't certain he liked: a possessive and protective streak that would send a woman like Erin running in the opposite direction.

If and when they got through this, he'd have some tough decisions to make. He'd either have to accept her as she was and live with the knowledge that there would be more dangerous missions. Or walk away.

He hit the outskirts of Santa Clara around 6:00.

It surprised him with its size. He'd expected a small, provincial town. Instead he found a sprawling industrial city. He drove into its heart, checking into the Hotel Santa Clara Libre.

The hotel was one of the larger in the city, though seedy and in need of restoration. He paid one of the hotel employees an exorbitant amount of money to watch his car, then set out on foot to find Padilla's shop. He knew it would be closed by now, but also that the shop owner lived alone in the apartment above his store.

As Alec had expected, the store had a large COME BACK TOMORROW sign in the dark window. Beside the building, however, he found the ragged concrete stairway behind an iron gate. Pressing the buzzer, he waited for a response from the second-floor apartment. When none came, he rang again.

He told himself Padilla could be out. He might have simply gone to get dinner or visit friends for the evening. Neither scenario, however, rang true. Things were critical for Padilla. He'd lost contact with Joe Roarke, had received alarming information from Erin, and was overdue to contact his own handler in Miami. Alec just couldn't envision the man out enjoying drinks with friends.

He glanced around.

Across the street, an old woman sat on a stoop, watching him. He'd noticed her when he'd first walked up, and she hadn't moved since.

Crossing the street, he gave her his broadest smile. *"Entiende el inglés?"*

She nodded.

"I'm looking for the owner of that shop." He gestured toward the building he'd just left. "My wife purchased something from him yesterday, and I need to pick it up."

She shook her head. *"No aquí."*

"He's not here?"

"No."

Alec frowned, wondering if her claim of speaking English had been just a polite response. Or whether she was enjoying making him struggle for information.

"Do you know where I can find him?" he asked.

She shrugged.

Then he remembered another of his quick CIA lessons on Cuba. American dollars were in short supply and thus a prime trading commodity. He pulled out his wallet and peeled off several dollar bills, watching for the old woman's reaction.

It was only after he'd offered a twenty that she smiled.

"They took him away this morning," she said in heavily accented but perfectly clear English.

"Took him away?" Alec handed her another twenty. "Where?"

Her smile turned thousand-volt. "His heart died in the night."

"His heart?" Alec frowned. "He's dead?"

"*Sí*. Very."

Alec stepped back, his worst fear confirmed.

Padilla was dead, and Alec doubted it had been an accidental or natural death. The only question was how much they'd gotten from him before they'd killed him.

"*Gracias,*" he said to the woman and moved off.

He walked quickly back to the hotel, deciding to move on to Santa Rosa tonight. He didn't want to take a chance on getting stuck here. If Padilla had been interrogated by the Cuban government, there was no telling what he'd told them. Erin could already be targeted for the same kind of treatment.

He considered driving straight to Casa de la Rosa and

the DFL camp. He could come up with some kind of story they'd buy. Then he could slip out with Erin in the middle of the night.

He stopped himself, because he was doing it again—assuming that she needed his help. When in fact, his showing up unannounced at the DFL camp could ultimately put her in more danger.

Better to stick to the plan. Better to trust her.

He'd drive into Santa Rosa tonight and find a room. Then tomorrow, as planned, he'd take Padilla's place and meet her at the market.

DAY SEVEN

CHAPTER FORTY-FOUR

Casa de la Rosa, Cuba

As dawn crept through the windows, Erin heard the hospital come alive below her. She'd already been awake an hour, pulling herself from bed, stretching her stiff muscles. Her side still ached, but as long as she moved carefully, it was bearable. Her father had tried giving her painkillers the night before, but she'd refused them.

She didn't want to cloud her mind.

She'd just pulled on the clothes Nancy had brought the night before when someone knocked softly on the door. It was one of the nurses bringing breakfast.

"You're up?" She set the tray down on the bedside table.

Erin grinned. "Yeah. I couldn't take lying around another minute."

"Are you sure? Does Dr.," the nurse hesitated, "I mean, does your father know?"

"He's sending me home today." Erin sat on the edge of the bed and poked around at the food on the breakfast tray. "So I expect he does."

The other woman frowned, evidently not certain this

was a valid reason for Erin to get out of bed so soon. "Okay, then. If you're sure."

"By the way," Erin asked, "what time is the flight back to Miami? I want to make sure I'm ready."

"It's not until this afternoon, around 1:00."

"Well then, everyone should be leaving fairly soon, shouldn't they? What is it," Erin calculated quickly, "a four-hour drive to Havana?"

"Oh, you're not flying out of Havana. DFL has arranged a charter flight out of the airport near Santa Clara."

"Really?" There had been nothing about private flights in Erin's briefing about DFL. "Is that normal?"

The nurse shrugged. "They've done it before. I think they get some kind of deal with the charter service. But no, most of the time the volunteers return on commercial flights out of Havana."

"Well . . ." Erin smiled, making light of this new information and turning her attention to the food. She wondered why no one else considered it odd that an international aid organization would spring for a charter flight for its volunteers. Unless of course, the plane was transporting something other than people, and someone else was footing the bill. "Thanks for letting me know."

"No problem." The nurse headed for the door, but stopped just before leaving. "Oh, I almost forgot. Dr. Taylor asked if you'd stop by and see her before you leave. That is, if you feel up to it."

"Sure." Erin couldn't imagine what Jean wanted, but she wouldn't mind having another conversation with the woman. "Where is she?"

"She's covering the office for Nancy today, who's getting ready to leave."

"I'll go see her."

As the nurse left, Erin abandoned her interest in breakfast.

Armando stuck his head in the door. His frown of disapproval spoke volumes.

"I'm fine," she said before he could voice his objection.

"Señor Diaz will not be happy about this."

"What is everyone expecting? That he's going to carry me to that plane?"

That seemed to confuse Armando, and she felt a little guilty. Since her father had brought her into the clinic, putting her in his own room upstairs, Armando and his brother had taken shifts by the door. Although nothing had ever come of it, she didn't doubt they would have protected her with their lives.

Smiling, she crossed the room to him. "Armando." She took his hand. "I'm fine. Really." Then she raised up on tiptoes and kissed his cheek. "Thank you for saving my life."

He blushed furiously and backed away. "It was Señor Diaz."

"Yes. I know my father fixed me up. But who found me in those woods?"

He couldn't deny it and didn't even try.

"Look," she said, "after I get back to the States, if there's anything I can ever do for you or your family. . . ." She let her voice, her offer, trail off. "Please, promise you'll contact me. They have my information in the office."

"You are very kind, Señorita."

Erin sighed. She didn't feel kind at all. Instead, she felt like a fraud. Something underhanded was going on here, but it had nothing to do with the people who made this place their home. They were good, they were honest, and they were at the mercy of not only their own government, but men like Gregory Helton. And she'd been lying to them all.

"Well," she said, putting a bit of a false smile in her voice. "I'm heading home in a few hours, so I'm going to go say my good-byes."

He looked doubtful, and she knew he'd go straight to her father. Which meant she had only a few minutes before she'd have to explain herself and get past Emilio. She needed to get moving, because she doubted her father would be as easy a subject to bluff.

She gathered up her things, grateful Nancy had thought to bring her bag from the PNR Jeep. However, without her Pocket PC, Erin had no way to contact the backup team. She knew Jensen would be worried, but she'd get Padilla to send another message today. Just outside the door, she stopped where someone had set up a chair and table. Armando's guard post. Leaning against the wall was a shotgun, and on the table, beneath a folded paper, a Colt .38 revolver.

She glanced around.

Armando had disappeared down the stairs, evidently in search of her father. No one else was around. She'd leave the shotgun, but she grabbed the revolver and slipped it into her bag. The weight reassured her. She wouldn't be caught unarmed again.

Outside, the morning air was clear and bright, washed

clean by the typical early morning showers. She'd known before coming here that these mountains had more rainfall than anyplace else on the island, but it had never registered until the last few days. Until she'd been caught in a nighttime shower, alone and in pain, stumbling through the woods.

Getting out of the camp was easier than she'd expected.

Half the staff was rushing around, packing, preparing to go home. While the other half was pulling double duty to cover for those leaving. Even the ever-present guards seemed to be absent. So she walked down the drive and headed for town without anyone even noticing her.

Santa Rosa was a small, mountain village, which a century earlier had grown up to support the La Rosa Plantation. Like most Cuban towns, it was built around a central square. This morning, it was alive with farmers and merchants setting up their booths.

She strolled through the displays, stopping to look at a trinket or two, then buying an orange to peel and eat. She didn't see Padilla, though she wasn't worried. It was still early, and he was coming in from Santa Clara, an hour's drive away.

After a while, she drifted over to the café on the square and ordered coffee. Hanging around the vendor stalls too long without purchasing anything would look suspicious. From here, though, she could see Padilla when he showed up.

The waitress delivered her coffee, and Erin thanked her, remembering to use her stilted Spanish. Then from behind her, a vaguely familiar male voice startled her.

"Are you American?"

She turned, and for the briefest moment didn't recognize him. He was so out of place, so out of context. Then it came to her in a rush, and she just barely resisted the urge to throw her arms around him.

"Mind if I join you?" Alec said. "I'd kill to hear English."

CHAPTER FORTY-FIVE

Casa de la Rosa, Cuba

Erin motioned to the seat across from her, unable to speak. It was the strangest feeling, seeing Alec here, hearing his voice. It sparked a riot of conflicting emotions churning inside her: excitement and pleasure at just seeing him, relief that she was no longer alone here, and irritation that he'd followed her.

Words escaped her.

"It's good to see you, too," he said quietly as he sat down.

The waitress returned, and Alec ordered coffee as if his being here was the most natural thing in the world.

By then, Erin had found her voice, and the questions spilled out in a rush. "Alec, what are you doing here?"

She couldn't let her feelings for this man, her desire to throw her arms around him, cloud her thoughts or compromise her mission. She had a job to do, and it must come first. "How did you even find me?"

"Jensen sent me."

"Jensen?" She shook her head. It didn't make sense. His being here didn't make sense. Why would Jensen send Alec into Cuba? How did they even know each other?

The waitress returned with Alec's coffee, and he smiled, that sexy, broad smile he saved for service personnel. Erin felt a very female stab of jealousy, along with the urge to grab Alec's hand and stake her claim before this other woman. Then, she quickly squished the reaction as totally inappropriate.

"Gracias," he said, in awful, heavily accented Spanish he didn't have to fake. Once the waitress had retreated again, he sipped the coffee and said, "You're in danger."

Erin nearly laughed aloud, still feeling off-kilter by his presence. "Tell me something I don't know."

"Is there somewhere we can talk?"

"Not now." She crossed her arms on the table and glanced toward the bevy of merchants on the square. Her mission came first, she reminded herself, like a mantra she'd forget if she didn't keep repeating it. "I'm waiting for someone."

"Padilla's dead, Erin."

She turned back to Alec, as again the ground seemed to shift out from beneath her. "What?"

"Are you done with your coffee?"

She looked down at the cup she hadn't touched since Alec had shown up. Then pulled herself together. "Yeah."

"Good, let's go for a walk."

They headed away from the square, out of town in the opposite direction from the DFL camp. The road quickly grew steep, and Erin stopped. She wasn't going to take a chance on ripping open her stitches by pushing herself too hard.

"Okay, this is far enough," she said, a bit of anger pushing aside the surprise and confusion. Alec had followed her to Cuba. "Now tell me what the hell you're doing here."

"I've come to get you out."

She shook her head. He wasn't making any sense. "Alec, you don't belong here. And how do you even know Jensen?"

He opened his mouth to answer, but she raised a hand to stop him. "Never mind. Just tell me why you're here and what you know about Padilla." Regret settled in her stomach at the thought she might have somehow betrayed the shop owner to Helton or his men.

"Look, we got your pictures of Taylor and Helton, and we figured out who they are." He settled his hands on his hips. "But when we went to pass the information on to Padilla, Jensen's people were unable to contact him. We—"

Again, she shook her head. "What are all these 'we's?" Alec shouldn't be part of any *we* involving Bill Jensen.

"Erin, are you going to listen to me?" He scowled, his own temper flaring. "Or worry about how I got involved? Because the way I see it, we don't have a lot of time."

For a moment she was totally unable to speak. He

should not be here under any circumstances, much less delivering lectures on her behavior. Then she took a deep breath, and another. He was right. Now was not the time. He was here, and he had information she needed. They'd deal with the rest later.

"Okay," she said. "Tell me about Padilla."

"When Jensen's people couldn't reach him, and you didn't check in, we were concerned. Someone had to come in. As a familiar face and someone you would instantly trust, I was the best candidate. My first stop was Padilla's shop. We feared something had happened to him, but we needed to make certain."

"So, you're sure he's dead?"

"I didn't see a body, but . . . I'm sorry, Erin."

She nodded, her face tight, controlled. "And Helton?"

He eyed her for a moment, as if gauging whether she was really ready to listen. Then he said, "Helton is a mercenary who's been on the run from military intelligence for nearly fifteen years." Alec hesitated. "He's dangerous, Erin, very dangerous."

With a frown, she shook her head. "No news there. So what about Jean?"

"Helton and Taylor are a strange combination, and we don't know what they're doing together." Alec took a deep breath before continuing. "Taylor's a virologist. A good one, with credentials that make the rest of us look like slouches."

"A virologist?" Erin worked through the possibilities. "So we're back to drugs?" Though it didn't feel right.

Alec shrugged. "Maybe. That might be all there is to it. There's a lot of money to be made in the drug trade."

"But you're not sure," Erin said.

"She worked at the World Health Organization," he continued, "until about a year ago. Her personnel file said the separation was mutual. However, right before I left Miami, Jensen's techies discovered the real reason. She'd been linked to several highly controversial and dangerous experiments involving antivirus creation." He paused, glancing away. "She was asked to leave."

"So you think she's angry?"

"I think she's unbalanced, and there's no telling what she's doing with Helton. After leaving WHO, she stalked the director for several days before pulling a gun on him in the driveway of his home."

Erin didn't trust the woman but couldn't imagine her threatening someone with a gun either. "Jean?"

"Evidently, he was able to talk her down, and she handed over the weapon. Then he agreed not to press charges if she got help." Alec shrugged. "She spent the next six months in a psychiatric hospital. Then she's off the radar, until you sent in a picture of her with Gregory Helton."

Erin turned away, not sure what to make of this. She'd known something was off with Jean, she'd just never guessed how far off. Still, it didn't explain what she was doing in Cuba, working for Helton.

"Something else you need to know." Alec's voice drew her back around. "Helton was in West Palm Beach in February." He visibly hesitated, then added, "Meeting with your father."

It felt like a punch to the gut. From her conversation with Nancy, Erin knew Helton had turned up at the camp in February. "So, the CIA thinks my father's involved."

"Don't you?"

She did. Or at least she had. Until he'd carried her off that mountain and posted a guard by her door. He'd saved her life, then protected her from Helton. Now, she didn't know what to believe.

"There must be more to it," she said. "If he's involved, it's because he has no choice." She folded her arms around her middle. "He's a good man, Alec, devoted to these people here. I won't believe he's willingly working with Helton."

Alec raised his hands in an obvious effort to placate her. "I'm just saying it's a possibility."

"I've been here the last week, Alec. I've grown to know this man."

"You're right," he said. "I don't know him. In fact, we really don't know anything. So, my instructions from Jensen are to get you out of Cuba."

She laughed shortly. "I don't think so."

"I've got a car parked back near the square. We're going to head to Havana, then catch the next flight off this island."

"I'm not going anywhere." She backed further. "I'm not finished here."

"Erin . . ."

"We still don't know what happened to Joe Roarke, and we don't know what Jean and Helton are doing in the camp. Maybe it is drugs, but we need to find out for sure."

"It's not your problem anymore." Alec reached for her arm, but she jerked away. "Jensen has turned this over to Military Intelligence."

"You're not listening to me." She couldn't believe they wanted her to leave. "I know where to look. It has to be the cabin. If this is about drugs, we need to know. If not . . ." She thought it through. "Well that's worse, and I need to get inside and see for myself what's going on."

"This is crazy, Erin."

"No, it's the only thing that makes sense. We can't wait on some bureaucrats back in the States. I'm here now."

He didn't answer her right away, then resignation washed his features. "You mean, *we* are here now."

"This isn't your fight, Alec."

"Don't be an idiot." He crossed his arms, stubborn as always. "You're not going in there alone. So, if you insist on going, I'm going with you."

Why didn't that surprise her?

CHAPTER FORTY-SIX

Casa de la Rosa, Cuba

Alec figured Jensen knew how this was going to play out.

All the CIA officer's talk about bringing Erin out of Cuba and letting Military Intelligence handle the possible threat had been just words. He'd known Erin would refuse to leave under the circumstances, and he'd sent Alec in to help her.

When he got back to Miami, Alec was going to have a little chat with the man. For now, though, he would have to concentrate on keeping them both alive.

"Any ideas on how we're going to get into this cabin?" he asked.

"We're going to walk through the front door," she said.

"Really?" This was going to be good. "I thought there was a security system."

She grinned and opened her bag just enough for him to see the flash of metal inside. "There is. But I know just the person who's going to disarm it for us."

Erin had then outlined her plan, and he had to admit, it wasn't altogether a bad one. Of course, there were only about a dozen ways it could go wrong and end up getting them both dead. But heck, what was the fun of going after the bad guys if there wasn't a risk or two? At least, now that Erin had made the decision to go in, that's how she seemed to see it. Alec, on the other hand, would have preferred something a lot less dangerous with more chances of success.

Now he stood with his back pressed against the rotting wood of an old barn, hoping he was in the right spot. Erin claimed it had been converted into an office where she'd find Jean Taylor. Then Erin had told him how to circle around through the woods and come up behind this building. After which, she'd headed directly back into camp. All he had to do was wait to hear her voice on the other side of the wall. And be ready.

As the screen door snapped shut, he tensed.

"I see you're feeling better," came an unfamiliar female voice from inside the building. It had to be Jean Taylor.

"Much." It was Erin, and he breathed a little easier.

"So have you come to say good-bye? I must admit I hate to see you go. You've kept things hopping around here."

"Well, I think they're about to get even livelier."

There was a slight gasp, and Alec imagined the unwieldy revolver in Erin's hand. "What are you doing with that gun?"

"Stand up and walk to the back storage room," Erin said. "And I suggest you do it quietly. If you make a sound, I have nothing to lose by pulling this trigger."

"I'm not going anywhere with you." There was definite indignance and defiance in the voice.

"Don't underestimate me, Jean." Erin's voice was cold, hard, and Alec wondered how anyone could question her resolve. "I will kill you. You won't be my first. Now, get up and move toward the back room."

"The back room?"

"We're going out the window."

"Let's talk about this, Erin."

"There's nothing to talk about. Now move."

He heard the scrape of a chair on wood, then the shuffle of feet coming closer.

"Out the window," Erin said.

"What? Are you crazy?"

"It's not hard. I've done it twice already without the helping hands you'll get from the other side."

"You're going to reopen that bullet wound," Jean said, still defiant.

Alec frowned, wondering what Jean meant. Erin hadn't said anything about being shot.

"Don't worry about me," Erin said. "Out the window."

A moment later Jean Taylor swung her legs over the edge.

Alec grabbed her and lowered her down, his hand sliding to her mouth. "Don't get any ideas about making noise," he said into her ear. "Your silence is the only thing keeping you alive."

A moment later Erin was beside them, a flash of pain in her eyes.

"What's wrong?" he asked, scanning Erin for blood or other signs of an injury. "What was she talking about? Have you been shot?"

"It's nothing," Erin said, dismissing him.

"Just a bullet wound," Jean Taylor said to Alec. "Someone tried to kill her." Then turning to Erin, she added, "Too bad they failed."

"Shut up, Jean."

"Erin . . ." Alec started.

"It's a flesh wound, and I'm fine." Erin shoved the gun against the other woman's spine and pushed her toward the woods. "Come on, let's get going."

After scrambling through the underbrush for a few minutes, they found a path leading through the trees. Erin kept Jean moving quickly, one hand gripping the woman's arm while another pressed the gun to her side. Alec followed, keeping his ears and eyes open for sounds of pursuit.

The cabin itself was unimpressive, roughly made and

small. Maybe this *was* about money, and it was drugs they were dealing with after all. He could only hope.

Jean crossed her arms, eyeing Erin with obvious disdain. "Now what?"

"You're going to get us inside," Erin answered.

"Whatever for? You going to steal drugs from DFL?"

"Just open the door," Erin commanded, pressing the .38 a little harder into Jean's side. "Unless you want to know what it feels like to have a bullet rip through your waist."

Jean shrugged, then entered a code on the keypad that opened the door. They all three stepped through, Alec closing the door behind them.

Inside, however, the building was even more disappointing. There were boxes stacked in neat rows, all labeled as medical equipment and supplies with DFL's logo.

"I told you," Jean said. "There's nothing here."

"There has to be something." Erin's eyes swept the room. "Look around, Alec. See what you can find."

He began his search, though he didn't know what exactly he was looking for. Maybe just some evidence of illegal drugs or contraband. Anything to explain Helton's and Jean Taylor's presence in this backwater part of Cuba. Then Alec spotted the scuff marks on the floor, heavy and consistent. Walking back to the front door, he followed them through the maze of boxes.

"What is it?" Erin asked.

"Wait a minute," he said, dropping to the floor. After brushing aside a small box, he found what he'd been looking for: a handle and cord embedded into the wood.

He pulled on it and the panel slid open easily, revealing a staircase beneath.

"Voilà," he said, meeting Erin's grin. "Looks like we found our cache."

"Come on," she said, shoving Jean toward the stairs.

"You don't know who you're messing with." Jean's voice held fear for the first time. "They'll kill you for this."

Erin sighed. "I've heard that before."

Down the stairs, it was like stepping into another world.

In front of them spread a large, ultramodern lab equipped with state-of-the-art equipment. Only this lab was no coke kitchen. He'd seen one like it once before. At the CDC in Atlanta.

It had all the elements of a P3 bio lab. Large freezers and nitrogen tanks lined the walls. There were showers and changing rooms with gowns, hoods, respirators, and protective clothing on hooks. And in the center was a biosafety cabinet. Whoever worked in this lab wasn't dealing drugs; they were working with dangerous organisms.

"Oh my God," Erin said. "Until now I didn't believe. I thought we'd find drugs." She turned angry eyes on Jean. Then, in a movement so quick Alec didn't see it coming, she slammed the other woman against a wall. "What the hell are you doing here?"

Jean laughed, a high-pitched, hysterical sound that sent shivers of dread down Alec's spine. "I've already done it," she said. "I'm finished. You're too late."

Erin pressed Jean harder into the wall, the Colt shoved beneath her chin. "Talk to me."

"Or what? Are you going to pull that trigger?" Jean shook her head. "I don't think so. Back at the camp, maybe, but here. . . ?" She grinned. "I'm the only one who can help you. And that hope alone will keep me alive."

Alec wasn't so sure. He saw the flash of fury in Erin's eyes and thought this must have been the way she looked last year, when she'd put a knife in the man who'd abducted her seven-year-old sister.

Grabbing her arm, Alec said, "It's not worth it, Erin. Let her go."

For a second, he didn't think she'd heard him. Then slowly, very slowly, she eased off. "Find something we can use to tie her up."

Alec paused, still unsure of what Erin had planned for Jean Taylor. Then he moved off, looking for rope of some kind. He didn't find any, but he returned a few minutes later with a phone cord.

"This will work," he said, pulling Jean's arms behind her. "There's a hallway with a bunch of rooms past that door." He nodded toward the far end of the lab. "We can lock her in one of them while we look around."

With Jean tied up behind locked doors, Alec took a deep breath. There was a warren of tunnels beyond the lab, carved into the ground. It would take days to explore them all. Days they didn't have.

"I want to take a look at this place," Erin said. "Maybe I can find something that will tell us either what happened to Joe or what she's created here."

Alec knew he couldn't stop her, though neither of them were qualified to effectively evaluate this site and its contents.

"Okay," he said. "But I don't think we should stay long. We need to get back and bring in reinforcements."

She nodded, obviously realizing herself that there was nothing much more they could do. "Okay. Give me ten minutes."

"I'll stay here and watch the stairs."

She handed him the gun. "Be careful."

CHAPTER FORTY-SEVEN

Casa de la Rosa, Cuba

Erin moved through the door at the back of the sterile room.

She knew she could hunt through the lab forever, even look through Jean's notes, and not know what she was seeing. This really was beyond her area of expertise. And if she touched the wrong thing, opened the wrong door, who knew what she could unleash?

This place needed to be explored by women and men in biocontainment suits. Microbiologists. Biochemists. Experts. People who knew what they were doing.

First, though, she wanted to see what was beyond the lab. If nothing else, maybe she could find weapons. The revolver she'd taken from Armando wouldn't do much if they met any opposition while trying to get away from here.

With caution, she opened one door after another along a deserted corridor. Most were sleeping quarters. She also discovered a small common room with a refrigerator, coffeemaker, microwave, and hot plate. She'd evidently found where Helton's men bunked.

Past the last unlocked room, the pathway deteriorated as she moved into an older section of the tunnels. Here there were no doors, just stone rooms cut into the mountain on either side of her. Rusted chains and manacles dripped from the walls. All empty. Still, the thought of what this place must have once been sent chills down her spine.

She glanced at her watch.

It had been nearly fifteen minutes since she'd left Alec. She needed to get back. One more empty room, then . . .

But it wasn't empty. A bloody body lay on a filthy mattress, an iron band securing one wrist and binding him to the stone. A man, beaten if not to death, then nearly so.

Joe.

She rushed forward, her heart hammering. She was too late. "Joe?" She gently lifted his head, and his eyes slowly blinked open. He was alive.

"Oh my God," she whispered. "What have they done to you?"

His lips turned up in a ghost of a smile and his words came out slow and measured. "So you're the cavalry, Erin. I thought you'd never get here."

She half laughed, half cried. "You're crazy. Let me see how I can get you out of this thing." She examined the ancient lock on the manacle. It would be easy to pick. She just needed a couple of long, thin pieces of metal. "Let me go see what I can find."

"There's no time, Erin."

"Hush. I have to get you out of here."

"Listen to me." He paused, licking his lips. "They've been developing some kind of biological weapon here. A virus of some kind."

She nodded, again looking at the lock. She had guessed as much, and Jean had pretty much confirmed it. "How are they going to use it?"

"I don't know." He eyes slipped shut. "But whatever they're planning, it's going to happen soon."

"Hang on," she said. "I'm going to get something to pick this lock." She stood and backed toward the door. "I'll just be a minute."

Then, death pressed against her temple.

Chilling, hard steel, small-caliber, but still lethal at this range. Sudden and unexpected, the gun and the man who held it had caught Erin off guard.

"Breathe," said the voice behind the weapon. "While you still can."

"Helton." Erin whispered the name. With it came a rush of air, and she steadied herself against the certainty of her own death. A gun to your head made it too easy to forget years of training, made all else but fear slip away.

She couldn't allow that to happen. There was too much at stake.

A second man came into her field of vision, a thick stripe of tape across the bridge of his swollen and discolored nose. Erin shivered when he looked at her, hate ripe in his eyes. One of Helton's hired guns. The last time she'd seen him, he'd been sprawled at her feet, cursing and grasping at his shattered face. Now, he seemed ready to return the favor, or worse, as he turned and aimed an automatic weapon at Joe.

"Don't," she said, willing to beg if necessary, though her pleas might be for a man already dead. Joe was so still.

"Your call," Helton said. "If you try anything, we'll put a bullet in his skull."

Erin nodded, barely, and felt death temporarily recede as the gun left her temple. Helton had no intention of letting either her or Joe out of here alive. It was just a matter of time, and she'd buy all she could get.

Where was Alec?

Had Helton killed him? The question, with its likely answer, caught at her, settling like a weight in her stomach. The only way Helton would have gotten past Alec was if he was already dead. The grief and guilt for bringing him into this momentarily wiped all other fear from her thoughts.

Not Alec. Please.

"Over by your friend." Helton nudged her with the gun, just a little left of her spine. It sent a sliver of pain up her side, snapping her back to the moment. "How's the wound?" he asked. "Still hurt?"

Erin moved slowly, ignoring the question, her mind scrambling for a way out of this.

There was always a way. Wasn't there?

Hadn't they taught her that at the CIA's Farm? Or maybe that was just Hollywood's version, and her own need to believe.

"What are you going to do with us?" she asked.

"Stupid question," Helton said. "The Cuban government doesn't take kindly to American spies."

"I'm not a spy. I was just—"

"Exploring. I think I've heard that one before. From you and Emilio."

"It's the truth."

"Spare me the lies, Erin. We both know good old Uncle Sam sent you. It's just a matter of which agency pulls your strings. Just like your friend there." He nodded to Joe's still body. "And the shop owner in Santa Clara."

Erin sucked in a breath. So Helton had killed Padilla as well. Had she somehow given him away, or had Helton known about Padilla's connections all along?

"My only question," Helton said, "is whether Emilio's really your father. I mean," he shrugged, "all we have is your word for that. How would *he* know after all these years?"

Again, Erin kept silent.

"Well, it's not important." Helton took a deep breath. "And I've had enough chitchat. On the floor."

Erin hesitated. Once they had her on the ground, it would be too late. If she was going to do something, it had to be now, while she still had her feet beneath her.

"Don't even think it, Erin." Helton must have read her mind. Or knew how he'd react if their positions were reversed. "You'll be dead before you take your next breath."

She looked into the man's eyes and saw her death. He was right. It was all over.

"Just tell me what you've created here," she said. "If I'm going to die, I deserve to know."

"Well, that's where we disagree. You'll have to go to your grave wondering." He nodded to the other man. "Go set the explosives."

Erin watched as Broken Nose hurried from the room.

"You're going to blow up the lab," she said, realizing that meant Helton's work here really was complete.

"With you in it," he confirmed. "We were going to turn both of you over to the Cubans. They would have enjoyed parading you in front of the world. But, they'll just have to do without. I'm not crazy about leaving evidence behind, and you know too much."

"But, what about—"

"Enough. You're too late. The package is already on its way."

Erin's mind raced. On its way? "Where?"

He flicked the gun in his hand. "On the floor. Now."

She backed up, and it struck her. Two dozen volunteers were returning to Miami this afternoon. "The virus is on that plane," she said. "That's why you've chartered a flight for the volunteers."

Helton smiled.

"I'm right, aren't I?"

"You'll never know."

Suddenly a noise came from the tunnel. A muffled thump, like something heavy hitting the floor.

Helton swung around.

Without hesitation Erin struck. A kick to his gun hand sent the weapon skittering across the floor. She dove for it, knowing she didn't stand a chance against this man in a hand-to-hand fight. He was too big. Too strong. Too well trained. Plus, one blow to the bullet wound in her side and she'd be at his mercy.

With a roar, Helton came after her, kicking the gun from her outstretched hand and grabbing her by the hair. "Stupid bitch."

She gasped for air as he yanked her to her feet, sending pain streaking across her scalp. His sheer physical size and strength intimidated the rational part of her brain, the martial arts–trained woman who should be looking for a weakness. Instead, she experienced a momentary urge to just give up, to stop fighting her inevitable death.

"Now what?" He twisted her hair in his fist, and another streak of pain banished her fatalistic thoughts.

She'd give up when she was dead. Not before.

"Fuck you," she said, wishing she could spit in his face.

He laughed, a low, sadistic sound that hardened her resolve further. "Don't have time for that."

Then, more commotion echoed from the tunnel, sounds of a scuffle.

Helton spun around again, dragging her with him this time.

Erin seized the split second with his attention divided and rammed an elbow into the hard muscle of his gut. He barely flinched, but his grip on her loosened just enough for her to throw her head back and up, connecting with his chin.

He grunted, his hold slipping as he staggered backward.

Erin twisted around and brought a knee up hard to

his groin. A simple move. Very female. And usually very effective.

Helton lost his breath, barely, stumbling back another half step, buying her a mere second or two.

She took them.

Again she threw herself at the gun, the stitches in her side tearing as she slid across the floor. She felt the wash of blood and pain as if from outside herself, her survival instincts in full force now, knowing that even a moment's hesitation or wrong move would mean her certain death.

Behind her, Helton growled like an injured animal. Nearly on her.

With all her will bent on reaching the gun first, the cold metal seemed to leap into her hand. She rolled, firing even before her eye registered her target. The bullet struck home, a shock of red darkening his upper torso, slowing him.

Still, he came at her.

She fired again.

The second shot froze him in place, his face registering shock, and the world slipped into slow motion. Taking careful aim now, she brought him down with the third bullet, the small hole in his forehead wiping all else from his face.

He fell, a large, suddenly clumsy mass of muscle and limbs. And as he hit the cold stone, her surroundings returned in a rush of sound and movement.

Near the door a tumble of bodies rolled across the floor. Broken Nose. And Alec.

She pushed to her feet, suddenly aware of her side, the pain of broken stitches and the blood staining her shirt, and of the gun in her hand, useless now. She couldn't make out where one man ended and the other started. If she took a shot, she could kill Alec as easily as the man he fought.

Then, a muffled shot as a bullet hit flesh at close range.

Alec?

Erin froze, everything inside her gone cold, her gun hand suddenly shaking. Broken Nose sprawled across Alec, blood soaking their clothes. Who had taken the bullet?

Then Alec's hand snaked out from beneath the other man and pushed the limp body aside. Relief flooded her and she staggered back, reaching toward the wall for support.

Alec scrambled to his feet and was at her side within seconds. "Are you okay?"

Erin nodded, not really sure. She pressed a hand to her waist and it came away bloody.

"You've been hurt."

"No." She shook her head. "I mean yes, but not now. The fighting, it just reopened the old wound. I'll be okay."

"But you're bleeding."

"I'm okay, Alec." She glanced toward the bodies on the floor, dark crimson pools forming beneath each. "They've set some kind of explosives," she said. "We've—"

"It's okay." Alec pulled her into his arms, held her close, and she allowed it. Needed it. For just a second or two. Unable, really, to pull away from this man she'd feared she'd lost. Not once, but twice. "Your friend set it up near the lab. I disconnected the fuse before following him here."

She pulled away. "Where were you? I was so worried." Then she remembered Joe and pushed past Alec to Joe's side.

"Still here," Joe whispered. "You're not getting rid of me that easy."

"Thank God." She pressed her hands to his face, trying to assess his injuries. "We're going to get you out of here."

Alec went through Helton's pockets and came up with a set of keys. As he worked them on Joe's iron band, he said, "I'm sorry, Erin, I didn't mean to scare you. When I heard them coming, I took cover. I figured it was better to surprise them from behind after I knew how many there were, and how heavily armed."

Joe's shackled hand came free.

"I didn't think it would be smart," Alec continued, "to get into a firefight, when I only had six bullets."

Erin laughed lightly, fighting back the tears. "I forgive you." She reached over and kissed him on the cheek, wishing she could do more. "I'm just glad. . . ." She shook her head. "Never mind. Help me get Joe on his feet."

"No," Joe said, the weakness in his voice tearing at her. "Leave me. You need to stop that plane."

"We can't leave you," Erin said.

Joe closed his eyes and settled his head against the wall. "You have to. I'll only slow you down."

"He's right, Erin," Alec said gently. "We have to get to that plane before it takes off."

"But, Joe—"

"We'll send someone back from the camp for him."
From his pocket, Alec pulled out a small handheld computer like the one Erin had carried into Cuba. "We'll send the backup team in for him and Jean Taylor."

Erin hesitated.

Alec stood and grabbed her arm. Reluctantly, she let him draw her to her feet. Though she knew they were right, leaving Joe in this condition was one of the hardest things she'd ever been asked to do.

"Go on," Joe said. "I'm not dead yet. But if you don't stop that plane, others will die."

CHAPTER FORTY-EIGHT

Casa de la Rosa, Cuba

Outside it had begun to rain.

Alec kept a firm grip on Erin's arm as they jogged along the path, afraid she'd turn back for Roarke. Alec understood her reluctance to leave the man, but he also knew they had no choice.

They'd picked up Helton's and the other man's semi-automatic handguns and left the fully automatic weapon for Roarke.

"What time is the plane scheduled to leave?" Alec asked as they neared the camp.

Erin glanced at her watch. "We have a little over an hour."

"Damn." Santa Clara was sixty minutes away on a good day, in good weather, when you knew the way. All they knew was that the flight was scheduled to leave out of Aeropuerto Internacional Abel Santamaría near Santa Clara.

When they reached the yard of the DFL camp, it seemed oddly deserted. "Is it always so quiet?" he asked.

"Never," Erin said, coming to a stop. "But with the rain and half the volunteers leaving today," she shook her head, "who knows?"

"Plus Helton's men are gone because they're done here."

"Yeah, that too. Come on, I'm going to send someone from the clinic to help Joe."

She darted across the yard toward the house and Alec followed, though he wasn't certain this was a good idea. If her father was still around, sending him to help Joe might be a mistake. However, Alec knew she wouldn't leave without at least making an attempt to get the man some help. And she didn't want to hear that her father was a potential threat. Plus, he'd sent a message to the backup team, so they'd be at the cabin within a few minutes.

Then Alec noticed again her blood-soaked shirt and shook his head. How like Erin to worry about someone else and ignore her own injury. "Get something to stop that bleeding while you're inside," he said.

"We don't have time."

"You can redress the wound yourself while we're in the car. But if you pass out from blood loss, you're no good to me."

Erin gave him a strange look, then grinned. "We wouldn't want that."

Within minutes she returned carrying a bag, a woman and man at her side. The man held a shotgun draped across one arm.

Quickly, Alec aimed his automatic at the other man. "Put down the weapon."

"It's okay." Erin stepped between them. "This is Armando and Sandy. They're going back to the cabin. She's a nurse, and he's going with her to keep her safe. He'll also watch over Jean until the others arrive to pick her up."

Alec glanced from Erin to the man behind her. Then he backed off, dropping the gun to his side. "Okay then, we need to go."

Ten minutes later they were headed for Santa Clara, driving too fast along slippery country roads. Alec concentrated on keeping his rental car from sliding off the mountain. Meanwhile, Erin stripped off her shirt and applied a fresh dressing to her side. Then she pulled on a clean top she'd brought from the clinic with the medical supplies.

"I brought you a clean shirt as well," she said.

He risked taking a quick look at his own bloody clothes. "Yeah, I guess I might raise a few eyebrows."

"You might," she added, her voice light. "You can change when we get to the airport."

"Are you going to tell me how that happened?" he asked. "The bullet wound, I mean."

"It's a long story."

"We have an hour."

She sighed, then with obvious reluctance told him a tale about a nighttime ambush, a dead driver, and her own flight through a wet mountain night. He realized how close he'd come to losing her. And again he had to wonder if he could live with this constant uncertainty. It was a weakness in himself that he didn't like, but overcoming it might not be possible.

For now though, he had to put such thoughts aside. Jean Taylor had created something deadly for Helton, or whoever had hired him. What, they didn't know. But it was on that plane, headed for Miami. That fact had to take precedence over any personal consideration or concerns. Just as Erin had had to leave an injured colleague behind, he had to put his thoughts about her aside. At least for now.

"You know," Alec said after she'd finished her story, "even if we get there on time, we need to let that plane take off."

"I know."

"If Castro's government is behind this, which seems likely, it won't do any good to keep the plane on Cuban soil." He threw her a glance. "They'll say all the right things, then transport the virus some other way at a later time."

For several long minutes Erin didn't respond. Finally she said, "Then we'll just have to search the plane in transit."

Alec wasn't sure that would work, either. "But first," he said, fighting the car as it fishtailed around a curve, "we have to get on that flight."

They arrived at the Santa Clara airport with a mere ten minutes to spare. Leaving the car at the curb, they raced inside, checking the boards for the correct departure gate.

Aeropuerto Internacional Abel Santamaría was a small airport by U.S. standards, so it was a quick run to the area for privately chartered flights. Still, if the plane hadn't been late taking off, they never would have made it. As it was, they hurried across the tarmac just as the attendants were retracting the boarding ramp.

"Stop," Erin yelled over the roar of the engines. "We're scheduled for this flight."

"It is too late," said the uniformed agent as he tried to usher them back to the terminal.

"We must get on that plane," Alec insisted, searching for an argument that would change this man's mind. None came to him. Like many officials, the agent was bogged down by policy and procedures he refused to question.

Then the plane's engines shut down, the props slowed, and the doorway opened. A man stood in the hatch. Alec recognized him right away. Emilio Diaz.

"I didn't realize he was on this flight," Erin said.

Alec kept quiet, knowing if he voiced his suspicions about her father, Erin would shut him out. Whether willing or not, Emilio Diaz had to know what Jean Taylor had created at the camp, and they couldn't just let him walk away. However, Erin had to come to the realization herself, and she would. Eventually. She wasn't stupid. Alec only hoped it wouldn't be too late.

Diaz yelled something to the ground attendant in rapid Spanish. The man answered, obviously unwilling to alter his course of action for anyone. But after another fiery exchange, the agent reluctantly motioned to the workers standing by, and they pushed the boarding ramp back to the plane.

Erin and Alec scrambled up the steps.

As the steward closed the door behind them, Erin wrapped her arms around her father. "I can't believe we almost missed the plane."

Diaz flushed but returned the brief hug before separating himself from her. "I was worried. You left the clinic and did not come back." Then, looking her over, he said, "How is your side?"

"I'm fine," Erin assured him, and Alec thought that those were her two favorite words. "I'll explain everything later. I didn't know you were going to be on this flight."

Diaz smiled tightly. "I wanted to make sure you got home safely."

Erin's smile lit her face, and Alec felt it like a weight in his gut. She'd found her father, and in true Erin fashion, she loved him unconditionally. It was going to destroy her if Diaz ended up being a willing part of Helton's scheme.

"You must take your seats now," the steward said.

Alec took Erin's arm, meeting Diaz's gaze, who looked at him with a question on his face. Who are you, the older man obviously wanted to ask, but the steward gave them no time.

Alec and Erin made their way to the back of the plane and sat in the last row. As they settled in and buckled their seat belts, Alec couldn't pretend any longer. He had to at least remind her of the possibilities, so that if the worst happened, she wouldn't be completely blindsided.

"Your father," he started.

"I know." She looked at him, a flash of anger in her eyes. "But we don't know anything for sure. Let's just wait and see."

Alec held her gaze briefly, then turned away. He couldn't face the pain in her eyes.

Once the plane was in the air, Erin said, "We need to talk."

Alec glanced around, wondering how they could carry on a private conversation on such a small aircraft. Somewhere on this plane, Helton had hidden vials of a deadly virus. In someone's luggage? In the cargo hold? Or an overhead compartment? There was no way to tell, and Alec knew they couldn't just start searching. The other passengers would shut them down within minutes.

Erin seemed to read his thoughts, or her own had traveled down the same path. She pulled a magazine from the pocket in front of her seat. Opening it, she wrote four words in one of the margins.

We need help. Search.

Alec considered. They could solicit help from the other passengers, all DFL volunteers, if Erin could get them to believe her. Or, the two of them could force a search. They were both armed—something they never would have gotten away with on a commercial flight, or even on a charter flight from a larger airport. However, the pilots couldn't be trusted. Helton had hired them, so if Erin and Alec raised a fuss with the passengers, the pilots could easily head back to Cuba.

He took the magazine from her and flipped to another page, writing just one word. Pilots?

Erin took a deep breath. And nodded.

So they needed to get on the ground, on U.S. soil, before they did anything. Then they'd take control of the plane before anyone or anything could be unloaded.

He reached over and took her hand.

It would be risky. All they needed was some hotshot with a rifle deciding to be a hero before Alec's and Erin's identities could be verified with the authorities. Still, he saw no other way.

It wasn't a long flight to Miami, which was fortunate because neither of them could relax. They were on edge the entire way. Then, as the plane landed and taxied in, Alec gave Erin's hand one final squeeze before unbuckling his seat belt and standing.

"Sir!" yelled the steward. "You must take your seat."

Alec ignored the command and made his way to the cockpit amid a murmuring from the other passengers. Thankfully, Helton had chartered this small private aircraft to carry his deadly weapon, otherwise Alec would never have gotten by the newly reinforced cockpit doors.

The copilot had turned to see about the commotion when Alec pulled his gun. "Stop the plane. Here."

The pilot glanced at Alec in alarm, while behind him, he heard the confusion as Erin pulled her weapon, positioning herself at his back.

"We're federal agents," she said. "Everyone stay calm and this will be over quickly."

Alec focused on the pilots. "Listen to the lady."

The pilot nodded. "What do you want?"

"Get the control tower on the radio."

When he complied, Alec spoke so everyone on and off the plane could hear. "This is Special Agent Alec Donovan with the FBI. I've taken control of this aircraft along with another federal officer until you can move us into quarantine." He paused, knowing his next words could very well cause a panic behind him. "We have reason to believe there's a dangerous biohazard on board."

Within minutes the plane was surrounded.

CHAPTER FORTY-NINE

Miami, Florida

For the next several hours, time crawled.

Both the plane and passengers were sequestered and searched, but the authorities found nothing. No suitcase filled with vials. No shipment of pharmaceuticals. Nothing supporting Erin's and Alec's fear of a biothreat. It looked like they were mistaken, or Helton had purposely pointed them in the wrong direction.

Finally, the passengers were allowed to leave, disgruntled and grumbling as they filed off the small aircraft. Alec went with the local authorities, discussing or explaining what had turned out to be a disaster.

Meanwhile, Erin waited quietly with her father.

He hadn't said anything since she and Alec had taken control of the plane, and his muteness echoed louder than any words. If he'd been totally innocent of Helton's plan, wouldn't he have questioned his daughter, demanded an explanation? He did neither, and his silence screamed a harsh reality. At the very least, he knew about the virus. Just the thought made Erin ache inside.

Alec, she knew, must have realized the same thing. So he'd backed off, allowing her to handle her father and ask the hard questions. And for that, she was grateful.

After all of his volunteers were off the plane, Emilio started down the stairs as well. Still silent. Erin followed, knowing she needed to stop him, yet wishing she could just let him walk away.

She caught up to him on the tarmac.

"Father." The word sounded stiff, formal, but somehow Papi no longer felt right either. "I need to speak with you."

He stopped, turning to face her.

"I . . ." She searched for the right words. What came out wasn't what she'd planned. "I'm sorry that I lied to you. I should have been truthful about my reason for coming to Cuba."

He glanced away, a distant look in his eyes. Then he said, "We all do what we must."

She started to smile, though it was forced. Then she went very still, remembering him saying these exact words in Cuba. Twice. Once when talking about the armed men. Then again when she'd questioned him about vaccinating the villagers and volunteers for dengue.

It hit her suddenly. Where he'd stored the virus.

"We've been looking in the wrong place," she said, almost to herself. "The virus isn't in a suitcase or vial. It's in the passengers, the volunteers." She met his gaze. "You didn't vaccinate them. You infected them."

Emilio shook his head, sadness in his eyes. "You were always bright, Erin. Maybe too bright."

"No." She took a backward step and pulled her gun. "Tell me I'm wrong about this." And she prayed he would.

"Put the weapon away, Erin."

"You knew all about this, didn't you?" Her stomach rolled, and she thought she might be sick. "You knew what Helton planned to do, you were a willing part of it."

He shrugged, a slight lift of his shoulders. "Yes, I knew."

She reached for the radio the local authorities had given her when they'd boarded the plane. "This is Officer Baker," she said into the speaker. "The passengers are carrying the virus."

"Come again."

Emilio started to walk away.

"The passengers," Erin said above the static. "Stop them. They're infected."

"Are you saying the passengers are infected?"

"Yes, stop them."

She raised her gun higher, calling to her father. "I can't let you walk away."

He turned to look at her again. "Do you really think you can stop me?"

"Why?" Fresh tears formed in Erin's eyes. How could he? How could she have been so wrong about him? "Why would you do this? You're a doctor. A healer."

For a moment she didn't think he'd answer. He'd looked so alone, so sad. Then something else sparked in his eyes. She could have sworn it was anger.

"This government, *your* government is killing my people," he said. "They are suffering."

"What are you talking about?"

"You know what I am talking about. The political agenda that keeps my country poor, its citizens hungry and without proper medical care."

Erin shook her head, not believing her ears. How could he sound so rational while uttering irrational words? "This is about the embargo?"

"No, this is about the Cuban people and the hardships your government imposes on them because of that embargo."

Again it made no sense to her. "So you're killing innocent people? Men and women who volunteered to help you?"

The sadness was back in his eyes. "Your leaders only pay attention to death." He sighed, looked away briefly, then focused on her again. "Those volunteers. They are vultures. They do not come to Cuba because of its people's need. They come to feel good about themselves. They are heroes because they spent a few weeks in a Third World country." Again he hesitated, a flash of anger, passion, wiping all regret from his face. "Does not your government, all governments, do the same thing? Do they not send their own people to war, to die for ideals that mean nothing to them?"

"That's different."

"Is it? I'm fighting for the survival of my people. Is that any less important, less worth dying for than your government's need to control other nations' ideals or resources?"

Erin couldn't speak, couldn't find words to wrap around the tightness in her chest. Was this the same man who'd carried her out of the woods two nights ago? The man who'd placed a guard by her door?

"Besides," Emilio said. "The volunteers will not get sick. The others, though, the ones they touch. Well . . ." He shrugged. "We all do what we must do."

"You're a monster." The words came out in a whisper, unbidden, unplanned. And they tore something inside her, broke a piece of her heart that might never heal.

He smiled, a sad, sad smile. "Sometimes it takes a monster to kill one." He turned and once again started to walk away.

"Stop," she said, her voice breaking on tears. "I can't let you walk away from this."

He kept on. "You will not shoot me, Erin. It is not in you."

She raised her gun, her hands and voice trembling. "Stop. Papi. Please."

"Good-bye, Erin."

Tears streaming down her face, her finger refused to pull the trigger. Because he was right. She couldn't do it.

From behind her came a rush of footfalls. "Diaz," Alec commanded, "stop where you are."

Emilio picked up his pace.

Then she saw it. In her father's hand, suddenly, a solid object, metal, catching and reflecting the sunlight. He had a gun.

She tried to call out, to warn Alec, but he'd seen the weapon and fired a warning shot. Erin flinched.

Emilio spun, taking aim, his gaze locked on hers.

A second shot burst the air, and for a long lingering second he stood, never taking his eyes from Erin. Then, her father fell.

And Erin sank to her knees, the gun in her hand still cold.

EPILOGUE

Miami, Florida

In a small, isolated room off Miami Airport's main concourse, Erin sat alone, a blanket draped over her shoulders and a cup of untouched coffee in her hands.

Everything inside her ached.

She tried to tell herself it didn't matter. A week ago, Emilio Diaz had been just a name. She hadn't known him, hardly even had any anger left for him. Yet in a few short days, she'd remembered how to love him.

Now, he was gone. Whether living or not. She'd lost him.

The door opened, and she looked up.

Alec stood on the threshold, his face reflecting the agony she felt. "I'm sorry," he said. "They couldn't save him."

Erin had braced herself for her father's death, feeling that it was inevitable. That maybe, considering he'd tried to release a bioweapon, it would be for the best. Still, the words spoken expressed a finality that seared her insides.

"What about the volunteers?" she asked.

Alec came closer, within reach, but seemed afraid to touch her. "The authorities were able to reach them in time. They've been put in quarantine by the CDC." He took a deep breath and slipped his hands into his pockets. "Fortunately, the preliminary tests look good. It seems they are carriers of a dormant virus that after a fourteen-day incubation period would have become active. Then they would have passed on the virus to everyone they came in contact with."

Erin took a deep breath, wondering if she'd ever feel normal again. Her father had done this. Her flesh and blood.

"And Helton? Who hired him?"

"The only person who might be able to tell us that is Jean Taylor. We're negotiating with the Cuban government to bring her out of Cuba, but I wouldn't hold my breath." He paused. "As it is, we may never know who was footing the bills for this."

She nodded, knowing it could be any one of a number of terrorist groups around the world. No doubt, if Helton and her father had succeeded, someone would have claimed responsibility. No one, however, wanted to take credit for a failure.

"Meanwhile," Alec said, "the Cuban government is claiming outrage and no knowledge of the incident or the lab at the DFL camp." Alec shrugged. "And of course, they're denying us access to the facility and demanding that the rest of the American volunteers leave Cuba."

"And Joe?"

"Your friends Sandy and Armando moved him to

town before the local authorities closed in, and your backup team got him out." Alec gave her a tight smile. "He's going to make it. You saved his life, Erin."

She tried to smile, tried to take comfort in that one act. Instead, all she felt was cold, bitterly cold, and sick.

"There's one other thing you need to know," Alec said.

She already knew too much, more than she wanted. But she couldn't bring herself to tell him no, either.

"Your father," Alec's voice broke. "He'd injected himself with the carrier strain as well."

She met his gaze then. It was one more piece of an incomprehensible puzzle. Another question she'd ask for the rest of her life.

"Like the others," Alec continued, "in a couple weeks, he would have infected everyone he came in contact with."

Erin nodded, hearing the words and holding herself together by a thread. "I couldn't shoot him," she said, as her control began to slip. "I just couldn't."

Alec closed the remaining distance between them, drawing her into his arms. "I know," he said, his voice no more than a whisper. "That's why I did it for you."

She felt the tears come, choking sobs that burned her throat and eyes, and she buried herself deeper within his embrace. Within the comfort he offered.

"We need each other, Erin," he said as he stroked her hair. "For all the things we can't do ourselves."

He was right. They faced too many demons. Alone, it would destroy them. Together? Maybe they stood a chance.

So for the first time since her sister had disappeared seventeen years ago, Erin let go. She collapsed in Alec's arms and let her tears come, letting someone else, Alec Donovan, carry her burdens. A man who needed her as much as she needed him, a man she thought she could love. For a lifetime.